MOSSAAN

Written by:
Neneh LouL'anne FayeKhan

Neneh LouL'anne Faye Khan can be contacted at

www.LouLanne.com

Copyright © 2012 Neneh LouL'anne FayeKhan

All rights reserved.

ISBN:
ISBN-13:987-1981608454

Table of Contents

DISTINCT COMMUNIQUE 7

DEDICATIONS 14

ACKNOWLEDGMENTS 16

CHAPTER ONE 19
   Steps 19

CHAPTER TWO 46
   Initiation 46

CHAPTER THREE 65
   Respire 65

CHAPTER FOUR 76
   The Push 76

CHAPTER FIVE 86
   Growing in Grace 86

CHAPTER SIX 110

Silhouettes 110

CHAPTER SEVEN 135
The Thirst 135

CHAPTER EIGHT 180
Evasion 180

CHAPTER NINE 191
Spurs 191

CHAPTER TEN 205
Child Bride 205

CHAPTER ELEVEN 224
Revolving 224

CHAPTER TWELVE 232
Exploration 232

CHAPTER THIRTEEN 237
Altruism 237

CHAPTER FOURTEEN 246
SHIELD 246

CHAPTER FIFTEEN 252

CHAPTER SIXTEEN 255
Ambitions 258

CHAPTER SEVENTEEN 267
Realisation 267

CHAPTER EIGHTEEN 278
The Lane 278

CHAPTER NINETEEN 287
Longing 287

FINAL QUOTES 364

TRIBUTES 365
Doyen George Christenson 366
Dr. Harr Freeya Njai 370

SPECIAL THANKS 374
NOTES 374
Find the Beautiful Things Hidden Underneath The Thorns 374

PROFILE OF MOSSAAN 377

ABOUT THE AUTHOR 379

DISTINCT COMMUNIQUE

When experience gives you hope, tragedies do not speak to you, but they have a way of talking to your soul. They shape you and put you in the picture to know what you did not understand before. We were taught to believe that it is the same as the many U-turns we come across when listening to stories, when watching films or even when indulging in the stories of our ancestors and their many struggles before their victories to settle into their respective kingdoms and regions. Every story has a way of shaping us. We enjoy listening to stories expecting to learn not just a few things from them but a great deal.

I want to take a moment and address the crux of my life that I gracefully name 'My Life Cap.' It consists of the right people in it that I call family and friends, coaches and mentors, teachers and guides, supporters and every well-wisher with whom I cross path. I often ask myself questions our mothers did not and will never find awkward to answer. Who am I? Both my parents and those who knew me were aware of my willingness to understand what was important about the lives of my loved ones. I made it clear to them that I did not want to know anything in vain.

I needed to be ready and in preparation for several volumes precisely of what I needed to write in the future. My late mother never dilly-dallied in answering that question when I asked her. She used all the sweet words of 'Chossaan' she knew just to tell me who I am.

I grew up showering myself with all the positive attributes you can ever know because, at a very young age, I knew that I could only develop good characters if I allow myself to be good and visualise being amongst the good people I call my role models. Our parents, especially mothers did that for us. It is called building your child's confidence, making them believe in themselves and telling them that anything is possible. Don't just stop at saying to yourself that you are a human being. Tell yourself that you are a human becoming somebody, taking many attempts to track everything that makes you feel that you are making your mark on this earth. That is why the Almighty Lord of Mankind sent you down to join the ones before you.

This maiden is written for a purpose to introduce myself as a child since the protagonist is a young woman who wishes to have a taste of the city life that she carved herself. I take the opportunity to talk about my inspirations. I wanted to share my humble beginnings, my journey and every story I have come across during this first phase of my life. Children learn very fast. They understand things very quickly. My 'Enfance' meaning childhood plays a huge part in this sequel that I wish to present and introduce the life of Mossaan. Who am I? I guess it is in a way asking what kind of seed is in me as they say in our local dialect, our roots. I pride myself in talking about my beliefs which is the leading quality belonging to me as I learn to be a better person. That includes becoming spiritual and putting the Almighty first. I believe that I am amongst those people who can openly say that I am part of a continuing change that carries a legacy and responsibilities. I am a believer in learning. To become an expert in something you must be willing to learn, to read the same thing repeatedly, understand it, test your knowledge on it and understand every aspect of what it is that you are learning. So, I take my time acquainting with people, but I watch with vigilance while doing that. I do not go into something and wait for my luck to unfold either. I am a confident believer who thinks positively knowing that fate is all about preparation and meeting opportunity.

If you consistently make yourself ready to receive grace, grace will fall into place, but because you were willing to accept it. Similarly, I say that God's hand is continuously present in our joy and our pain. I want to be able to honestly share the most crucial facet of my life with our audience.

My childhood experience shaped me into what I have become, and I can happily say that I have become a feminist, a woman who still tries to find her way for journeys do not end. They only stop when you pass over. That is what I believe happens. To call for success only is not the person that I am. I call for strength, spirituality and the ability, grace and be gifted with the most desired attributes - showing gratitude to my Creator, even when in pain. Alhamdullilah! I praise the Lord of Mankind.

We have all got stories to tell, and we cannot achieve a thing if we lack the zeal to document anything that makes a story sound intriguing or come out to be meaningful. Growing up in Africa, the people I knew who have contributed a lot to my upbringing inspired me. I am not only referring to my parents who have passed away but the people in their lives. These people make up a whole community of great men and women who value family spirit, relatives, community members, friends and everything that brings people together. This kind of bond is what they knew and raised us in, which made their environment so conducive and friendly for all generations; ours and the next. I ride with them in thoughts, and I go to bed feeling thankful that they are the reason why I say Ubuntu.

We would like to say that their times and ours are different, but the values do not change at all. We always refer ourselves to think of the way they lived and did things as a community. They lived a very healthy life free from all this; the contemporary world and its myriad of the artificial charade. It is funny that we always run back to those values when we seek inspirations. It shows that we cannot do without them. It is without a doubt the same as what history dictates. That is why we need to put a great deal of importance on our traditions and cultures wherever we may find ourselves. Life is a sketch that briefly encompasses all kinds. It is up to us to draw our maps from those drafts.

The anecdotes highlight the nuance between cities, villages and their populaces. Two different worlds and yet speak through the same voice, see things through the same unique lenses. Here is a muse, an inspirational story, a guide to our dreams. It depicts the way of life, childhood, upbringing, ambitions, and faith or every young woman growing up in Africa.

From inception, I wanted it to write it as the memoir of an African girl child with all the necessary details, but I decided to commence the sequel with my account of things and make it my vision. It is how I envisage the young women I met from when I was nine years old emphasising on my encounter and friendship everyone that welcomed me with open arms. I became an enigma to many of my peers for quickly falling in love with the village setting that I found richer than the cities. I have always been, an open-minded person, some of the qualities that I think people lack in our society today and I would like to reiterate that with that lacking, we can never perform well because it feeds paranoia. My personal experience fits in nicely, and I focus on the nuance between myself and the protagonist mainly because I began to understand at an early age that one should always be grateful, loyal and having integrity is the icing on the cake. Traveling from end to end made me appreciate my life much better even though I used to think that I have had a tough time. I spent my childhood moving around countries, meeting and acquainting with new people who taught me so much good to add to whatever I already had in me.

With these discoveries, I began to understand my lineage that I put no importance to because I was a child and all I needed was to be a child. Luckily for me, there was a lot I would come to understand, and the many years spent in those new environments helped me throughout my life, and I am forever going to be grateful for my experience and thankful to the elders who are still alive to remind me of my trail and my roots. I would not have been able to talk about history this much or write such stories if I did not get the exposure that I had, and the time spent bounding from village to village.

Today, I feel so proud just because I can share what I know, and I appreciate every bit of both environments I call homes to my ancestors and my parents not to talk about my lineage. It has given me realms of opportunities, and I thank everyone involved throughout these distinct phases. It is not about who is involved in this story but rather what is in it to gauge a personal trivet.

Writing Mossaan's story is a reminder of everything that I have been through and thankful for then, and now. I am grateful because the people I came across showed me so much love and allowed me to learn so much about myself, our different worlds and everything that matters. Though the story is a fiction, there is a lot of real-life happenings vis a vis culture and tradition especially the child bride who is part of what I saw going on in my childhood which I incorporated in it.

Reminiscence brings joy and joy it is all that I desire to achieve with this book to the extreme. I want you to be part of this sequel. I also want you to be able to document every step of your journey. Even if you do not want to, try to enjoy putting your story in chronological order because it certainly pays off. I am an avid storyteller, and I aspire to be a great one someday. Let us share this journey.

DEDICATIONS

To my darling Boy, my Jewel, Edriss Bijou Khan as always

My son Edriss inspired me to venture out on this journey to share my work with the rest of the world. He makes us feel proud for becoming one of UK Young Writers. I was in awe when I learned that he got selected for his creative work and they started publishing his beautiful write-ups. That was enough for a child to be motivated and to improve. I am a proud mother for this inspiration will go a long way.

As young as he is, Edriss already believes in education and what it can do for him. School is a prerequisite, and we are taught to understand that it can open realms of opportunities for us. He is growing up into a beautiful person, a gallant young man with a lot of potentials. His spirituality and beliefs in learning give me hope about the future, and I ask The Lord of Mankind to make His Angels and Prophets his shield; to guide him and his friends and even the establishments he attends for both his Quranic lessons and schooling. I hope that my words remain his inspiration.

I dedicate this book to you Edriss, my young Sultan as I fondly you. You are my raison de Vivre. Your tremendous support and understanding got me here. I know that you are now very pleased with this achievement. It is our project, and we have made it happen. I always remind myself of the blessing of having you as my son. In your own words "When you encourage me to be confident and do what will help me grow as a person, I will do nothing but the same for you, and it makes me feel happy to see you achieve your goals. Because you deserve it".

I thank you, son. It is about funding our dreams.

The words are enough to feed us with more ideas. These collections of words of encouragement are far from being a vanity. I am just happy that I have now found the enthusiasm that I needed to write stories that I know from my childhood, my many tracks and other fictional ones based on what our African society presents to us.

 I am forever grateful to The Lord for blessing me with such an amazing 'Boy.' I pray that Allah The Almighty protects you for us and cover your every path with His abundant blessings. Edriss Khan, here I want to show how much you mean to Mama.

Thank you for the person that you are. You make me live wholly and speak highly of me. Your love, trust, respect and adoration are enough for me to live in hope. What's more, the jokes you share with me trying to make me look so cool and I do it so oddly. It is impossible for me to express all the right things and the pride of having you as a blessing in my life. I just want to seal this by saying how much you are loved. You are my L.O.V.E & J.O.Y. Love always wins.

Thank you for also teaching me the modern style of a thing called D.A.B.B.I.N.G [Smiles…]

I bless you this day and all days my child with everything good in life. No man will detect your destiny. You are in the cocoon and the hands of the Lord. I thank my Creator boundlessly for, without His guidance, this would have been a dream, and that would be it. We are heading to the finishing line together. I cannot thank you enough, but I wish you enough SON.

#DontLetTimePassYou

Mommy

Though the book is a special dedication to my son, I will use the opportunity to give special tribute to these two remarkable persons, two of the greatest I have known in my professional life. They left this world at a time when their savviness was most needed. But, who are we to say that they should be here with us today? They are in a better place, and we pray that The Lord of Mankind places them in His most beautiful Gardens in Heaven. Amen!

"The Dream has to be bigger than the fear."

Speak Or Be Spoken To.

ACKNOWLEDGMENTS

Writing is a lonely profession said many of my peers, and I agree. So, I say thank you to everyone who keeps me company along the way. My very special acknowledgements and thanks go to all the powerful and smart and knowledgeable women out there, candid and passionate about feminism, education, leadership, community development, community enhancement and community involvement. I credit this to all those who have revealed the yearnings, pleasures of their new desires for success in life through; motivating, coaching or teaching others to become empowered in a male-dominated world, the rigid environment in Africa and the world at large.

I am grateful to so many of my dear ones who have always believed in me. When I candidly said that I felt it was too premature for me to write a whole book, many of you kept reminding me of the stories you have enjoyed hearing from me and everything I believe in and speak about in various platforms.

I know that you have been waiting for too long, but with patience comes notable achievements and this is the product that is born out of that virtue called 'Sabr' which is patience. I am hoping that this is not one that will give you shudders because it touches on so many things we lack to understand is our society today, but the joy relatively.

Your enthusiasm has genuinely pushed me to this stage, and it is like nudging a slanting door to make sure it closes well. I got a few suggestions when I wanted to make it a film and what I heard most of the time was, why not books first then a documentary? After good thinking, I finally put the transcript 'en elan' with velocity, sent it to publishers who gave positive feedback that was so encouraging. This positive feedback was accompanied by the siren that I needed to hear. Here we are. It is the beginning of the sequel.

I am thanking you for your unflagging support and for making me understand the true meaning of friendship, acquaintance and most of all, the family life and its serendipity.

Our thinking defines our life and blessings establish our trust in our Creator. Together, we show our gratitude as you have always taught me to comprehend. I am because you are referring to the providence in everything I do and for that, I ask myself this question all the time.

How can we live on this planet without 'Ubuntu'? It is 'Ubuntu' at its best.

'The nests must be built from broken branches.' If you can build that you can deal with anything that does not look fixable. We are each other's twig. May we always see the positive side of everything we face.

CHAPTER ONE
Steps

Focusing on the first ten to one hundred levels at a very young age into my early adulthood, I started travelling within the Senegambian region beginning from Senegal and then the neighbouring countries. I had to move to another country for my secondary education because the Gambia did not have a French secondary school yet. I flew far and wide during that time, visiting relatives in many towns, cities, and villages in and around Senegal where both my parents originated. I must say, I enjoyed the discoveries I have made that guided me throughout my adult life. I have also found myself discovering my imaginary chaperon throughout, and that gave me the ability to seek for further knowledge on what will mould me into becoming. As I fondly say to myself; I am a human being jumping into my mode of 'human becoming.' This notion granted me what I needed to be successful in fighting the enemy within which was fear itself.

Through the lenses, everything is seen, and I made learning vital and my priority. I wanted to gain a lot and winning was my goal. I did not feel comfortable in situations that I could not handle. Little did I know was that the Almighty, my Allah watched over me all the time and pushed me into my destiny. God will make you feel so uncomfortable in a situation that it will propel you into your future, but fear keeps you, hostage.

I never allowed worrywarts to keep me captive and stagnant. I knew from inception that the temptation was going to be too much, but I was at the same time aware that it is going to make me disconnected to circles that did not allow me to tap into my inner positivity. Nothing destructive could be my comfort zone. I am a firm believer, and I am sure whatever happens to me, it is Him catapulting me into my destiny.

I have also seen and experienced so much while interacting with the people that I looked at and fearlessly embraced and call them my inspiration. These are people from all walks of life. They were always so keen to tell me stories that, even my parents did not find the need nor the time to share with me for fear of having me become infatuated. Who would not be obsessed with beauty and even challenging stories that have got everything good in them?

Knowing how inquisitive a child I was, my parents never bothered themselves to tell me much about the history I was interested to know in the beginning. I had the smallest hunch of my origins. Like any other young person, it is essential to know that you have relatives/relations outside the family home and members you have known since birth; the siblings such as sisters and brothers you see and your two parents. I have always felt lonely at heart that I did not have a significant family, a big family around me in the Gambia. I used to be envious of our friends during festive seasons when they go to their extended families and ours were all the way beyond the borders. We saw them three times a year or once most of the time.

Even though I was the lucky one in the family, I have been frequently on the go, never had time for leisure and at times on my own with strangers who were assigned to look after me. I was known as the most prone to homesick. What is more, I was always depressed during my teen years.

Travelling to Senegal did allow me to see, learn and embrace who I am. What I knew then was enough for me to hold onto until I embarked on my many voyages meeting relatives in the villages, towns and cities located near the town where I resided with my regal and very popular grandmother who was a humble local politician. She raised other young men and women. I was a happy girl and lucky to have been treated as the 'chaat' of the gang. I got used to being treated as a 'chaat', the last born/youngest that I was not. But to my grandma, I was her youngest, and everyone called me by that name.

As a middle child, I always wanted my parents' attention that is why I drown in my books just to make Papa happy. He believed in education and wanted the best for his girls. I managed to win everyone's loyalty and care due to the bond that I had with my father who taught me how to speak French properly removing me from expressing it anyhow. Everybody in my family in Senegal thought that I had extra tuition at home. I told them it was Papa from whom I learned the art of speaking well with proper elocution taught to me. He also made sure that I said the words correctly so that I can impress my teachers and anyone in my family in Senegal.

These family members I got to meet and grew up to know were there to give me advice and my Allah, as usual, was always present to guide me. They were all older than me, and grandma ordered them to teach me, train me well and she reminded them that she was watching through the eyes of her security guards who were 'Peul Njenguel.' They were these no-nonsense guys, Fulas from the border between Senegal and Mauritania.

My frequent interactions with them and the elders gave me clues to everything that I wanted to know. They introduced me to many people I could consult for anything as and when I needed. I had always informed them of my school projects' due dates so that they know that their help was needed. They made sure that I get what I wanted from elders' gatherings, etc. I did tell them tales just to get more information about stories I would have otherwise spent hours in the library researching without any luck. As usual, I buy Kola nuts for everything. I am an old soul and I believe that the Kola can do anything for us. A lot is said about it.

We do tend to blame our generation for not documenting events nowadays, and our elders or ancestors did not make things easy for us either. But we cannot blame them. The resources were limited; however, they have always done their best, that is why we are enjoying what we have got today and the help of the griots who spent their time leading from what they have learned and what their elders passed on to them. In the Wolof term, 'guewel' means griots. It comes from the same Wolof word 'gaywal' meaning, seated in circles to learn or to listen to stories. Usually, the storytellers assign someone with a good memory the tasks of taking notes carefully so that they will be able to narrate the same stories with accuracy when they are gone. This is the reason why Kings always had the best of griots in their camps and they never went to war or to the battlefield without them.

Griots do play a significant part in the history of Senegambia and are termed as very noble because they are loyal, and they can die for protecting the kings and people of the kingdom. Griots are known to lead all the battles of the kings they serve.

I had a way of luring everyone into getting me the information I needed so that I could write the stories as they were. I used my homework to cheat my older cousins to give me the best of guidance to document my stories. I had the wisest cousins especially the older ones. They always wanted to help me do my homework. It took them a bit of time to know how mischievous I was. But I could get away because I was the kid sister they did not have. As soon as I uttered project, the storytelling began. I enjoyed every bit of it. I can laugh about it today, but they laughed more when I speak with them calling me all kinds of names under the sun.

Who am I not to allow them to say whatever they want to say to me today? I still find it hilarious that they used to believe every word I said to them. I gave them a tough time looking after me which was not a bother to them. Who would have imagined that I was that much of a troublemaker indeed, but in a subtle way? As a grandchild and great-grandchild to these elders, I could cheat, and get away with it. I am theirs, and they are the people I confidently call my blood and the ones who will always enjoy anything that comes from me no matter what I said or did. These are the same people that taught me everything about oneness apart from my parents.

I see what I see in my parents in them, for they had my best interest at heart and made it their duties to instill the Ubuntu concept that is now in me.

I recall one of my uncles once told me that he wanted to give me something that I could use to start my school projects. That was in case I wished to know what my parents thought that I could not comprehend at an early age. So, they did not trouble themselves and warned everyone around me not to abuse my adolescent brain by giving too much information I could not handle and exposing me to things that would make no sense to me.

As usual, parents always think that it is necessary to wait until we reach a certain age for them to inform us of what they think we need to know. It is not that they do not understand better, of course, they do, but knowledge is power, and it cannot be what it is without wisdom. They did not know that everything made sense to me. I did not stop being inquisitive, and they knew that about me. There was nothing wrong with the stories they had to tell me. It was just about the horror that many stories were termed as. Other than that, the darkest parts were to use of oracles to exterminate whoever that was there hindering their progress.

I loved the horror and discoveries of the dark sides of African Kingdoms and their kings. But the role women played, I mean the unsung heroines, gave me the zeal to keep on pushing to know about their influence. I was more interested in being in the know of their stance and responsibilities. Their work had an impact on everything women do in society today, but nobody talks about these great women that much. All they talk about is that there were sturdy women called 'Lingueres,' kings and princes and the importance of their warrior sons, hunters, griots and so on.

Knowing what women did then when men were busy negotiating and fighting for their kingdoms and rearing children were essential to me. That is what I wanted to have information about before going on and asking about my great grandparents whom I heard used all kinds of oracles to win their wars or battles. The 'Tchieddo' in them is in each one of their breeds. I was young, and I had no clue what feminism was all about. However, girls are naturally inspired by their mothers and grandmothers. In my case, I was very close to my father, but my interest in who my great grandmothers were and what they represented to their communities. I remember teasing my father. That is the kind of relationship I had with him, that he is different from the ones that I had met in Saassaara,

Djilor, Bilori, Gandiaye, Ngoiy whom their people almost worshipped and bowed down to when greeting them. I came home with witty stories that made him laugh. I did get away with a lot of things.

Some of the things I said to him made him laugh so hard, and I usually glanced him shaking his head. I bet he thought that I was too much. I stated that I would never bow down to anyone when I visited Ngoye. It is a village I went to and what I saw there amazed me. I met senior women and men who thought that everything they did for me would mean rekindling their relationship with my great-grandparents. I had to ask them what had that got to do with me and them bowing down to me? I had to run away, and they kept chasing me around. It is one of the big stories I had ever explained to my father. His advice was not to go there anymore because elders should not bow to you. It is not good.

I tried once to curtesy for my great aunt in Saassara, and she quickly held me by the shoulders and said 'Mook waay mook waay Faye Biram Mbenda Waaggaan. Waaggaan Tchillas Wassyla' God forbid she meant. I just said, whatever Tanti. To me, I just wanted to follow on everyone's behaviour, and that was it. Was it because everyone called me 'Juddu Njerri' and I did not belong there? I took offence that they did not accept my greetings. That is how I saw it which was contrary to what they knew. Besides, I did not have a formal induction apart from the time I first went with my mother. The whole Saassara came to see us, brought so much food, even gave us goats, chickens, they offered me two cows (male and female) and offered a lot of blessings to us from the Diouf and Faye clan as they say it. I felt blessed and welcomed into this family that I have always belonged to but had a little knowledge about them. They are hardworking working people that I can shout about to the top of my voice. My great uncle was my banker. He provided everything for me. I felt lucky to have them in my life. They were all very proud to have met me and hearing my mother introduced me to them as Coumba Ndoffene made them love me more. Hmmm! It was a name that I did not like when I was younger, but I started enjoying it because of them. It was an important thing to them especially my great uncle, Oumar Diouf. Nothing beats tradition. You cannot know its magnitude until you share the same room or sit in the same area and hear people talk about it.

My cheeky cousins always laughed and spoke in their Serere accent and Wolof that they have never met any girl named after Maam Bour Sine Coumba Ndoffene. No wonder she behaves like a boy they said to each other. I always added that I had many namesakes which makes me feel unique and I laughed too instead of being laughed at; I laughed with them to show them that it did not bother me. In my cheeky demeanour, I did not find it funny when they kept talking about the same thing. I replied that there is always a first and that they should live with it. I am your 'Bourette' then I cheekily said. I was a cheeky cousin and niece from the Gambia.

Africa is mystic and what I loved about the stories they told me was that everything they said that sounded dangerous was not to me. I audaciously waited until no one was looking, and I went on my adventures and sneaky peekaboo moments. They must have thought that I had something in my small head that prevented me from being scared. It was merely innocence, and my spirituality at an early age helped me a lot. My father said to me that I should not fear anything. Whatever happens to me I should know that it is my Allah's decision and He has the final say in my life. Nobody knows my destiny, but Him alone and that I should believe that. That is how I still am.

When I succeed at something, it is Allah. When I fail at something, it is He who is not ready for me to have what I seek to achieve. It is as simple as that. The way I was with my new families helped me know so much about myself. If I were timid, I would not have had the best of the experience. Timidity does not help in anything. It does not help you achieve anything at all.

As most of you would know, Serere people are known to be very strong, and elders are rigid. I was lucky to have a father who was never going to allow me to be a softy for anybody. He trained me early, and I thank the people who insisted that even though they thought I was too young to attend secondary school in Senegal, he should let me go and he did. I still laugh about the escort from the Gambia to Senegal. My mom, my father, my two uncles to also meet their old friends in Senegal to let them know that I was there so that they can keep an eye on me, which was very nice of them to do. The love you grow up to know is ingrained in you from a very young age. That is all I have ever known, and that is all I have to say. The reason why I feel the need to give out love and share it is because we are told that to love another person is to see the face of God. It does not cost much to love your fellow human beings and to show gratitude to the people around you. It is nothing but following what Allah recommends for us to do as human beings. We must love one another to have a better life.

My uncles, left everything behind to accompany my parents to take me to my new home/country that I had never been. Leaving my siblings behind was the saddest moment for me because I was about to leap into the unknown. They wanted to make sure that they spoke to whoever they knew in Kaolack where I began in Lycee Gaston Berger to look after me. I believed that Allah was always watching over me. I loved every bit of my fact-finding mission shenanigans. Nothing could stop me from going on my exploration. I made it my point of duty.

All the strange stories did not stop me from asking about the rooms they forbade women from entering and the tall trees that children did not walk or go under to play. That included my ancestors who were 'Tchieddo' not believers and non-Muslims. They utilised all kinds of protections to win their wars against Muslim leaders. How the kings fought their battles wetted my appetite, and I wanted to hear more about my great-grandparents, especially Salmon Faye and Bour Sine Coumba Ndoffene who eventually became a hero by facing the administrators of Ndarr to stand as a witness to Khadim Rassoul Cheikh Ahmadou Bamba. I must say that bearing his name gives me boundless joy that his works have gained him a great spot in the Mbacke-Mbacke household. Today, people celebrate him in Diakhao, and a big annual conference is held to celebrate the date when he went to the administrators to stand as a witness to this nobleman whose mission was to teach the Islamic religion to his disciples and nothing more. It is called 'Le Temoignage De Bour Sine.' It is held every year on June 14th in the main house in Diakhao. That is another big story on its own that I always find myself talking to the small screens whenever I hear people give their numerous diluted versions. I would go like, that is not how it happened as if I was there. I was not there, but I sat with elders who knew so much about the stories, and theirs is almost one hundred percent accurate. They even told me how Djakhao came to be for finding the way into the village. The messages get diluted with time because not many people can tell you that they witnessed any of the events.

I was lucky to know one of my great uncles Mame Omar Diouf who lived up to 100 plus. Senior men in the surrounding villages consulted him for stories they wanted to share on television. Somehow, he was the only person I have ever feared because he did not talk too much. His height was too intimidating for me. He was also tall, and every time people looked up to have a word with him, he commanded them to bring their gaze down. He did not like to be looked at which was my weakness. I always looked at him right in the eyes which made him wonder what kind of upbringing I had.

Nobody dared speak loudly in his presence. My mother was his favourite niece because she looked like her great-grandfather Mahecor. Mother and Mame Omar always chatted the evening away, and he still made sure that all the rooms were well kept for her every time she was in the village. That is why I loved him too, but he was not an ordinary man with whom to you can acquaint with easily. I tried to get to know him well, but the fence between us was too high, and I took advantage when my mother was around visiting the family. She came to see me every month to make sure that I had all my needs. She did not pay for my cost of living, but since she had a good business going on at that time, it was necessary for her to bring me stuff like clothes every month including groceries and some cash whenever she was coming.

I looked at Mame Omar from the corner of my eyes, and he often said, I see you looking at me. Do you want to know me Faye Birame? I did not say much. I just laughed. He was kind of strange, but I promised myself that I was not going to bother with this one. My sisters still laugh whenever I tell them about him. I only managed to make him laugh once when he gave me a protection belt and said, you young girls do not like this but have it. It is going to protect you. I told him, MameBoye I am not a wrestler. Why would I wear this? Now, that took him off guard. He called me MameBoye too, because of my namesake. Bless him, he looked after me very well and prayed for me a lot. I always wondered if he was not from Gabou himself and I used to tell people that I often saw him in my dreams.

I am so proud of my heritage. I recently learned about how we are all interconnected from Senegambia to Gabou Kansala where all the Mannehs and Sannehs derived. Mansa Wally Jaxhateh Manneh eventually became Mansa Wally Dione. No matter what, I have always said that we need to write our stories. I will help the younger generation grow up and become knowledgeable of their backgrounds. These tales can be passed onto the next generations to come. They serve as lessons, guidance, etc.

I learned to build something from nothing and how to appreciate trivial things. Most of all, how to allow my fate to manifest itself. I use the 'I am,' and 'I will' analogy to be able to gauge myself amid my philosophies. Being told stories and reminded of the Jezebel Spirit was a gateway for me from inception. Knowing those anecdotes does help one become humble and steadfast. I have always referred my thoughts to those lines whenever I found myself grappling with issues that are concerning to myself and my environment. It has reconnected me to the very essence of trust, what the world can become if you allow yourself to confide in anyone you meet.

It is true that I became fully aware of my surroundings from inception, but that does not mean not making 'faux pas.' This spirit of Jezebel I can honestly vouch that what I know about it is that it is used to find its traits in everything, especially when I try to fathom something out. It was one of the skills I can say that helped me distinguish between the twenty percent of the ninety that you give your all out. The same thing applies to the work of the mind and the heart. The brain works harder than the centre part of our body, but everything well is credited to the core. C'est la vie and the understanding that we do have. I run into all kinds, but most of the time, into good people who loved me for the Almighty's sake and my late parents' sake. I found peace in the many lessons I have learned and from what they teach me. As they always reminded me, Life is about finding peace. To see an order, you must be willing to lose your connection with the people, places, and things that create all the noise in your life. In my head, I needed to keep pushing to know where I belong. With this positive advice, I started concentrating more on the things that matter. In them, I found people with beautiful aura, hardworking, giving, appreciative, grateful, humble to the core. I call them the blessings that coat my soul. Every time I think of them, I want to do better. They had so much to share, and the love they had for me helped me step into the world, I had no clue what it had in store for me.

The modest and significant words of wisdom filled my heart and put my mind to work. I envied the young people living in the village. I did not know the reason then, but now I see it. I just craved to be easy going like them. My initial steps were about getting to know the environment I was in that I loved so much, then the acquaintances, listening and learning along the way.

I heard so many exciting things about the villages, our ancestors and their plight, everything that can make a child feel proud of the people that they call kinsfolks. I also witnessed what happened in some gatherings called 'Pentcha' in Wolof or 'Baantabaa' in Mandinka. I equally heard of so many sad events, for example, incidents that occurred to people very dear to my parents and the communities. Elders do refer to those occasions when they give the advice to warn their offspring but to instil in them the best they can.

For anything to come out correctly, we must provide the challenges with the assessment they need, and if we are lucky, we can fix our physical problems with our spiritual solutions. That is if we are fortunate. Life is about ten percent of what you deal with every day and ten percent of how you deal with things that life throws at you. I have always said that with all the condition that I have that sometimes act up like they are a predicament, I think of the rest of what is excellent for me to give me a push. My wellness and my determination help me deal with my limitations. The latter is abstract to me. That is what I use my mind for; to block out unpleasant happenings that can drive me crazy. We are all in this world on a mission. We must accept our destiny by understanding that we are not in control of anything but have something in common which is putting God first. We must continue to seek God and put Him first.

I set my life the way I wanted it and broke into a barrier to doing what people thought I could never do. I push forward to compete with myself to reach the finishing line. That has always been my goal and drive. I set my boundary without asking permission from anybody but from my Creator. Life is a test I have always said to myself, and I embrace all challenges.

Sometimes, events that happen to you can discourage you, but you must be strong to pull through. I grew up learning about acceptance and thanking the Lord of humanity for everything that happened to me; good and evil. Because I have leaned towards learning, encouraging words and the wisdom of our elders and even young people that I emulate. They are my muse for everything happens for a reason. I feel great having that level of patience, and I learn a great deal through the constant rerouting of my life that I often do and that makes me feel safer than ever.

This ampule called life, as they say, is a nearby reservoir or even a container in which you must create so many spaces to start compartmentalising different things in it. In my head, I believe in creating a pigeon hole where I have precious information in their respective holes to consult. Things you need to tackle daily and in doing so, have orderly in mind. Whatever they are, it is crucial to avoid allowing sorrow, anger, sadness, and futility to overshadow everything right that is supposed to be occupying the most massive space. Never replace the joy, peace, confidence, and creativity with pain, and worry. There should not be any room for worry.

I enjoyed the experience I was associating with my relatives, with the new friends that I adopted in the villages and towns I visited. Though we have different upbringing, we share the same lineage, and that mattered a lot to me. I felt good meeting new people who regarded me as one of theirs. Besides, most of them were my cousins, younger and older uncles and aunties, etc.

I have always said that because I was the newest, making me the family's sweetheart was natural because they were ever so loving. Getting used to them was very easy. I did not struggle to fit in at all due to their nature and their love for humanity. The kind of love they showered me made it easy for me to feel that I belonged to them and I freely asked questions. No wonder they called me their own. I was glad no one considered me a stranger. I quickly got used to their environment and never felt like a newcomer, but the ghost 'Juddu Njerri' meaning the foreign-born that I never was. They meant what they said but used their wisdom to make it sound like a joke. I accepted it because I did not want to upset anyone. They were all I had, and I felt good being around them especially being away from Mother and Father and my siblings. People have diverse ways of acquainting with others. What baffled me most was the secret they always kept. But, I wanted to know. It did not disturb me not to understand. I was just eager to be in the know.

My beautiful mother was still thrilled to see me follow my young aunties in their kitchens in the evenings when preparing/cooking the most delicious foods (Baasseh akk Tcherreh) Couscous and peanut butter sauce that I loved so much. Knowing how I am with everyone, worrying was not what I often did. Nothing is a bother to me, especially when I am around kind folks like my mother's people. Nothing annoys me that much if you reciprocate the respect I have for you and particularly when you mean well.

Mother loved the way I was with everyone; they were her family members and mine too because we share the same bloodline. I got used to their ideas and was also familiar with their names and the significance of each one of them as they are always keen to explain what their names meant. I found out that becoming friends with people who aren't my age and hanging out with people whose usual first languages aren't the same as mine did encourage me to be open-minded. It allowed me to grow up fast. Their first word was automatically mine, but I did not speak it, and I do know why. It is because both mother and father did not talk Serere to us.

Meeting new people from divergent backgrounds allows you to see beyond what you know. I grew up exposed to learning. Educating myself was the only choice that I had, and I am glad that I embraced learning very well. I discovered very fast in looking at everything through the same lenses with others, even though at times, people think that I live in a bubble. I did not see it that way and still do not see it like that. I focus more on what interests me to dissuade myself from eyeing what others have their interests focused. I go with all the traditional names they call me, the names of the heroes I learned to understand and the heroines I lived to emulate and see as my role models.

For anyone who is familiar with African traditions, names played a considerable part in a child's life. Even today, you hear parents name their children after people they believe are worth naming their offspring after. It is unlike naming your child after a celebrity/Star you follow or a football Star who plays well and has gotten himself many snazzy awards. In those days, things were different. There is so much of history to tell about the rich Serere culture and where I belong. Their way of life has moulded every one of their children. Sereres are very humble people, but very proud of their traditions and cultures. Our elders have always referred to the customs to give their daughters' hands in marriage. I take pride in the fact that I love my people and I give myself targets to learn, to know, spread the messages and stories that can fortify the younger generation for I already love storytelling.

These people from whom I have learned a lot of things of valour remain in my heart. How everything worthy that I see inspires me is a question I always ask myself. The answer is that I know positivity in everything, even when the negativity tries to overshadow the possibility of enjoying good things as little as they are. I believe that sadness does not last long. I feel lucky to be one of those people that have overcome depression. It is the strength that I discovered very young. What I always have in my mind is that everything has got a lifespan and that any situation will come to pass. Good or bad, nothing lasts forever. Oh, how much I think in that mode.

I allow little negativity to overshadow my life considering what I used to see in the villages and remembering how people smiled under the sun and trying circumstances. These things taught me a lot. They taught me how to save my tears, contain my pain/sorrows and how to learn to accept my fate. When people refer to how fast I had to grow up, I want them to know that my interest lies in walking on the same path as them. I wish them the possibilities to meet the same kind of people I met along the way before now. I have always embraced goodness since I was a little girl, and I could differentiate tolerance and kindness, patience and laziness, eagerness and greed. That is how I got inspired to share the stories that I know choosing from my beliefs as a woman.

Nobody should wait for anything to happen for them to be motivated. Everyone should know that they are influential, and that motivation comes from the heart. Every good deed, every good thought is motivational. Compared to how we are today, building a future begins when you realise that you must come out of your comfort zone and disregard your excuses, do yourself a favour and push yourself harder. There remain the lines that I often hear the little voice in my head tells me. Working towards the attainment of the goal should be something everyone uses to attain the vision. There are times in life when we think that we are going through circles without a hint about anything. When you are faithful in a routine and, something is happening, all you see is whatever gives tranquility. You develop, you are ready, and you are to witness rarity. Yearn for progress even when you do not see it coming.

My grandmother once said to me that I must live to remember that no matter what, I should stay faithful in the routine. Nothing should be considered mundane. There is no such thing, and I still live with that notion that nothing is futile unless you make it seem so. I remember that because she did so much work for me, to help me grow by inculcating all that she thought was crucial in my upbringing. She had me for nine months every year, and failing was her fear. As Victor Hugo had said, "Adversity makes men - Conspiracy makes monsters." She wanted to groom a virtuous woman. If you're going to ask me if she has been successful in doing that, I would answer yes for I AM what my mother lived for she once said to me. That gave me hope because my mother was like her too. Blessed are those that learn from the best or try to imagine themselves as one of the best. When you raise children, you want to make sure that you tell them how good they are and that you do daily. That's how you get the best out of them because they will always be ashamed to go wrong.

Having read so much about history taught me enough to

comprehend how society worked then and how it does today. There exists a significant nuance, but that is how we can gauge everything today and make ourselves open to learning just for the sake of what we are about to take out of life. That is how the world is. We must not accept any excuses. The bolted chains should be released.

In the remote villages in Africa, as much as we would like to think that people know little, I found myself relying a lot on my relatives whenever I wished to embark on a fact-finding mission. Hats off to the elders. Nothing escapes them. There are few that I met thirty years ago who are still in decent shape and living well as they say. They are in their late nineties. I remember talking to one of them, and I expressed how envious I was. He asked why, and my response was 'How I wanted my late father to be here with us guiding me through every step. Papa too would have been ninety-two if he was still alive. Sadly, he left us when he was about sixty-three years old. His demise was shocking.

I enjoyed sitting with them even though the girls my age were always indoors or in the kitchen helping their mothers. I replace my old habits for the better, although I can never allow myself to regret having those practices in the first place because they have made me what I am and ushering me towards what I am about to be. The activation energy comes from the love I have for humanity, and I am contributing in my little way. I embrace discipline and take it as a self-training. The system in my head that helps me shape up my entire life. Doing a lot more does not mean getting a lot more done. My movement does not mean progress, but I am grateful for being able to think that I am progressing step by step while claiming immensity and trying to make today count. It is vital to learn to make a difference and not just to live. I follow what energises me to remain unique and I live each day with the hope that my contribution towards becoming better remains the goal never forgetting that the 'I AM' analogy used is concrete and real. If you do not care for yourself and live by your rules, somebody will impose a law on how to live on you.

I usually refer to the elders' words of wisdom to get up, shake up and go. Whenever I am on a quest for something, doing my research, especially on historical events, I look no further. All I do is consult the Papas (our elders) who freely give me the information that I need. I never get stuck because they are there to guide and share with me all that they have. They share willingly. There is so much that needs sharing, and we must keep asking.

I encourage more write-ups to tell Africa's stories. Most stories I learned transpired during the 'Ngonals' or Soiree. Ngonal is one of the best moments after sunset or after dinner. People usually gather in numbers, and when it is the weekend, the children join in as well. The best time to listen to funny jokes, folktales that younger ones enjoy a lot. Today, I see that there are many television programs created to do the same. It is informative, and if you are an avid follower, you will learn a great deal.

People organise it in turns. If it is your turn, you are responsible for cooking, providing a variety of savoury and sweet snacks and drinks to entertain visitors, next door neighbours or even people like me who enjoyed it so much. I never wanted to miss a single weekend since I did not go out clubbing. I was too young then, going out after dark for prohibited. That is why I enjoyed going to Saassaara or Bilori and Gandiaye and even Fatick in the end. They provided drinks such as Attaaya (Chinese green tea), lait (hot milk), for snacks they had; Guerrteh baxhal or Guerrteh saaf (boiled fresh nuts or roasted nuts) Pangkett (doughnuts), Fataayas (pies).

I did not rely on books alone to know about my ancestors and the life of women in remote villages. These moments shared with peers around the evening circles, sitting around the fire covered in blankets, eating snacks and sharing jokes were remarkable moments. I was able to learn and have fun at the same time. I was never one to just listen and laugh at jokes. I made sure I asked questions that sparked great discussions through the nights with my notepad and pen in hand.

I usually travelled with a lot of goodies to share with my cousins and everyone present. If I relied only on books to learn about what I know today, the chances are that I will still be living in the dark. I chose to write this story using very notable names to share with the rest of the world. It is my way of inviting people into a new space that I have created to tell the many stories that I have written and how to share them. The cultural and traditional aspect including the usage of the Wolof language I believe will wet everyone's appetite. It is equally encouraging. A mixture of the dialect is the drive to motivate. I found this hopeful, especially with people that do not speak the Wolof language. What we do have in our society today is, young people who do not speak their parents' native language because they are born in the West; Europe, Australia, USA, or even in areas where people have another vehicular or vernacular language they use to run their businesses.

I know that to understand my roots, I had to show my willingness and belief in learning, wanting to belong and showing utmost humility for that is key to our elders' hearts. It helps to learn the culture and traditions and link them to the languages and stories. We have more powerful influence in the world and traditions dictates every aspect of our life. When you hope, you must seek help, and through breaking yourself away from negativity, you will push to hit the limit and beyond the adaptation response.

There are beautiful names in the story, chosen because they deem fit. It is due to the geographical situation and the place where events took place. I visited often and what I am proud of is the fact that recollecting my life then, the girls I befriended in the village, the elders I managed to have on my side who loved me dearly and my understanding of how young men think. So, when it comes to chauvinism, I saw it all. If you ask my young cousins who are big men now, they will tell you she was born ready as a feminist because she learned about feminism from her roots, the people who made kings, princes and helped hold the fort when men went in the battlefields. I do not believe that feminism is about burning bras. You burn bras to make a case. Feminism is about loving yourself as a woman and fighting with everything you have got in your power to voice out your opinion as a woman. That is all that it is.

CHAPTER TWO
Initiation

The names used in the story are ones you hear in Africa, especially in the chosen regions and villages in and around Saassaara, located in Sine. My late mother, the beautiful, regal Linguere Gnilane Diouf, daughter of Singg Mahecor Diouf is a native of Diakhao situated in Sine with strong ties in Saassaara, Bilori, Gandiaye and the rest. They are very historical places that most people know. I love the history that I know about the area and the brave men that come out of Sine.

The traditional and cultural happenings left me in awe. Everything I learned filled my heart with joy, for it was new to me in the beginning. But I embraced it well and gelled with everyone and quickly made the environment my own. I became a regular visitor because of the way I was always welcomed and entertained. It was something I thought was not going to last for long, but to my surprise, no one had ever thought of treating me differently even in the absence of my late mother. People were always as jolly as they were during our first visit. That was not just encouraging. It was unique. When you grow up around people like that, you emulate them, and you would want to be just like them. I still sing praises about them, and I refer to the places, the people of all the villages and the environment as my School of Life. I do not need to look further for inspiration. I look up to the women and even the girls in the village and their ways of living, bearing all burdens and still laugh. They have a prosperous life even better than many in the cities. The only difference is the location which is normal.

The people of Saassaara make a habit of initiating new family members into the clan, and as a Guelawaar which is my maternal clan, I automatically became, and they were proud to have me, and on top of that, I loved it there which was my winning point. The initiation is simple; it is like a getting to know you; an icebreaker is presented and puts the fence down for you to get in. No one can leave the wall up when you need to get in. If you do not jump over, they will make you jump by force. There is a way they say it in Serere. They want you to know that you have a say in the environment which demonstrates your position in the family to make you feel proud. Most times they put a test for you to answer every question to see if you know your ancestors and the vital members of your clan. I cannot say that I passed all the tests, but my charm made everyone be on my side, and we laughed throughout the day into the evening. Of course, my beautiful mother was there to help me answer most of the questions. As she used to say to me, always be generous with your words and the little you have. It will help win their hearts. It does not mean that you must buy friendship, but to show people how to do things. When you give, people will always remember you as the giver. But you must stop at what you can offer because you are giving for the sake of the Almighty as recommended. I can never forget my initiation day when everyone made their way to the main compound. Those that came first heard of my mother's arrival and called one another. It was an exciting moment. I felt the love they had for my mother. The reason why I have never left them. I still communicate with them, and I have always wanted to know how I can keep doing what she used to do for them, with them and even more. They had a perfect relationship. It was always a give and take. My mother did not just make things to give to them. I have never seen anything like that. Giving was their thing and that I grew up to know and I am learning to be just like them. I had always told my classmates that when I needed money and I did not need all the questions about what it is for, I run to my great uncle that we all called Mameboye. He just asked how much you need and there you are with the amount of money that you needed. All he wanted to know was when you needed it. If I did not visit with my mother, I would not have known their generosity especially my chosen and favourite Mameboye. I had two of them; Mame Ousmane Diouf and Mame Oumar Diouf.

At first, I did not understand why they had to come in numbers just for my mother, the humble and kind lady. She later explained to me that her people live on celebrating their own. It is simply that. Honouring each other is essential. In the Saassaara, everyone was happy to meet me because none of them ever travelled to see us except a few of my great-uncles and great-aunts. They are too many. It is a huge family, and sometimes I forget names. So, I called everyone MameBoye; men and women, even some of my older aunties. They had to stop me from calling them Mameboye by explaining what they were to me. What I had said was that I guessed it was not yet their turn to meet any of my siblings; Momo, Fatoumata, Khadijatou and Mariatou. I did not have to mention the rest of my siblings who are not with us anymore; Ndey, Papa Demba, Tessanou and Coura.

It is natural to have a massive family if you come from such families. Most women have many children that is why they ask us why when we settle with one or two kids.

There are so many cities, towns and villages to visit that one cannot just do it in one trip and even a dozen of trips. Our clan is enormous, and many of us do not know each other. That is what we are blessed with as my grandmother used to put it. It is no one's fault that we are a huge family and that we know little about each other. But when time permits us to meet and mingle, acquaint, we do our initiations happily. That is the order, and it is an enjoyable one.

Mother's people in Saassaara never met any of her children before me, at least in that village and they were delighted with their 'Juddu Njerri' as they fondly called us being born outside the territory where most members of the clan reside.

She explained to them that I was the first one to visit because she took me to one of the big cities for my secondary education which was Kaolack/Senegal. They were all surprised because I was too young to start secondary school at nine. But I was tall enough, and that helped, and I had a mouth on me. So, I was safe. I was able to tag along because the school was off. Going to school in Senegal made it possible for me to know most of my relatives. She needed to visit them quite often. I went on my own, occasionally because I felt so welcomed. Those occasional visits became frequent and the dozens of times because of the love I have for not just my mother's family up there in Saassaara, but for humanity. Being around the right people is a blessing, and it is healthy for a young person. I was in my developing years, and all I needed is reassurance and being around people who treasure my life. They gave me all that that money cannot buy. Part of what moulded me, as my late father had always emphasised upon, is the fact that I had new people in my life. People filled with wisdom and knowledge. If you know people of our tribe, you will also know how they do not spare you the truth. They can show love and care, but when it comes to telling you the truth, they will do without a second thought. I enjoy meeting new people, especially people who can teach me a lot. They showed me nothing, but love and the importance of my presence were so evident that I always felt great to be around them. As young as I was, they gave me the respect I did not feel was necessary and they addressed me like I was an adult. Often, they tell me stories about my great grandfathers from both my parents' families. That is how much they knew. Even the young women who motivated me to think of the struggle of young women in that region knew so far. But they do not have the ability,

I enjoy meeting new people, especially people who can teach me a lot. They showed me nothing, but love and the importance of my presence were so evident that I always felt great to be around them. As young as I was, they gave me the respect I did not feel was necessary and they addressed me like I was an adult. Often, they tell me stories about my great grandfathers from both my parents' families. That is how much they knew. Even the young women who motivated me to think of the struggle of young women in that region knew so far. But they do not have the ability, access, and resources in place to take the stories beyond the 'Ngonal.' They are very knowledgeable about everything concerning their environment. I was amazed at their level of wisdom and thoughtfulness.

What I saw every time I visited was envy in a very positive way. They have always wanted to have the liberty and the freedom to roam. I was able to travel back and forth, and they could not. They still expressed their envy to me, and I found that overwhelming. I was young, and I could travel on my own to visit them and got picked up whenever I needed to go back to the city where my school was.

I saw them as my peers, and they should be allowed to be free. I used to laugh when I got asked how my father could let me be that free. To their surprise, I told them I was not free before I left to come to Senegal. I had to be honest. I was not born free and fled the nest. The only choice they had was to let me, allow me to grow up and trust the Almighty, whose job is to cover us with the hand of the Holy Ghost. I became very prayerful, and I believe that spirit has stuck with me. I thank my Creator for that. It was an opportunity for me to be myself, to be strong, to be independent, to be confident in my skin, to grow and to develop into a sensible woman. From then on, I started to give credit to my father that I used to call traditional, primitive and too cultured because he did not give me the chance to grow up when I was living with him and mom. I called all those names whenever he denied me permission to go out to hang out with my friends as far as the 'Boppi Kogn', the junction where we loved to meet every afternoon. Oh yes, I remember that very well. It was nothing extraordinary. We usually hang out there to watch people pass by and all. I started appreciating him a lot more because he could have acted differently. Papa almost denied me the opportunity to go to Senegal at the age of nine because I was too young. That could have had me stay stayed behind for two more years for nothing. Thanks to Monsieur Gaye, Doyen Mbaye Ababakarr Gaye who had my best interest at heart. These two men were good friends. They called each other 'Tom' for having the same name, Abubakar. He told my father that he should not underestimate me. I was super alert, and I laughed when people remind me of the way I used to be. My big brother calls me 'Aunty for All' whatever that means. Things went alright as he wished. He trusted me and encouraged Papa to let me go. Papa had to wait until the last minute though to agree to do the necessary paperwork so that I could finally go and the rest is history.

My siblings still remind me of my free-spirited self. Something Papa instilled in me. The thing is that they could not be, and they were not free to choose. I always thought about them because they were vibrant, brilliant young and beautiful women who did not have the opportunity to be selective or have their plans and vision. The kind of idea that I could have even though I was too young. What they lived for being the dream of having someone come and visit and pop the question, ask for their hand in marriage, and they will then leave to go to the city for good. It is a different world, but things have now changed. However, this story is written to address issues that women still grapple with, which is the lack of freedom. The question here is not only about time. It is about morals, values, traditions, culture and all the possibilities to preserve a family name.

Sassara and Gandiaye where many of my mother's family members live in a place where I can honestly say that I found young women, I still talk about due to their level of obedience, their beliefs in tradition and culture, kindness, magnificence, grace, and honour. My aunty Baassine always asks for permission to go to the market which I find very old fashioned. She thinks that I am a 'Saassouman' as she fondly called me, and I called her the same. She feels that I am too free and that I was lucky to be born outside the parameters of Saassaara. It is nice to remember her and her ways that I do not mind seeing her children follow.

I felt like I was one of cousins and aunts the moment my mom introduced us. I remembered the entire neighbourhood passing by in the evening to meet me and introduced themselves to me. Some of my grandmother's friends called me their 'Woujja' co-spouse because, in our culture, your granddaughter is your co-spouse. It is banter that people love having. I believe that it is because every grandparent yearns to have grandchildren and they look after them like diamonds. The bond between granddaughters and grandfathers is always captivating. Some of them came to visit my mother accompanied by their children my age then. I felt respected. I reciprocated that importance and respect they accorded me, and I still do talk about them and my numerous visits.

The people in the town, the villages knew me so well because I enjoyed visiting. I took goods over now and then. Much was given to me, and the opportunities were many. Learning about the culture and the tradition cannot be matched. I learned to embrace the rich culture with gratitude. It is beyond imaginable. I still gush about the love they show me and even hearing my voice over the phone. Amongst the many areas, they have taught me were grace, fulfilment, recognition, and acceptance of fate and conviction. I appreciate those that give without taking. Most of the things I had learned when I visited my relatives in the village are stories that we can narrate in all forms. The data gathered can last us a lifetime of sharing stories, making documentaries, you name it. As my great uncle, Omar said, you will not find these levels of storytelling in libraries or museums. You must be part of this clan to know. He jokingly told me once that I should be buying them a lot of Kola nuts to have them seated down in a circle to tell me more stories. For those who do not the meaningful thing about Kola nut should be thrilled to learn its powerful meaning that symbolises covenant, unity, love, and peace. People share it in christenings, weddings and other sacred events. I asked him why he didn't ask for money. He replied and said, the money is used to buy the kola nuts, therefore, buying them and bringing them spares us time. We use our time in the field. They make a lot of money in their areas, cultivating their yearly food. They amazed me. I used to wonder why they had so many workers. That too, I asked why they had many people working for them coming from different towns and villages.

Naturally, they do not tell you everything, but Mam Oumar replied again and said to me. "When you finally come to reside here, I will find you a large allotment and many workers to work for you. But, you will have to pay them well so that they can feed their families." He was something else; a man of high stature; smart, God fearing and very spiritual. He was a 'Toubbenn' a converted from the 'Tchieddo' that he was, Mame became very religious amongst the seniors consulted all around Senegal because he knew his history well. I never had a second thought about trusting him with my affairs. However, I was a little watchful or mindful of his characteristics. He spoke little and never wasted time on anything futile. I noticed something very early on. When the women gathered and talked loudly, they stopped and dispersed the moment he walked into the compound. I usually go around to give them false alarm that Mam Oumar was coming. They took off without wasting any second. It amazed me how much they feared him.

My cousins used to be wonder how I got to have this old man too fond of me. I often told them how he should not be fond of his favourite niece's daughter. He never allowed the girls to sit where he rested. But I guess I was the darling great niece, his lookalike. My friendship with him lasts for a very long time. He was my paternal grandfather Waaggaan Wassyla Faye and Singg Mahecor Diouf that I did not know. Being my mother's uncle gave him that elevated position in our life. He was a gentleman and a nobleman whom everyone consulted. I believed that he had to be the way he was to keep his graciousness intact.

I often told him what I wanted to be when I grow up and we prayed about doing better than that. As you know, young people dream of all sorts, and I used to tell him that I wanted to become an Air Hostess or a Model. He will add and own a big farm to serve every family. That was his wish. Today, looking at what I am doing mainly on the humanitarian side, I see myself doing all that he wished for me. My interest lies in this work that I do, the stories I want to keep writing that I make my priority due to my love to see success for women and excellence for all. Before embarking on the storytelling journey, I consulted my knowledge pad about the great ancestors and what they have done to make their mark in society. I will step in to give Mossaan a proper initiation. I will take the opportunity to present her in the best way I can.

Being part of the story makes you understand the way you live your life, and how vital it is to have 'Sabr' (patience). This sequel is not a collection of fables, but a book of life, a school of life and it can take you back to your childhood as it has done for me.

I wanted to showcase a contrast and make the comparison myself. Wherever or whenever you think you are suffering, others are rejoicing. I learned from a very early age that we cannot have it all and that when we lose something, it is because bigger and better things are coming. This story has given me the courage to talk a little bit about me, to embark on these exciting things that everyone is anticipating.

My experience once again has helped me see the world beyond the sphere that I know is already there and tap into my inner spirituality to guide me through and into understanding everything that surrounds me.

My mother, whom I like to use the present tense when talking about her is a lady I emulate. She is my reference to everything I do or think of doing. Although she is no more, I hear her voice in everything that I do. My father being my silhouette is never far away. My siblings think that I am weird when I tell them I will consult Papa, and I sincerely do ask him when I am seriously in need of someone to talk to, and sometimes I laugh at myself when I do. Doing weird things like that is better than talking to every Tom, Dick and Harry. I always want to know where he is. It is all in the head. I also believe that when you see nothing lesser than right, it does not matter where the place you learned the best is, you will always run back to that spot to seek for inspiration or help.

My late mother is a lady I emulate, and I repeat that I loved everything about her, the people in her life, what she meant to them and represented in our family. She was a true Linguere, a true-blue Blood coming from a family of Kings and Royals that she did not even enjoy because kingdoms in Senegal were no more by the time she was born, but the griots praise them using those words linked to their surnames and parents' works. They are recognised by their fathers' or mothers' names or surnames. They normally asked who our mothers are, and then that is followed by who is your mother's mother and that mother's mother etc. I did not know why they had to ask all of that, but I eventually gathered that it is how they know who you are and that is how our Sereres griots do it to tell you your 'Chossaani Maam' about your ancestors' roots.

You must be born with the best to know better and sprinkle the goodness all around you. All that is left now is the surnames and birthplaces, the links, the ties, the relatives with a myriad of perks to indulge in for being from the noble clans. There are also the perks being from that genealogical tree of Sine-Sine, now the histories of all Guelewaar.

There is only one thing I love to boast about which is the grace topped with the etiquettes of these women. They have it all, but they do not see it because they know the best in what they do not have, which is ironic. They are regal and polished. These women teach their sons and daughters how to treat their fellow human beings, and that is enough to build a kingdom. If you ask me who is the real feminist, I will tell you these women are, and it is what we were born to witness, to know and to grace their presence is utter luck that we cannot find anywhere.

I had always admired how they spoke so highly of Mama Diouf, my mother when she was alive. She meant a lot to everyone. As young as she was when she got married to my late father, they found themselves raising my uncles, Djouma, Njook, Djogoy, Sedar. They were all my mother's brothers, whom we regarded as brothers because Papa had them as his. She was only seventeen when her mother passed away. Supported by her aunt even though she was already married, she considered her as her very own mother. In her family, every daughter must have several mothers for security reason. In fact, the matriarch of the family has a role to look after everyone. Her mother's sister was the one who represented her in everything. That is my Nana Aminatta Diouf, the politician whom I lived with when I was going to school in Senegal. She made me one of her own and never wanted to let me go. She was almost obsessed with me and knowing me; I complained a lot about that because she wanted me all to herself. Everybody laughed about the way she monitored my every step, but I did not complain to her face. I did to others thought which she knew about and gave me a good telling off. It is nice to have a family like that. Mom is my unspoken Heroine. Diouf Gnokho Baye, Linguere of Sine, I lauded you yesterday. I will commend you today and will always do. Your story inspires me though it cannot be this time since there is a lot to tell about you the beautiful daughter of Diakhao, Sine. In this book, I have you in my thoughts, and I know your blessings are sent down as always. Many people I consulted think that Mossaan is me. I shake my head and tell them if you feel that you know me and that I am Mossaan, you should try and see a story about my late mother. She was more than what Mossaan's story tells us. That is the main reason why I begin the story with a mini-memoir about one portion of my life. Enface pronounced (ang-fangs) which is a French word for childhood. It is also one of the reasons why I use this book to be one that educates, inspires and motivates. Educative, Inspirational, Motivational are the three combination words that are guiding the narrative.

I love storytelling, and this is if you like to put it, an infusion of non-fiction mixed with the fiction that I deliberately wanted to introduce as my way of stepping into this writing world. My empathy lies with the many young women I often saw in the villages looking at me as the black little European lookalike or even better the 'Juddu Njerri' as elders called me. I was this savvy little girl who always visited with a lot of nice to have goodies they wished they had. For me, those goodies were nothing compared to how they treated me, and I was not a little black European as I emphasised. The only difference between us was that I was born in Bakau and they were born in Saassaara, Bilori or even Djilor. Other than that, there was nothing different about our backgrounds.

They did not know that the only time I travelled abroad was when we had intercontinental events. But to them, they yearned for the things I took for granted. Things like living in the city alone were big. I can recall having my young aunties coming home to the town in The Gambia to live with us. That happened very often. Every time Mama went to her village, she will return home with one or two young people given to her. She never said no. I used to look at her, and I saw only blessings in her eyes for being trusted to look after these young people to stay with us for a while. She never refused to bring them home with her. What a brave woman she was.

The part I did not enjoy was the way she looked after them more than her own as we used to say. I was never jealous, but one of us was, and I do not want to mention her name. But, now I understand her. They were her responsibility. She had to be the one to care more and to protect them until they return home to their parents. Bravo Mama!!!

Without a mention of what inspired me would be a betrayal to my conscience. I wrote the film with the thought of what I saw in my parents' native towns and villages. Kudos to those young women who have been my source of inspiration. I will sing their praises year in, year out. They are the brave sisters; I do not talk about often. But, my love for writing and the ability to jot down some lines will allow me to describe or tell stories that I loved about my people. They are the best. The excellent quality in them is still the virtues their children; sons and daughters, nieces and nephews like to outdo. They were the real sons and daughters of the noble warriors, kings, and queens of Sine. Their stories get told in the fields, at sea, in the meadows and even in the museums and local gatherings. Should we adopt their ways? Can we reach their level? Should we keep dreaming? Yes, there is nothing wrong with doing just that. What we need is to understand that though we cannot reach their level, we owe it to ourselves to live up to their standard in unifying the forces to become one, or to try to be how they were to make our environment a better place.

To all the women of the world, inspired by our mothers and every good woman worth matching, there is a Mossaan which depicts the concoction of beauty, a sophisticated experience, and grace in each one of us that we must investigate. I know, one can read this story and gush about how similar she is someone you know who is in you. That is what happened to many of my friends I have asked to look at the storyline. We all need outstanding virtues respectively, and this is a constant wish for every woman. Mossaan portrays beauty and elegance coated around anything that calls for grace. You can take us out of Mossaan, but you cannot take away her aura from us. There is a Mossaan in each one of us, in every woman. I give props to this concoction of the fiction - mix, my way of introducing my stories/ write-ups with an abstract spiral. The praising should begin with us because that is how we can encourage you to have a go at discovering whatever tickles your fancy. I know that personally, I read books that give me some inspiration. I buy magazines to get inspiration in the styling department, food to cook and many other things. But, reading real-life stories have also played a huge part in everything I do. I get to learn to write my own even if it is not this one. Stories help you carve your path. They also help you pave ways for your progress leading to success.

I have learned that I cannot satisfy everyone. I cannot be on the same page with everyone, nor make everyone laugh, enjoy what I contribute in this world of storytelling and literature, but I am chuffed to bits with my ability to devote my time and effort to share the journey I have grown into my adult life. It might not be much to others, but to me, it is a mega leap that folded hands and laziness will never give me. Writers do not just write for the sake of writing. They think about what they write, and my experience has shown and taught me that, I could not have written anything about these stories had I not experienced anything similar. I write it with passion and add what could have, what should have and what would have been. Call me meticulous for I have been, and I smiled at each stage because I had a delightful moment with the people I call family. I had also to mention some crucial moments about my childhood. I must say the beautiful people and everything else about life. You cannot do anything without motives, inspirations. This book happens to give me the opportunity to highlight a little about my memoirs, young female adults, ambitions, vision, opportunities, learning, progress, stature and splendour, achievement and every facet of triumph and failure. Let's remember this following adage if you are versed in Wolof. 'Doyyaadi mi ngui kommaasseh chi kiiy wakh ni gnyeppa bonn bemm dess momm.' The person you call crazy might saner than you that is why you never call someone mad leaving yourself out. Saying that the rest of the world is insane except you is an absurdity.

I am one with the highest walls and indeed possess the most profound love of writing, listening, understanding and educating. I gain more in return for your input is anticipated. We learn as we grow. I do not take this reassurance lightly. The insertion of adages from Wolof gives the story the traditional and cultural edge you look forward to from the onset and hearing this favourite name as a title. Mossaan means beauty, but beauty is not only about how you see things on the outside or the beautiful things you say or would like people to see. Beauty is something that is innate. Beauty is all about purity, and even morality does get stained at some point. What makes it stain is the influence.

CHAPTER THREE
Respire

As the impossible broken-down states, I am possible, and it is about planning. In describing the woman can be comfortable, but, giving her all the attributes, the true 'raison d'etre,' the definite and laudable meanings can be a daunting task. We know why. Because there is always going to be some, who would oppose the majority. The fact of the matter is that it is possible for the woman to be everything she wants to be. It is what it is.

The power of a woman is irrefutable. Many of our male counterparts have preferred referring to women as the 'Daughters of Eve, which is not a sad thing at all. Though, to the powerful women in the world, rich or poor, the best description they give themselves is the following; Holders of Forts, Homemakers, Advisors, Community Leaders, Mothers of humanity, Sisters, and Breakers of barriers. It can never be too much of a hassle to define women. What women are, is sacred. It is a gift from above. Even time cannot change that. The road to life is straight and narrow, that is what they say, and discipline helps us reach our goal. But to say any negative word to describe a woman is something that even people that try so hard to win, accede to the opposite and they eventually revert it. That is how powerful women are. Women had more power before than now especially African women.

'Kann moiy Djigguenn'? - As our elders describe women in our society, the African society then regards women as the fort holders, child bearer, soldiers, homemakers and decision makers. In the process, the scenario changed, and hell started to break loose. It was not the women's doing. It is a society with everyone's contribution to what makes it become what it is today. Aha! They say. 'Yaaw Djigguenn, Yaaddi Kii gnepp wakh ni ammuut dolleh, teh gni amm dolleh Yepp Munn Nga Lenna yengal" "Yaa amm nyamm tay Barri dolleh."

Who is the WOMAN? "You are the one everyone says is powerless, but still you have the strength and ability to shake anyone with power."

People want their lives to make sense. They want to sit back like cosmic detectives and examine what is happening to them so far, identifying the critical turning points that shaped them and retroactively imbuing these moments with a mystical aura like the heavenly forces of the universe. Don't take a right person for granted and do not miss out on the right things that people around you have to offer you daily. Realize that there are always possibilities that can make you yield excellent outcomes.

What an excellent person offers you daily; man or woman, gives you the opportunity to stand out amongst your peers and when you fail you can rise and come out stronger. If a woman gives you too much care, attention and value you, respect that and reciprocate that respect. Just consider yourself lucky for having all that time and energy given to you. Women have limited time. The same way people say that a woman's chance to flourish is short-lived, especially when her responsibilities are so big needless to mention all the different chores and issues she has on her plate to deal with daily.

Consider yourself lucky that she loves you and that she does not want anyone else to take her place in your life. If a woman says sorry to you even though it was not her fault, do not think that she fears to lose you, but she considers her relationship worth another chance, and she does not want anyone to have your heart. It is vice versa.

Amongst the many women whose imperishable records the Holy books have, there are a few who are conspicuous, too visible for their pure and commendable characters. There are examples of womanhood at its best, and like nothing any failure, they have had. It would seem as if theirs was the "white flower of a blameless life." The women of this 'Duniya' meaning the world will and shall never compare themselves with men. Let us recall, ponder a little bit. It is certain that although time lets us overlook so much, togetherness and all it encompasses such as the procedural, respiring is what women did together. Women, everywhere they met, sang, and danced along, felt cheerful together, cried together at every sound of the sphere. It is all about their emotions and how to conquer the negative energy around them. Women sang songs of creations. It is natural for the woman to believe that it is her job to be responsible and to allow everybody to perch on her back. It has always been called the maternal instinct. Sometimes it is on display without realising it.

Women danced to the ethics of nature when the rain falls when the cattle graze in the meadow. It is all about the woman, her feelings and her positive instinct and connotation on everything around her. But we cannot go back to that time. It is a wish for every woman. Accepting where they came from and moved forward with velocity to find the spot they are yearning. All the creativity then is unforgotten, but new phase is respectfully emerging. It is no more a ritual that anyone dares communicate to us, and there is no going back. We, women, are on an unearthing expedition and we need ample liberation to build palpable relationships. This concept has always been there. It is reawakened in this story as we follow and learn how events unfold. We must keep exploring to the end. Anything that is worth doing is worth doing wrong until we do it right. I am no other than a woman with a vision, explicit or not; I choose to think and believe that it is crystal clear that I am working towards reaching it.

Part of what we need is knowledge, talent to do what we love to do. We make it essential to the understanding that life changes unexpectedly. As for me, I like to write, and the story of Mossaan is where my heart is. I keep my commitment to make my commitment to finishing the sequel that the readers will enjoy and to contribute. Every story must start from somewhere; the beginning, the middle and the end. Sometimes the term becomes a continuity as we tend to reinvent ourselves gradually and everything around us. C'est la vie.

FOUNDATIONAL

Every year we pass through is a book from which we make our sketches, draw and map out different chapters. The same goes for stories. Writing a book does not only give you the opportunity to tell a story. It gives you the edge of researching, to think and to challenge yourself and even doubt yourself too at times. What makes this one accessible to address is the three most crucial areas featured in each chapter from the steps to the script and flashbacks. With the latter, the story is something that we experience in life. We share the experience and connect with it because everything is about our daily lives flukes features that are in it.

Fundamental truth does not need to be provable beyond a shadow of the doubt. In this case, this story you are indulging in is holding real events to highlight the contrast between the real-life and fictionalised stories that give it a whirlwind change and memorable episodes filled with cultural, traditional, and historical moments from which to learn a thing or two. You will have the chance to be in the know of so many beautiful stories that you never knew. Having a landing space is essential for it encourages you to leap. My instruction is to get a smooth one.

Good stories are inspirational, motivational, lessons filled, guiding and what is more, they are captivating and cajoling. They also help you walk through the darkness to find the lit torches leading to abundance. Wherever you are, there will come a time when you cannot rely on miracles to change your life. What you must do is make peace with the mirror in which you will find your reflection and watch it transform into what your heart desires. There will be no need to keep torturing your soul. You will find the comfort in readjusting yourself and finding the inner self that is indeed in need of you to grab whatever that is a hindrance to you by the horn and be in charge.

Using the basic principles that I have in mind guides me to address the different areas I need to speak about carefully. The intention is to educate about the little I know of the world around me starting from the traditional, cultural aspects of where I come from, my childhood experience that has made it possible for me to be. My wish for a better life for all is not contrasting the kind of life the young women in the story have. It talks about ambitions, environment, traditional norms, care, living, obedience, gratitude, humility, patience, acceptance, willingness, and evolution. It is purely that and more that do not swerve from what our initial intentions seem to be.

DESIRE

Desire - The attractiveness of hope, as they say, is that from the period, it considers being the period of actualisation progression, a process that dictates time. It will be utterly improbable to think that one could wish something this very moment and achieve it the very moment as well without having concrete plans and understanding the game in executing and mastering every step. It recognises that a series of events must take place first, for nothing happens overnight, and if that were the case, nobody would have suffered or said they have been hurt trying to achieve a goal.

Knowing what you want, and recognising are two different things one must consider often. The desire matches with a vision you have for the goal to become a reality. Things will become more comfortable when you know what you want, what you dream to grow, to have and to experience. Never leave behind your aspirations for having them planted is key to everything you wish to do for the planted seeds to become ripped.

Mossaan never asked why she was where she was. Amongst many young African women, she lived to obey orders and does not question herself about the many stripes she was born with and the designing in every phase she passes through. But, she had a vision and her plans to become what she thought would be beneficial to her and her whole community. It did not stop her from pushing the envelope, neither did it prevent her from being herself in the environment God has already chosen for her. She had a purposeful life and never wished to relent on what steps to take to get to where she wanted to be. Her environment was not conducive to her but had the stamina to get on with it and see how things will pan out. The seed that she allowed to grow in the tank that is already in place for her. It was a cradle filled with goodness at the same time the challenges she must endure.

ANGUISH

Anguish - Positive thinking is not about expecting the best to happen every time but accepting that whatever happens is the best for this moment. Often, we speak for ourselves as a second person ready to hear, heal and guide and even encourage. 'Look into my eyes and tell me what you see' Does that ring a bell? Standing in front of the mirror talking to ourselves, we believe is a lot in deciding, from how we look at what we need to do about what we do not like about ourselves. We all agree that and very often that is the very situation in which we find ourselves. However, we do not wake up daily, yearning for our lives to be one filled with sufferings and terrible experiences.

Expecting greatness always helps us to achieve greatness. That's the beauty of having dreams. We must continue to coat our lives with positivity, sign a pact with ourselves and understand the contentment that is in having dreams. Many of us do use our goals to find the best of solutions. It is ever so important to have in mind what life can give you and that it is not always extraordinary. Our eyes show the depth of our soul. Sometimes our eyes betray us by not being able to hide what we feel inside. There is always a story behind the eyes. Some sweet and some filled with so much pain, some so captivating you feel like you have fallen into a trance. It is not enough to just look for the sake of seeing. Look deep into the depth of your soul. Do not wish. Use your eyes and act like you can capture everything that you meet. Insist on making eye contact with everyone you spend time with because your eyes reflect your spirit. Finally, do not take for granted the depth in which your eyes can. It leads to the comfort I chose to make the protagonist and even where I often find myself to be in for it is crucial to allow everything that is good in and share.

SOLACE

Solace - They teach us about that which to expect of the future. Like the way, the wise ones would put it. "Always expect the unexpected." We are not in control of our destiny, and we cannot shy away from the truth when it finally knocks at our doors. It is a reality that each one of us lives through without any choice of rejecting it. It is because we can never be able to choose what to have or what not to have when it comes to the myriad of gifts, fortunes, misfortunes, and mixed issues the future holds. It bears down upon each one of us with all the hazards of the unknown. That's life, and we have no other choice but to sail on it, gel with it, reap what it comes with and not anything like what we sow. Just because it never belonged to any of us.

The key to life is to expect everything on a silver platter coming from no other place than above, yet to be genuinely surprised and forever grateful when everything falls into place. Assuming all good things to be ours, while not knowing how to take anything for granted, is predictable and we are not perfect. If there may be a key in life, this is the key, and we cannot say no to that. It is the solace and the spot where I often wish to find myself hiding in. It is a place I call my ampule. I want to own it forever. It is an excellent place to be whenever possible. That is a constant wish for me, and I believe that it is attainable should I try a little bit more. By giving peace to others, an order will be in and with you. This rule shall begin with me with everything I would like Mossaan to achieve in her life.

*Never force helping others, but just do what feels right in your heart.

*Never think of feeling the need for taking a break from being the right thing happening to others.

*Never rely on the good things you do to receive the best treatments from others.

*Never hold back when it comes to serving your Creator.

We all deserve beautiful things in our lives. We deserve everything that is wonderful in life. Therefore, learn to cultivate a new mind - a mind that can give you a lot. Learn to develop a modern mind, a mind that can provide you with everything you want for yourself and even the very best thing which is pure love. You can find that you or your children if you feel unlucky to have tried many times and did not see anyone that tells you what your worth is.

Solace is not something one can invent. It is an inner feeling that can only develop through what the gathered thoughts can give. With my actual beliefs, I ask for my Lord to give me comfort. To make me comfortable. To make me wiser to see the wonders of His creations and to let me speak of the truth and reveal His promises to me and everyone around me so that the peace and tranquillity we achieve become everything that we seek.

We do deserve everything that is wonderful in our life. Our new mind can give us everything we want for ourselves even the very best thing, once again. In each one of us, we have that urge to create an inventory. The latter is a reminder to forgive ourselves to move on to a newer level.

CHAPTER FOUR
The Push

Perfection is the most motivating of attributes. I never look at people and judge their level of genuineness. If I ever find the need to decide, I withdraw from their space even when I have all the reasons to do so. It is not me to have any intentions of spoiling those qualities that already possess. If anything, working on my weaknesses is all I have time to do especially now. Everything I have today, I have ever hoped to achieve. Thus, I will never feel the need to desiring what I do not have.

There is something a friend told me some years ago. She said that spoiling what you have by wanting what you do not have shown how ungrateful you are to your Creator. The prove is that you smile, and you are not continually crying. Be grateful. Show gratitude. Yearn for more while being appreciative. Nothing ever comes to you at the wrong moment. Try your utmost best to give all the positive energy and motivation to people who were down and out that was ready to quit. Be jubilant for being chosen to bring the light out to people, and most of all, never mind and don't you ever be bothered by the same people that will let it out when you need the light to be brought out to you. You may be the chosen one for them, but they are not the ones for you. When you have a hiccup, don't feel it is necessary for them to be the ones to stand with you on the road to rectify the situation. They do not have your light. Yours is with someone else and somewhere else. You can never appear as an empty vessel when you are a firm believer in yourself as you have a reminder that you always get what you give. It does not have to be from the same people. Be motivated by fairness, and that will help you get to the right destination.

In a nutshell, your energy is what makes you what you become. It is what separates you from what can harm you as well. The sense in me tells me to do what is best even though I put a wrong foot and that is quite often. I can hear myself saying this kind of thing. Make it a habit not to follow pessimists, people with the way they see or take things. Never judge them though for being that way either. Pessimists individuals do not raise their hopes high for all the right reasons they have in the world. It does not make them cynical. That is how they are and respecting that is where your motivational self will flourish. It means being a realist.

Action proves why words mean nothing. Intentions, they say, without actions are just ideas and ideas without actions are just thoughts. So, if you wish to make a momentous change in your life and you have no idea where to begin, embark on a journey filled with motivation and everything that can keep you focused until you meet your goals.

Spiritually, many of us miss out on the excellent guidance in the messages given to us daily. We witness all kinds happening in our world today; we still ignore the anecdotes, and that is why we complain about searching endlessly without solutions. They are there; we are just not looking in the right place. There is a universal force that permeates within everything and everyone. This energy through the actions of connectedness and effect, circumstances and events, directly and indirectly, bring people and things together. The reason why we say that our meetings are not by design is real. It is not accidental.

We all know that this force is divine. It is a force which acts without bias. It only knows energy because energy is all there is where the motivation also is. Never waste the precious time given to search beyond where you should be searching. I base my thoughts on these areas and in everything in which I find myself engaged. I share what I do.

I press on to hold on to the helm of the garment of the King of kings, on my knees, I ask for guidance and 'Secours.' Everyone needs rescue now and then.

Written to comfortably portray the life of traditional girls living in environments that do not just control them, to have their best interest at heart is the right thing to do for them. It uplifts them. This literature is a learning tool geared towards formations, wishing to present the nuance between young women living in different environments but pursuing the same free dreams.

As they say, it is a Man's World with a place for each one of us. Let us face it, it is the truth that raising girls/daughters in an African society comes with a lot of unexpected challenges, but they also come with significant and positive outcomes. I have seen my mother go through it all. When my father past away, our aunties from Senegal thought that taking us all back to Senegal was the best solution. To them, it was going to be more comfortable for my late mother for she would have had all the help she needed to have us in control. As you have heard me say a myriad of times, the reason why I love that woman, so much is that she openly told everyone that even if she were going to eat sand with us, so be it there was no way she was going to giving us up. She made it her work to raise her daughters on her own without having to send us to our aunties because they thought that she was not going to be able to cope without a father figure around to guide us. It was not a pleasant moment for her, and from then on, she became the enemy for all the wrong reasons. But, I am glad that she didn't give us away. Would I have forgiven her? I do not know about that, but I am happy that she showed us that you have been elegant, regal and still be fierce. Everyone knew about that in her family. She was supportive, a confidant to everyone but she lived by the truth. She brought us into this world and what I did not understand was why on earth they felt they had a say in our upbringing when they did not the time father was still alive. I did not want to understand that, and I remember when one of my aunties approached me trying to talk me into agreeing to go with them because she knew how much I loved going to my father's home. I quickly said no because there was no way I was going to leave my lonely mother who was grieved. I thought they were heartless and did not feel sorry for a woman who was so loved by their brother.

The stories here do not aim to portray the unhealthy lifestyle of a traditional and cultural African family but to candidly showcase what has been happening in our world before and now. With this contemporary approach taken, I have decided to start narrating a fictional story of a girl child, a daughter and a young adult female, Mossaan fondly called Moss by her loved ones and those around her. Moss is an epitome of a beautiful woman. Even at her youthful age, she represented everything that is beautiful; regal, gracious and everything a woman would want to be.

As an author, I won't say this is the first time I have seen a fiction mixed with a true story, but I guess that it is what gives Mossaan an exciting edge. I feel that it comes with a lot of the new slice to enjoy. The contrast has got a high substance from which the motivation derives.

With a lot to be considered, the narratives are talking about the predicaments every girl child goes through in her life growing up in Africa. It is just to show how young girls/women live with their elders. Furthermore, it is the twenty-first century, and a lot has changed. We must go with the era and what it requires; the 'do's and Don'ts we must not fail to mention. Agreeing that it comes with a lot of challenges, our research and resources and the props in place will be of assistance to make this happen. It is the tool we need to design and efficiently gauge where we were as it relates to the advancement of women and girls, and how we may achieve a desirable future for them. We would be able to address the myriad of challenges faced daily, but also the hope we have in working together to eradicate the fear we wake up to in dealing with issues that are of concern to us. Being born in Sub-Saharan Africa and a highly-cultured environment, rich in its ways, I cannot help but to boldly say that I count myself amongst the luckiest young women of my generation who grew up from an affluent traditional background with astute parents. The judiciousness in them was not at all a wrong path. They raised my siblings and me with the knack to understand the world around us from childhood. No one can deny that we have the best culture and tradition in Africa worthy of pride. We are fighting against certain norms that society has for us. There are many reasons why this happens. The times have changed, and the world with it. It is called evolution. But some traditional custodians of certain norms have refused to change with the times, and this often leads to tension in the modern society.

When I mention African culture and tradition, it is the best of my experiences, I am genuinely and solely referring to and what I do know growing up. I am proud to be counted amongst the young African women who want to see change happen. Needing change is never intruding, and it should not be for anyone that does not have an African custom. The customs in Africa offers an exceptional lifestyle, in which society and nature blend seamlessly. If you have never encountered such a story, this is the perfect opportunity to engage in learning as this is the best insight you can refer to when it comes to an understanding of the life of a cultured West African young woman in the modern world.

The life of a young is obedient and honoured of a woman who yearns and dreams of becoming a decision maker, a contributor to serve her people, to take part in any decision-making procedures that concerns her life and those of others. Her participation in societal affairs is not considered unique. It is reasonable to the people she lives with, and they do not see it as extraordinary but laudable behaviour. They praise her but is that enough for her to rise above what she sees as challenges are the question we ask. Her challenging environment is one that she should consider a lot when making decisions.

What do the traditional norms offer? We hear people say that the society has a set of expectations regarding how prospects or affiliates should and should not behave. A typical way of talking when addressing women in our community. That is the standard as they call it. A norm is a guideline or expectation for behaviour. It is without a doubt that each society makes up its own rules of conduct and decides what constitutes a violation of those laws and the steps to ensure a redress when they become transgressed. Norms do change persistently, and there is nothing anyone can do about that. It is as transformational as the rules of laws in constitutions. It is worth exploring every area of traditional and cultural norms, which I think is going to bring excitement.

There is nothing like a rigid set of rules in it that is off-putting, or anything that you will be expecting to see or come across that is unheard of. It is the freedom to abide by some fundamental rules combined with the freedom to adhere to the demands or requirements of an evolving society. For this reason, when the traditional norms meet our society's myriad of elements, those living in it must pay attention to think of the most necessary things. It must be that need for development - a change for the better. Inspiring stories keep us going and wanting to do better for ourselves.

Mossaan wanted to have a taste of city life. The same world is what some of us are tired of having. So, the contrast is clear. I found the need to commence with how I discovered the protagonist, my life, my path and what I can recall up to the time I became a young adult. The different layers of this story and the principles go unnoticed, and that is how it becomes a fiction-mix. One of first, but very alluring.

It is a tale of our beloved and chosen woman of substance; we should establish a relationship with the character that is the professional pianist and the page-turner. We often hear that "Every professional pianist needs a page-turner." As the page-turner, I owe it to the protagonist to tell her story in a just way and a very delightful manner. It is an exciting way that encourages every reader to create a moment between them and the main characters they have a choice to pick from and call it a 'Rendezvous Avec Mossaan.

As I pen down this story, my brief experience which could have taken another journey in the form of memoirs is better off being presented as the life of this regal young woman Mossaan.

I would like to present it the way mine could have been. That is my goal, and that is precisely how it should be. The Mossaan in me will not fail to show herself. I am sure yours will show up too in a matter of time. We cannot avoid blaming ourselves

Wading with you is our aim. I have chosen to be the storyteller, telling you a story that accompanies all that we have journeyed into since childhood. Contrasting Mossaan's and mine, even yours, we can understand the many denotations of the glass ceiling in its multiple forms, interpretations that have been here from day one.

The heroine is none other than Mossaan, who has lived through every facet of change. She complains little and takes in a lot but perseveres beyond our imagination. Some exciting events topped with all that makes life electrifying after all, challenges, the quest for change and freedom. Because of her journey, we can change how we see things as women. Stressing on how learning never ceases when opportunities arise, we must buckle up and rise with every breakthrough availed to us. It merely is an ambition which is a common thing we have with men. We all try to pursue the same things; the hunt for contentment, the expedition for modification and a better life. This is the kind of life that is beneficial to anyone around us. That said, we must think of Mossaan's background as a young African woman and what life has in store for her. The environment she lives in gives her a little of that possibility to excel and exhale like any other girl with a bit of freedom.

Compared to other nearby villages Mossaan cannot complain much, but with all the resources available when found, she wants to go on to find out what is available that she can do to give her what she has ever wanted. Even though the environment does not allow her to make her own choices independently, Mossaan will continue to live in hope. She is left to abide by the rules of her background and the people in it. The story depicts, for the most part, the life of a woman in Africa. The vest with multiple stripes we are born with cannot be ignored nor embraced, but a lot can be done to turn those lines into borderlines and make them respected. In our culture, family members have rights to make decisions. We are obliged to adhere to the rules. People like our uncles and paternal aunties and brothers make important decisions for us, and that control has never ceased. Even when we try to be rebellious, we will always go back to those essential roots because they what made us what we are today.

CHAPTER FIVE
Growing in Grace

It is all about time - when times are tough, many get tempted to withdraw, cut their losses, and weigh things out. In some ways, this can be a valid strategy. However, you must also pursue a path of growth if you are to survive and thrive during those tough times. Famous psychologist Abraham Maslow said: One can choose to go backwards toward safety or forward toward growth. We select extension again and again; fear must be overcome again and again" What I take from this is that, in the process of becoming, you have to accept yourself as you are, so you can better transform yourself into what you are called to become. No matter how much you go through or have gone through, you must stay upright, unshaken and work on being in love with the person who has been through a lot but is still standing. That person is you.

I have learned to develop positive rituals and routines that support resilience during those tough times. The tough times are going to throw punches your way and the rituals and routines that helped you during boom times may not be enough to provide you with the resilience necessary to choose growth and overcome fear day after day during tough times. We define resistance as the ability to recover quickly from depression, illness, or misfortune. The key is to improve back to a more positive, productive and active state. In the end, we must understand that resilience is not just about enduring adversity, but about overcoming misfortune.

Many people end up creating routines and rituals like overeating, talking too much, getting into all sorts and blaming society for everything they deem wrong without finding a better solution. But, then again this is what our fellowship with the community, in which culture features, does to us. We all have a way of blaming our culture and not the people who make decisions. The same people we feel we must run to when something is troubling us. It is not our nation, nor our society. Well, we avoid blaming anyone, but we can cut that and face up so that we can feel the real us in us. People in our respective communities have a way of making things unbearable when we allow it. But, there is always a will when there is a way. We choose the latter and peaceful approach that makes way for composure.

Stability of the mind is another important thing that I have come across and have paid so much attention. If we designate something as natural, then we are inclined to think that it is most unlikely to have mostly to do with society. Mossaan here is continuously in search of herself and all the possibilities that await her to make her the person she wants to become. She does that with utter patience, with excellent characteristics in the eyes of her peers, before the elders of the village and not to mention her very own relatives who think the world of her.

I elaborate on what she yearns to become. It is not rocket science, and everyone knows that is what she wants to do to change her life. It is not a tall order and not too much to ask, but people in her life make it impossible to give her what she needs. Tasks become difficult to execute without snags with many predicaments. She is not one of those people that ask for help, and that is not how you want to be a young woman trying to survive in a male-dominated environment.

Being grateful is one of the best virtues one could possess. Always be thankful that you do not have everything you want and that means you still have an opportunity to be happier tomorrow than you are today. There are a lot of dissimilarities in her story compared to ours, but not to all of us due to our diverse backgrounds. However, the story remains one of a kind, of a young African adult, a woman whom we expect to achieve her dream because we love good endings.

Experience proves that nothing is easy to reach. There is no problem that faith cannot solve. Each one of us has an ability within us and around us to find a way, every day. I have always dreamed of writing stories that are inspirational. I refer to myself steps to becoming bold. Not waiting until I know it all to embark on journeys I have always wanted to adventure out has encouraged me to start pondering on the next steps. Becoming Bold - I step out in courage every day, even when I feel lethargic, defeated, trampled upon, discouraged and sad.

I always ask myself this question. How do I follow these orders daily? Step out in courage today; your life story is someone else's hope. Keep shaming the negativity that is bolted in your mind refusing to let you be. Keep shaming the cultural shame. Keep sharing. Keep giving. I also tell myself to think of the futility of going through it all alone and keeping it to myself. When it comes to beautiful thoughts about stories, I think straight away about sharing with all my heart because what you take for granted might be educative and entertaining to someone else.

'Me & Mossaan' once again – It is a 'Rendezvous,' and it is nothing less than an exciting matter 'C'est Une Histoire d'Amour' 'A Tale of Acquaintance.' It is enthralling. What an elating moment to have to share the same page with a fictional character that tells the typical life experience of an innocent, and still a very ambitious young woman somewhere in Africa in this 21st century. It does not matter how difficult it is; you will finally fulfil your dreams. What is important is the planning, the wills, wishes, and purposes. With time, one must be able to visualise things backed with good intentions.

When you know what your key goals and aims are, you can align them with your core purpose in life and provide motivation and inspiration in the context of your current challenges. No one is immune to problems. In fact, they make us discover our innermost self and ability to address issues or learn to tackle every issue that lands in our laps. Once we can visualise the achievement of our goals and objectives, we will find the inner peace ready to come out. We will start enjoying the peace, success, and progress on our journey.

With time also, comes everything we grapple with, all the goodness life offers, the ambitions, plans, success, failures, the falls, and rise. We go through pinnacles of life, and none of its distinct stages is avoidable. It is a gate each one of us must go through. It is as simple as that. Some have it easier than others, but it still it is a pinnacle of life. We seek potent inspirations and act towards our goals daily with affirmative action that creates confidence, momentum, and progress for a brighter future.

At the commencement of each day, the minutes we take to identify the compelling primary steps that are present to move us forward should always be what determines our success or achievement during the day. Therefore, it is vital to consider what route we wish to take daily. Finding inspiring individuals or actions to guide us is crucial because the openness to other activities can lead one to a destination that yields all the goodness one needs.

Today, choosing those that inspire us and committing to adhering to the aspirations can make the actions efficiently completed. I cannot avoid talking about or reminding us of what is motivating in this story. It is the fact that everything revolves around someone who is one of us and yes, a woman. She is an African woman. She is a feminist. She is a young African woman who has big ambitions just like any young woman. Let us not forget about the tests we go through as women. Nowadays, women are facing a lot of tests. The free process of the African woman is a daunting task; eventful, serendipitous. Take women and run a series of assessments on them to see if they will give your wishes and wants willfully. Stories of the Suffragettes and the women of Walo - Talataiye Nderr in Senegal and Aline Sitoe Diatta will guide you on how these individuals and groups of women taught us how to value life centuries and decades ago. Women are the backbone of society. Let us all take pride in that; men and women since one cannot live without the other.

I do remember often telling people how they should not see my spirituality as anything new. It has always been there, but I preferred keeping it to myself when I needed not to prove to anyone what my belief is. You can speak something into existence all you want, but if it is not part of God's plan, it is not going to happen. Saying that I do not do less self and more worshipping will be far from the truth. I do less personal, but that does not stop me from inserting what I see as a disparity to the main character in the story. It starts with me as the woman who has lived under similar circumstances to be able to tell her story as it is. It feels good to communicate with the world in a myriad of ways when telling stories about something that has touched your life through fiction.

The importance of sharing stories and presenting them in ways that inspire others to follow suit. It highlights the needs for pressing forward. We are interconnected even when we refuse to accept it. Every story we hear has an impact on our lives. We often relate to someone's delightful tale, upbringing, characteristics in both positive and negative ways. One thing we must know is that God will put you in positions you did not apply for to test you. Quite often, I hear people speak kindly about others' achievements. Those are true believers who understand that each one of us has got something good going on even when we prefer not to notice our blessings but eyeing others' blessings.

It feels good to know yourself and what you wish to share. Finding myself in every situation and any stories, as an African child does not go beyond feeling blessed to know that I am a real believer. I feel on top form, and it is the connection that leads to the "Chossaan and Aada." that is the culture and tradition where we pride ourselves. The same as Mossaan and any other woman we share the same culture and tradition with, I understand the many stripes I was born with; being a woman and being African. It means grappling with a lot, and it goes on until the end of time.

Time is significant, but it is more important to live it for nothing is in vain in this life. That is the belief I wake up to daily and what I like most is that my spirituality does not allow me to think of anything too weighty on me. Who am I to believe that it is all rosy or it shall be so always.

Who am I? I am an African woman born in a culture and tradition that reminds me of when to understand that I am about to derail and that it is the time when to think of the key for my rescue to happen. We are born to strive. I use my highest muscle and my worst enemy to work on anything that is around me. Yes, it is what I am taught to believe. The mind is the most active muscle. You use it for everything. That is the fact. Wisdom is what we need to use it astutely. Amazing things happen when I use my mind the way I should do, and that is beneficial to me. I try to be as realistic as possible to myself and do what I loved then which was being highly informed and listening to my parents, and even disagreeing with them as part of doing what I was encouraged to do.

My late father, according to my mother was the culprit. Everything that I was that she did not like was my father's doing. I loved her for giving all the credits to herself. I relished doing what made me happy, and I still do. Yes, I emphasise that those wondrous things happen when you are honest with everyone around you, with your surroundings, yourself and start living, doing what you love and not what others like you to do. If not, your life slows down. Life dictates you to stop wishing for anything that has no time attached to it. It is possible that you can end up waiting for days to arrive because you have developed a habit of being patient and using the allow-analogy to go on happily. That helps you also to cease looking forward to extraordinary events because you have that unique soul within embellished with everything that describes the joy, and everything protrusive you want to share with people. You start to live in each moment and ironically living like a human being again. Hooray!!! You just ride the wave that is life, and with this feeling of contentment and joy, you have never expected. We are all learning and doing that sailing through and moving fluidly, steadily, calmly and gratefully without any disruption. You will feel relieved and ready to embrace the lightness of your thoughts; the mind becomes clearer because you have lifted the veil.

Life without the layers is life without hopes and stories do describe our voyage and penetrate deep into our depths. Behind every lucky person is himself/herself. Knowledge gives us power. But experience is nothing without wisdom. Knowing my culture heals every part of me. My culture and tradition are my Raison de Vivre, my 'Laissez-passer' for they add to my etiquettes, values and the morals in which I am born and raised.

We grow up thinking that we cannot survive without the freedom we need; being boundless and becoming highly open-minded. I feel grateful for the lessons I had learned from peers, elders and the women before us whose stories our mothers and grandmothers told us. It makes me think how eager I am to wake up every morning with a zing in my feet, knowing that my every word is going to be aimed at making a difference in society. Now that is promising and heartwarming. The elders we emulate did that work for us. We owe it to them for instilling that magnitude of greatness in us.

We cannot address our culture in Africa without a mention of her supernatural properties. I will take this opportunity to discuss an incident that unfolded before my eyes briefly. It reminds me of one of my closest friends, a girl with a heart of gold. Her name is Awa Rose. What a beautiful soul she is; very kind and giving. Her name describes her perfectly. Awa had gone through an episode that was very scary to all of us. I remember seeing her go through a lot of pain. The pain was indescribable, and I was awed by the myth that surrounded it. Something happened to her that made me more cautious about the mystic Africa that I have always denied myself to believe that it existed or still exists. I do not want to think it yet, but I am careful, wary at the same time.

It is unfortunate enough to live in a society that does not spare innocent people, but worse when you do not take precaution about anything. We were carefree, and when we were told not to walk the streets around the Maghreb, we brushed it off and accused our elders as primitive. They knew what they were saying.

I did not know how she got her foot infected like it was without having a single wound on it. From the bottom, the top of her foot had a whole we heard from stepping on something that was not aimed at her. Who would harm an innocent young woman who was still going to school? This is how we used to think. Awa told us several times she did not recall stepping on anything sharp or hard to cause her pain. She did not notice stepping on anything that could cause her that much pain. That was too mysterious for an ordinary man to understand. Our elders used to tease us that if we did not stop wandering around Maghreb time, we would one day meet with the wicked jinn and mysterious winds that will destroy us. It is called 'Thielly werr' in wollof, and it looks like a twister.

I used to wonder how the wind can change my life for the worse or how on earth can one step on stone have a leg the size of a ship? Not that her foot was a size of a boat, but she had a tough time to walk, and it also took longer to heal. I remember people saying it is 'Korrteh' as in a spell meant for someone else and not her. They always told us that if it is not intended for you, you will survive with the pain. If not, you die. Isn't the pain better? But it was uncomfortable and unbearable. I do not want to wish that on anyone even if you were about to chop my head off. It was all a mystery to me.

I spoke to my father about it. Out of the blue, we were chatting at night, and I just said to him. Why do you always tell us that it is a bad omen to walk around Crepuscule/Maghreb? He explained, but I have had my reservations. Does it come from where we least expected it?

I never wanted to believe in it until I got sick myself. Before my parents' discovery of my heart condition, I jokingly said to my Papa that 'Domma ammut' meaning sorcery does not exist. I was a gabby adolescent in a sense that I had a lot to say, but only at home with my family, and when I think of that, it makes me laugh. As much I'd like to say I was a polite young lady, those moments deny me the politeness I claim for especially in front of my sisters. They still laugh at how I used to challenge them a lot and Papa who was my best friend. My mother used to sit in her corner with her usual smile telling Papa that it is his fault that I was the way that I was. 'You told her to challenge everything people say to her. Now, she is doing just that' You trained her to be your Aline Sitoe Diatta. Live with it now'. But Papa did not bother listening to everyone laughing about how I always tried to challenge him innocently. I was just used to asking too many questions and did not agree to anything I did not trust, nor believed in those things. Not that I was too young and naïve, but I have never seen anyone affected by their hexes.

Now I see in films' stories of the ancient and modern times in countries where people still practice the darkest of spirits of voodoos if I may say. I still think that you cannot have victory by exercising evil deeds. And those practices show nothing but darkness and sad endings.

My own experience made me finally realise that it was happening to me. Dark spirits attacked me. Someone had put a spell on me. I was confused because I was too young. I was always throwing up, I did not sleep at night, and I did not put on weight either. I was just skin and bone even in my early twenties, and there was nothing my parents did not do to try and heal me. From then on, I promised myself that I would never take myself where I should not be. Do you see why I trust the power of my ancestors and their traditional and herbal remedies? One of my great uncles travelled down and whatever he brought with him was what healed me. He used some of his ancient/old dried leaves as a remedy which I would like to know about but never mind.

I was grateful, and I started taking heed. Knowing that my father needed to have peace with his family, I asked him if that was the reason he left Senegal to come live in the Gambia. But he always clarified to me that evil spirits are everywhere. My role is to be careful, mind my steps and avoid arguments. I had that in me from then on, and I still see beyond what people think I know. My mind was and always filled with so many 'what ifs' to avoid saying the wrong things to people who will not hesitate to harm me. The level of grudge someone can hold against an innocent person does not have to be about any vital thing. People can destroy you quickly without sweating about it. To be on the safe side, you must keep pressing on and asking God to make your destiny unknown to man, because if they do, you will not reach the street you walk on let alone where you want to be in life.

My lack of belief in sorcery still deepened. We quickly forget, and that is humane. I felt that I was living it myself. I was living it bizarrely: the problematic sleepless nights, and frequent nightmares, pains, etc. I still cannot stop thinking about the mystique Africa where I was born and grew up. There are some unanswered questions, and I spoke to my parents about my worries about the culture and tradition. But how does one know about something that no man created? Is it sudden? However, a girl like me did not allow a day to pass without the urge to know. I have this enthusiasm for learning, and that is what saves me daily. I asked questions, and sometimes I get answers and other times I get laughed at because I did not leave it until I get at least an encouragement from my elders. My father was in awe and my mother who has always shown how mindful she was, never said anything. But I just waited in distress. They all thought that I was not going to make it. As they said, I am like a cat with nine lives. I was not ready to give up. I grabbed the evil spirit by the horn. I will tell you by not going to sleep at night if you ask me how I successfully come out unharmed. When everyone was sleeping, this young lady watches the imaginary stars on the ceiling. Even now, I do the same. I stay awake all night when I feel scared in my home.

I can recall the first days I started walking correctly again. I got better and felt stronger with a lot of mental bruises and little physical one hence being diagnosed. I took it in my stride, and that has helped me embrace life much better. Feeling positive is not something I say or write daily to please anyone. It is indeed how I think I should live every day even when things get stormy. Attractive stuff for life are hidden under thorns, and I go by that. I will keep repeating that as I always do at home. I believe in what life throws at me is what I should use as a lesson and move on grew up. There are some unanswered questions, and I spoke to my parents about my worries about the culture and tradition. But how does one know about something that no man created? Is it sudden? However, a girl like me did not allow a day to pass without the urge to know. I have this passion for learning, and that is what saves me daily. I asked questions, and sometimes I get answers and other times I get laughed at because I did not leave it until I get at least an encouragement from my elders. My father was in awe and my mother who has always shown how mindful she was, never said anything. But I just waited in distress. They all thought that I was not going to make it. As they said, I am like a cat with nine lives. I was not ready to give up. I grabbed the evil spirit by the horn. I will tell you by not going to sleep at night if you ask me how I managed to come out unharmed. When everyone was sleeping, this young lady watches the imaginary stars on the ceiling. Even now, I do the same. I stay awake all night when I feel scared in my home.

I can recall the first days I started walking correctly again. I got better and felt stronger with a lot of mental bruises and little physical one hence being diagnosed. I took it in my stride, and that has helped me embrace life much better. Feeling positive is not something I say or write daily to please anyone. It is indeed how I think I should live every day even when things get stormy. Attractive things of life are hidden under thorns, and I go by that. I will keep repeating that as I always do at home. I believe in what life throws at me is what I should use as a lesson and move on to the next stage. No matter what, I must remain grateful to my Lord. He Subhanna wa Ta'ala has always been there for me. He is for everyone and that I know very well. But it does not stop me from calling Him my Allah for the mercy he has bestowed upon me. I shall forever keep pressing on to hold on to the helms of His garment.

The role of the jinn is to find stubborn people to destroy. You know that it is what they tell us hiding the core reason why our parents tell us to avoid walking certain times of the day or leaving the windows open around the Maghreb. It would have been easier if they informed us explicitly of what to avoid and why. Young people are too straightforward and difficult to lure into any mysterious happenings. There are good jinn and evil jinn. I believe that people do just like how I spoke about our ancestors and their ways of fighting their so-called enemies to win their battles. It is dark, and it is important to fight that rather than women and feminism. Our children must live in a better world and trust the continent they equally call home.

We cannot escape from falling victims this mystical happening, but as believers, we can always run to seek deliverance and through powerful prayers. With prayers, we can save ourselves from these unpleasant and scary experiences.

Talking to Awa Rose about her experience and those mysteries recently and reliving those moments is an eye-opener. Our children must understand this spiritual side that no one wants to address seriously. It does exist, and we must do our best to avoid it. What happened to us was not usual, but I keep telling myself that they have had a go at me and that was their last chance because My Allah is watching, and my gate is locked with the most robust padlock no one can open except Him. That is how confident I feel. The fence is high up there, where no man can reach because it can only be if I do evil to anyone which is not within my remit. I let go of anything to the point of silliness. I do not know vengeance, and I do not retaliate because I do not give anyone the chance to do wrong to me that will make me want to harm you.

Our elders had always said that it gets worse when the 'Korrteh' is not for you. Ah! Africa, Africa, Africa. What is exciting about this rich continent is that no amount of tradition, culture in the books can prepare you for anything. Therefore, it is essential to keep learning everything you think might be of importance to you.

We do have what it takes to succeed more than our western counterparts, as my old man said to me on the bus, commuting home from work. He asked where home is? I told him what he wanted to know about me. He immediately asked me why I didn't hesitate to respond. My response was that I did not have any second thought in telling you because I am a proud daughter of the most beautiful continent, and I smiled. It was not a cheap smile. I did with pride written all over my face. And yes, Africa is rich in culture and tradition. He looked at me and smiled too. I smiled back at him again. I did not laugh for the sake of it. I genuinely smiled right back at him. We connected, but I did not know why I even spoke to him. He was an old man with grey hair. I do not get suspicious of anyone nor anything. I am careful, but I do not judge anyone. He wanted to know, and I told him what he needed to know. There was no harm to that nor ignorance to it. I do not condemn societal expectations in its entirety, but I measure my triumph with my ruler. I believe that I get guidance from my Lord in everything I do. Even in my moments of pain, catastrophe, I think that He guides me. He never fails me.

When people believe in staying away from strangers in public, I do not because it is not my fault for being approached by strangers who want to have a word with me. I do not allow the ruler that the society uses to make me feel short or intimidated. Our struggles are different, and so is our individuality. What you are denying, another person might not want to touch with a two-meter pole.

If you feel that compliments settle you and give life to your self-confidence, spare others the prognosis, forecast because there are some who do not link their sureness to another person's endorsement. Fear never decides your safety. That is clear.

The old man happily chatted with me about the system but never had he mentioned anything to do with God. It took me a few hours later to realise that he was only talking to me. I found him seated with many other people but was not talking to anyone else but me. Was I the only one he had seen or was I talking to an imaginary friend? I still asked that question. But I take it as it was. It was a moment though the page is open. It did not matter; I felt I did what my parents always said that I should do. Be kind but do not be silly or naïve. It is about using my graceful self to be approached with kindness and respect for these matters to me. Respecting elders and responding to people when they are talking to me.

So, it is necessary to know that you should never pretend to be bigger than anyone because of the Almighty, we are all equal. Not knowing who that old man was is still bothering me. If only I could see him again, that could help me come out of my misery. It will be a relief. I tried finding him without any luck. Hopefully, someday I will cross path with him again. The mission I now have is to see the same old man and I do try to find him every time I got on the same bus number. It could have been easier for me to know where he was from if he saw me on the bus. But I found him there when I got in. His face I remember, but his image I do not think that I will ever see again. I left it to my imagination, whatever I think he was.

Our parents never stopped finding ways and resolutions to our worries, to protect us from the supernatural beings. We always wanted to be free like birds when we were growing up, but the mystical stories made it impossible to live freely. I have seen many of our sisters, and I smile, knowing how they used to live life to the fullest. People talk and tell you stories that make you want to be more careful and mindful of your environment. Where you go is important and knowing your path saves you from meeting unwanted spell.

For many of us, living in the West has made us forget those mysterious events we used to hear. Now and then, we revisit moments where events such as what happened to Rose come to mind. That is when the carefree hat gets thrown away for a moment. What happened to Rose caused us fear beyond imaginable. There is darkness, but one we fear not because we must live life fully and deal with issues with the innovation that is in us, in our way.

The liberation we all crave for, a new breed of modern women is not at all a new thing, nor simple attainment. It is not something that belongs to Europeans as many would think. It is not just an attribute. It is a way of living. Some call it emancipation. Some say feminism and I believe that being feminist is about loving yourself as a woman as I have mentioned previously and many times. Therefore, I have always had in mind that looking good and feeling the feminine side in me is as core as the values expected from the feminism world. I shall repeat this many time to emphasise my beliefs. To most of us, being a feminist is not a new thing. Feminism is about loving yourself as a woman and wanting to use everything that gives you a better life and future to continue nurturing the environment and everything in it. That is all and nothing less. With that comes the responsibility of knowing how to get what we are craving, how to find ourselves and others to engage in enjoyable activities. We need to be involved in causes that can yield positive results.

Many people think that the feminism concept is about women taking power from men or women overpowering men. The need to lift the glass ceiling is a must, and a bright idea needs to be understood. The concept of feminism, when followed, cannot derail us. Growing up, I have learned how to listen, consult, empathise and work hard to match the good things that I can add to my repertoire of 'nice to keep attributes and not just skills.'

I have always wanted to be a contributor. Life is not a journey, but a practice run filled with stumbles. There is a natural aura that vindictive people who go out of their way to hurt others will end up with ugliness, alone, broke and lost. If you give a good thing to the world, then over time your karma will be right, and you will receive well. It is only right for whatever that is good, and what we are anticipating in this feminism concept, is going to be collected. Nothing ugly has ever come out of their plight to success. If anything, the idea has had the best continuity and women rise by the day.

In Senegal, the stories of 'Talaataye Nderr' et Aline Sitoe Diatta and many other influential women is the best example to give. It is a runway we must value, for there are so many things we learn along the way, no matter how short, or long we live.

From childhood to adulthood, there is a reminder that we cannot afford to derail, and we must keep on doing what it takes to lift whatever is going to prevent us from becoming free-spirited. We owe it to ourselves to feel our presence and amongst those that are for the enhancement of the goodness that society must offer. It does not matter how much we grapple with things, the quality of life we deserve to live does not have to be spared for the strong ones, the wealthy and affluent or educated ones. It must be for everyone from all walks of life.

Unity has always been part of us even when we grow apart, in various regions of the continents; Africa, Europe, Asia, Australia, and the Americas. We were born to be united. I evoke the times we steadily and forcefully emphasise how crucial it is to keep negotiating with our parents for playtime. These were moments that were very vital to us. Many of us did not have too much, but were rich in culture, enjoyed the love of families and had enough resources that today, in the modern world, is considered support networks. These were my mother's words as she continually reminded us of how everything is ready for us to grab and make our lives better.

It is the love of family and parents who were always present. That alone is enough to make a child grow up and be happy and confident. It is not still the reality that wealthy parents never had time for their offspring. The cases differ, and I am aware of what our modern world grants us today. We are teaching our family, our life experiences and what we endured. You must aim for it.

Culture and tradition help us find ourselves in diverse ways. It includes how they could contribute towards anything that yields positive and fruitful outcomes in the lives of humans through looking back the different steps taken. It is a universal dictum in the Wolof language which says, "you can only know your destination if you are truly aware of where you come from." We live in a time where each one of us owes it to society to contribute towards what creates a significant, substantial change and advancement.

For everyone to get involved in societal innovations is vital. It is possible to look at things in ways that describe this era of ours as something different. We should willingly see at one or two things and assure ourselves that we will be doing something about what makes living exciting, especially when we feel that there is something that lacks in us. The ever so present thing that deters us from progressing the way we wish to need to be out of our lives. That something alone will be beneficial to our communities, regardless of wherever we call home. For example, investment in research and using the findings, making time out of our busy schedules to inform policy decisions on girls, women's deprivation. Doing something about our verdicts is an important starting point. No amount of work is enough when it comes to making things happen.

Each one of us will do what is within reach. No matter

how we do it. What is important is how well we are chipping in. It does not have to be just for our gains and only for those that we know. It is about finding your niche in society, finding your forte and using it.

In conclusion, we can promise that finding yourself is to lose yourself in the service of others. Oh! How quickly I see myself n it is beyond belief. The littlest thing or act gets me excited about life and its myriad of positive accomplishments, hopes, challenges, opportunities not to talk of the many avenues to tap in. Not that I am the most adventurous person but, I admire the fact that opportunities will always be available to those who never stop seeking them. I must say this, several times, again and again. I don't know how this has become hereditary to me and where I got it from, but I do know one thing for sure. It is not by accident. It is not something I had in my adolescent years to be precise, but I do know that I have learned few things that keep growing. I cannot say that I was not a rebellious young adolescent girl, but I was obedient to the core to whatever my elders had to say. I have always been the daughter who believed that I could only excel with the full support of the people who loved me more than anything. To date, even though my parents are no more, I still spiritually consult them. It is in me, and it makes me feel guarded. That's my bluff. What is yours? Remember that we are discovering the story together.

CHAPTER SIX
Silhouettes

I usually tease myself about how I gauge or address my every situation, but it is therapeutic to me just like the way the character in the book is and in the ones to follow. I would say things like 'I have hundred and one problems to solve and adjust myself', ironically, my childhood explains all of them. Just like that, the answers are right there staring at me. How did that happen? I asked myself, and then the responses in many forms suddenly appear. Again, just like that in front of me.

I do a lot of remembrance of my path, and I show gratitude too many a time for if I did not have a childhood, I would not have been able to say anything relating to it. So, I am thankful that I could be a child, yes with a difference and can repeat myself on this subject. Some people do not have much to say about theirs because pain is all they have known all their lives. They do not wish to revisit those moments because either they have had it all or they were not allowed to be children nor allowed to express themselves. I have known pain, disappointment and I have gone through a lot but, I have known grace, gratitude, happiness for everyone around me felt the need to flatter me.

My childhood fascination had been seasoned using burning issues that affect women and girls in society. I have never felt that I have done more than digging deep into the many reporting on what happens to women globally, especially girls on the African continent and other parts of the world. Women go through all sorts for all the wrong reasons.

My spirituality is somehow guiding me to continue to go on a routine fact-finding mission. With that always lingering on my mind, I learned, and I am still learning a lot of things; reading and watching so many stories, following up on issues internationally, researching and digging deep into intergenerational dialogues to be in the know of my world. Yes, the world in which I live and want to contribute immensely to the little knowledge that God has bestowed upon me. I grew up thinking, this is it. I am here, and I am ready to learn and to know everything that I need to know.

I do not wish to stay in the dark since it is not something the movement allows us to do as a people. Somehow, I live in the arms of the sleuth of the religious guru who happily granted me space in his or her spiritual mind. I exhale rapidly following my imaginary guru and his noble princess. The purity of the brain and the soul that I yearn to attain promised to make it easy for me or anyone seeking to reach the level. I follow wholeheartedly, and I listen.

I keep emphasising on talking about what moulded me into what I have become not just as a woman but as a person. From my childhood, all I knew then was love for humanity, and I live by what they instilled in me. That is all

I have ever known. These are good qualities to keep, and if what I give or do is not enough, I shall make this my duty to keep searching for a better version of myself. These were what I grew up to believe that I can receive in return when I practice giving, caring and loving others. It is something that my father had taught me to think from inception. He was our teacher, and he had the patience to do what he had to do with us from the beginning. I just start with what I can finish. He inspired me to love my fellow human being, not more than I like myself, but to show the love and care that I would want to reciprocate. Surprisingly, as he had always said, you can only love people if you successfully love yourself because you must know that people would not care about you if you do not care about them. There was intelligence, but there were fate and people that he can attest to that too. He could not present everything for us on a silver platter, but he introduced us with so much to learn. Patience and contentment lead us through until today, all the way much here or now. Alhamdullilah! It is enough for now. The unity in us is enough for each one of us.

Compared to the many issues I mentioned in platforms and meetings, my parents were the kind of people that give up on their children so easy to follow their traditional and societal norms. They were never ready to give us away or give up on us without putting up the fight to make us walk the path that pleases our Creator. They did even when it was tough for them because they wanted the best for us.

Of course, nothing can happen without reason. Bringing us closer to Allah first and they saved us, and for Papa, it was worth it even when he had nothing left to protect the children he brought into this world. Teaching us about our tradition briefly, our Serere culture, about good ethics and societal norms topped with family values. We did nothing on our own without consulting them. They did everything as a family. They did so much for us like any other family and explored all possible avenues that we can remember when we trace them back.

The learning began at a very early age, which is standard regardless of the size or resources we had in place. We stuck together in the bumpiest of times. But, the harmony we had in our home in the presence of both mother and father was enough for a child to grow up thinking in and believing that everything is going to be alright and all rosy if you work hard. Nevertheless, that is a poor contrast to what the realities of the world are. I know that people close to me regarded me as a people pleaser because I never wanted to see anyone angry with me. What they think makes me laugh. It makes me feel fantastic though knowing that people look at me that way, then I know that I do it naturally. If only those who say it know that what I had time for growing up in the harshest of conditions that weren't necessary, they will understand why love and care are all I had known to keep me in shape. I did not have the time to dislike. All I had time for was to accept my fate, to do what I had to do to stay safe and healthy. We had to live under the conditions Papa wanted. I had to be the learner he had seen in me and accepted all his firm orders for learning was all he wanted me to do.

These two first human beings, which is how I would like to address them, were concerned about us. So, they made us ready to tackle the storms. They had always mentioned the days when they would be no more. The sound of that used to give me sleepless nights thinking about that. As I was very young, I used to cover my ears and called Papa insensitive 'warrehkatt' meaning preacher. How can you tell me about the day you will die and leave me behind knowing that I believe that without you I won't survive? He used to give me amusing responses. "But is it your death Neh?" That is heartless Papa. That is heartless and insensitive. I made him listen, and everyone knew that about me. He looked to me with all my complaints about what people did to me and what everyone complained about him. Nothing major but you know how parents are, and Papa was jovial, but you cannot have a piggy ride on his back. He was not that easy, but I had my ways to make him listen. He must have thought that he raised a crazy little woman in me. Indeed, I was his 'Awa Manneh' his best first cousin. Amongst my siblings, I was the hot-headed one that everyone loved. That is why I cannot deal with hate nor troubles. I get affected, so I do not try to be a hater to any living soul. That would be insulting to the values and virtues I have ever known.

As I grew older, I began to understand every little thing they said to us. Papa particularly, always said that it is not going to be easy for any of us facing this world alone without parents to guide us and they are not going to be around forever. However, The Creator that chose to bring us into this temporary universe will always provide for us, show us the way and guide us to walk through those the maps that are exclusively for us. I say this because we do know that we had so much to deal with both spiritually and physically. That was our fate, and we accepted it. Now I know very well how scared he was thinking about us being girls, being born away from the clan with only one brother who travelled and lived abroad and a young family of his own. We fend for ourselves, and we survive the storms. Nonetheless, we did manage, and we are still here being guided by 'Baba Oluwa' as my Yoruba friend says every time she feels the need to celebrate me for one thing or another. I am glad that He is watching over us. My father's fear then had become our solace because we are cautious about everything he had said to us. Papa did not have it easy, but 'Bagn Katt la wonn.' I understand the kind of family he comes from and what I know is enough to understand all the things he had gone through. He was a tough nut to crack. The family he came from needed him, but he needed to see his children live and grow into adolescence and adulthood. That was his dream and Allah's plan. He successfully had that at least before his premature demise after his endless fights to save us. He lost his firstborns Tessanou and Papa Demba, and that was enough trauma for a young man who tried to live modestly. With Mo, our big brother, they travelled to the Gambia where we, the girls were born, living his fourth child that his mom snatched from him. She later died from childbirth together with her twins. I was still very young when she died. I did not get to know her well for I only met her once when I was still in primary school.

The family Papa came from is big and very well known in Senegal. It is a large family from which, if he had to go for what his lineage accorded him, he would have lived longer and happier. But that is another story about LouLanne Waggaan Faye Ababakarr Bukkar Tchillas who happened to be a Loul according to my research on our family. But that was him. With pride, he told us his story but often omitted a lot. We never knew him well. Mom only smiled when we asked her who her husband was. I remember nagging her all the time about anything because she was easy going and it was it was to her I went to when I needed to know something. I would go, Mama Diouf, I see that you do not want to tell me much about Papa LouLanne and his family, but I do know a lot. Can you describe him just a little for us? Mama, not just the person you know that we know and see daily here with us, the dotted father. But, the person you knew well before we were born. She just smiled and jokingly chased me away to get off her back. Mama always thought that I heard things that I did not like about Papa. But that was not the case. I wanted reassurance because I was baffled by what the griots told me and his chosen way of life in The Gambia. I was proud of him and the humility he displayed.

I was intrigued by his personality at the same time. Going to school in Senegal, people that knew him well always felt the need to share the moments they had with him, and everything they said was right. They told me about the times he used to buy boxes of shoes to drop them off at the gates of many Mosques in Senegal without revealing his identity. He did many other good things that I would reflect on and feel so happy that he was my father. That makes me smile. As a child, I was not interested in all of that. Mom always said that I should be proud. "Money is not everything to him. You, especially NennJallo, you have the right person for a father." Of course, I knew that. But, my frustration was that they never told me anything about him that I wanted to know. I eventually stopped asking and wanting to know more about him. I settled on what was there for me to know about him, which was the person I saw, living humbly with us and the wisdom that any man would want to have.

He was knowledgeable, loving, caring and a no-nonsense man that everyone saw in him. What a Wiseman he was. He is still my 'Ezzemo' the Wiseman I learned to know a little about, but felt I knew through my late mother and others. Today, I am glad that I have settled for that knowing that his family and friends honoured him. He would have been ninety-two (93) years old in June. His friends are all old now, but still very alert. Tonton Ousmane Lougar always tells us all the beautiful things about him to make us smile. But he also explained the bravery in him, and that is enough for me. They have not forgotten anything about their days. Well, they cannot remember everything, but from what they tell me, the love they have for him and hearing them speak so highly of him is more than enough. Mom wouldn't have known Papa so well because she married young too." Always do what you need to be informed of the pass of your loved ones and leave it at that NennJallo". That is what she said to me. Mama Diouf had always told me that, Papa was a nobleman. I miss him because our world is empty without our branch. I used to try so hard to find someone in our family to hold on to, to cling onto but all I get is a disappointment and people who cannot show us the kind of love he had for us. But we are grateful that we have Allah. I always refer to what Mom told us before she died. She said that we should remain grateful and that the opposite of grateful is not ungrateful. It is in fact worry. If you worry that there is no one to solve your problems, then you are not thankful to your Creator the Almighty. She wanted us to know all the things about our father but some things she felt the need to protect us from especially me. I love my discoveries, and everybody knows that about my family in Senegal. I am a detective, always super sleuthing on people.

He was a man of honour. Someone who did so much good for people. I had always considered him retired by the time he went to the Gambia where we were born. I teased him a lot and said, I will retire early like him when I reach thirty.

Today, I am elated about what my late mother used to tell

me. "Always try and know what you need to know." In a way, she was indirectly telling me to keep being my own Super Sleuth. She told me never to stop asking. I will one day know and when I do, I know I will be more inspired to be just like him. Mother knew how fond of Papa I was. I was his 'Takanderr' the silhouette. Who wouldn't want to be? He had his flaws, but his nobility never failed to show especially when his friends and cousins came to visit us. I wish I had the filming wits that I have today.

My silhouette had his characteristics. He was giving, hardworking, soft-hearted, witty, charismatic and wise. He cried a lot for us. But he prayed for us too and asked us not to keep our emotions within. "It is OK to cry" but it is better not to do all the time. He added that we should not be dependent on anyone. He did press on that. I still do not know why. But he did.

Mom's advice then has helped me to sometimes look at the most complicated aspect of life as a simple thing easy to tackle. Life is what you make it. I learn to take things at my own pace and sail away even when I am finding it difficult to cope. An awkward situation never deters me from being the determined person that I am. In fact, I learn from it. No matter how difficult a job has become, I tell myself that the power within, topped with what God has given me, shall stay with me and I remain undefeated handling anything thrown at me with grace.

I manage everything through prayers, taking criticism positively, because, in the final run, it is not people's opinions that matter, but what my Creator says about me when I stand before Him on the day of Judgement. I am not perfect, but the sympathetic character in me suffices.

I was taught to believe in myself and that as a young woman, grace was all that my parents thrust upon me. I could not do otherwise, for it will be contrary to their wishes for us. How I should behave and what people expect of me remain my burden. That is why I will feel ashamed of my involvement in anything that will bring me shame. My sisters still laugh about some of the things I did and funny enough, I still do.

Whenever I disagree with someone and say hurtful things to retaliate, I end up feeling sick because I have made someone feel unhappy and hurt with my words. Sometimes, I get sick over it even when I am the one who is right.

One day, mom found me crying after fighting with a friend who followed me home on vacation. She was aware of what my friend did to me and wondered why I was the way I was. "NennJallo you know arguing is not for you. Why do you have to when you know that you will feel like this?" I do not have the energy nor the heart to harbour malice, no matter how much I try to be vengeful. Contrary to what I live with today in a society where you come across people who think the best of themselves and the worse of others. "Doyaddi wessou woul nitt kouy neh momm rekka baakh. Gneppa Bonn" I find it hilarious, but Nana was always right. A person who thinks that he/she is the best thing since sliced bread and that the rest of humanity is worthless. That person needs rehabilitation to get better. It is a sign, and that a person that thinks like that needs help to gain sanity.

Life is all about learning new things, getting inspired and aspiring to change things that do not work for you. I have a habit of using every good act I come across or any experience to map out my journey. It does not matter from whom that inspiration comes. You can draw inspiration from children as young as Five, Six or Seven…. I take pride in coming across people with excellent attributes that can rub off on me, both honourable and virtuous deeds. These charitable acts are like stencils. Once they are ingrained, they will never leave you. Obliteration will only be a word.

I never forget those who did well for people not to talk of people I am grateful to God for blessing me with their kinds. Even with those, I do not see any more due to distance; I want to remember the kind words said, good relationships we had and moments we shared with all the nice to remember things worthy of recollection.

The malicious bit can be put to rest when there is no more communication happening. That is if there was any malice in the first place. That is how many people find peace with and within themselves. I guess I fall into that category. That is the reason why I keep my cocoon safe to use for rainy days. I can always grab it when it is in need. It is ever so important to give without expecting anything in return. I care genuinely, but I talk a little. I have also learned that when you show grace and gratitude, you will receive all of that back. You can only see yourself in people and whatever you say to others is what you are as a person. I relate to every person I meet mirroring my acts in everything I do or say.

The good friends and sisters I have met along the way have inspired me a lot. I am not one to wage war with anyone. I can argue with a friend and smile when I see them achieve something because they remain inspiring. I cannot befriend anybody that does not inspire me due to a scarcity of time. One must have a goal in life if not nothing gets done the way they should.

I do hang out a lot with younger friends because of the inspiration I draw from their conversations and their easy-going nature.

The kind of motto that I will never part with is the one that encourages me to stay true to myself. It is the one that is always going to help me as a reminder to be better, do good, to speak well of others and apologise when I unintentionally say something wrong that can cause emotional consequence.

Making things better is what I wake up to, again it is that zing under my feet that I get up and wake up to daily. Acts of kindness in whatever I embark on for generosity is a foundation of inspiration, and it gives more than we can imagine. Since I do not like being hurt, I work my socks off to create a harmonious environment wherever I am. I do my hardest not to hurt anyone around me, and I quickly apologise when I feel someone's malaise around me. My compassion towards other people is marvelous. Wouldn't you say the same? Come on, smile at me. On a serious note, it is without a doubt a reason to wake up every day to find something positive to share with everyone. I encourage learning, starting with myself and then with my closest. Remember that knowledge is not just about the books, pen and paper. One cannot learn virtues in the classrooms. They are the essential skills that help you and the backbone of your soul.

If I were to choose another career for myself and the gift that comes with it, I would go for the idea of being an entertainer, someone who will make everyone laugh to help people see the brighter side of life. As the saying goes, coming back to the judging that people do…No one can judge you for we are all the same before God. We get judged by our deeds, and we should emulate one another and use each other as references, not rivals. We must not judge each other as our elders teach us. Only our Creator can judge us. When people do, just take it in your stride and continue fighting for causes that are worth giving your precious time to and do it for the society that needs progress in every aspect.

Our mentors and coaches tell us and remind us of how we are needed regardless of what we can do for society, big or small. A lot needs to be done based on our resources and capability. There are many amongst us with crushed dreams. But the good thing is that there is always a way to bring hope back. Failing is not the end because we can still find a helping hand in friends and families. Many people wake up daily with nothing much to focus their energy on. It can happen to any of us. My humble prayers always refer to unity and grace for all of us and helping one another to celebrate life and to be a helping hand to each. How much you have or give is not essential. We live on a day to day basis, and our destiny is not in our hands.'

The relentless search on an attempt to find good people to look up to for inspiration is vital. We may not always be lucky, but it is critical that we learn to move away from what deters us from succeeding both in virtues and everything that can make an enormous difference to our life and our society. One should master the art of penetrating through barriers that try to stop us from yearning for better things in life. Being around influential people do not mean to be people with wealth. It is everything to do with people who can teach you moral values because they are our tickets to success. That does not also mean people who can give you what you need but people who can show you the way.

Nobody needs handouts. People who can help you heal and give you moral support can help you come out of a dark phase where you do not wish your enemy to be. You will grow up in a person wanting to be amongst that category of people, and only society can benefit from the person you have to become in the end.

What I keep remembering and talking about is my incident in addressing a topic with a young member of one of our mentoring teams. This young lady is very eloquent and poetic. She always called herself 'Society.' Yes, she does call herself S.O.C.I.E.T.Y. But I prefer the name I gave her, which is F.E.L.I.C.I.T.Y.

She introduces herself that way at every meeting we organise. She is one elegant young woman who always thinks about what she can do for people who crave for transformation in their lives. She does live up to the name though, I give her credit for that, and it is very promising to see such a young person with so much to offer. I look at her, and I say to myself that I want to be just like you. She says the same thing to me, and that is very nice of her for she uplifts everyone she meets. Her peers say positive things about her as well. Only twenty-four years old, but she already has a mind of an old woman. Indeed, very astute to say the least. I guess we human beings or 'human-becoming' as my mentor says, we do not always want to appreciate what we are in the open for fear of people judging us as being arrogant. We look outward which makes us interesting. I become fond of her because she gives me joy knowing that she is going to make it in life. She has got a myriad of plans and innovative ideas to execute. She inspires me to do more in our communities. Surround yourself with people that help you grow. They do not have to be your friends, age mates or top influential people. All you need is level-headed people who you find interesting. Make yourself available to be part of the groups of people who strive on changing lives. Your energy is a currency and not have to be your friends, age mates or top influential people. All you need is level-headed people who you find interesting. Make yourself available to be part of the groups of people who strive on changing lives. Your energy is a currency and what you must do is use it wisely. I make it a point of duty to keep my search broader and going for those I can look up to and suck up positive energies. That is my mission.

The many silhouettes I desire to see in the shade are on the up. We shall keep counting because I have seen so many young women who are doing justice to why they are on earth. It is early days, but things will fall into place and society shall benefit immensely. It is never enough to stick to just one thing. That is not fashionable anymore.

Embarking on different discovery missions is what every person believes in nowadays. We do need those energy bulbs to keep pushing the envelope.

Working on women issues is both terrifying and amazing that is why we pursue the cause. It is a rewarding movement that is for all women to be and take part in developing themselves. If you want to guess what it is, do not go too far. It is to do with the female gender. That's right. It is the famous word that most people think that it comes with all the negative connotations which are wrong.

I often heard my grandmother said that every woman is born feminist, like it or not. I am lucky to be a daughter of a man whose peers described as feminist for the love he had for his daughters and how he was eager to see all women including us feel worthy and have the rightful place in society. Yes, that is the kind of man he was. He was not amongst those men who made too much noise about having too many female children. Papa did not make that his worry at all. He happily named all his daughters after his sisters except me. He jokingly called me the lone black bean in a pot, and that is precisely what I was. I used to be jealous of that, but I was just a kid then, and it does not matter anymore. My parents gave me an additional name which is my great grandfather's name. People considered as one of the greatest men in Sine. That was enough for me to say when everybody teased me. We had fun about that. Papa did not like seeing me get into arguments, but I did anyway. It is funny when people think of me as a reticent person. I mind my business, and I am also quite shy but not to the point that people can ride on my back to have a picnic. He always wanted me to know that good people do not argue or talk too much. Good people do have a giving heart, generous and kind. They are equally beautiful inside and out in every sense of the word, but they are principled too, and that is what our parents advise their children to become.

He would often speak to me about one beautiful woman in

Kaolack, Senegal. Her name was Coura Thiaw (Chaw). Coura was a beautiful woman, trendy and well appreciated by her community especially the men. Hmmm! Yes, the men enjoyed her beauty very much. Beauty is not everything, and those lines come from men, but they never settle for anything that is not beautiful. Correct me if I am what you must do is use it wisely. I make it a point of duty to keep my search broader and going for those I can look up to and suck up positive energies from. That is my mission.

The many silhouettes I desire to see in the shade are on the up. We shall keep counting because I have seen so many young women who are doing justice to what they are on earth for. It is early days, but things will fall into place and society shall benefit immensely. It is never enough to stick to just one thing. That is not fashionable anymore.

Embarking on different discovery missions is what every person believes in nowadays. We do need those energy bulbs to keep pushing the envelope.

Working on women issues is both terrifying and amazing that is why we pursue the cause. It is a rewarding movement that is for all women to be in. If you want to guess what it is, do not go too far. It is to do with the female gender. That's right. It is the famous word that most people think that it comes with all the negative connotations which are wrong.

I often heard my grandmother said that every woman is born feminist, like it or not. I am lucky to be a daughter of a man whose peers described as feminist for the love he had for his daughters and how he was eager to see all women including us feel worthy and have the rightful place in society. Yes, that is the kind of man he was. He was not amongst those men who made too much noise about having too many female children. Papa did not make that his worry at all. He happily named all his daughters after his sisters except me. He jokingly called me the lone black bean in a pot, and that is exactly what I was. I used to be jealous of that, but I was just a kid then, and it does not matter anymore. I am named after the greatest, and I say that to my sisters just to flatter myself when I argued with them. Papa did not like seeing me get into arguments, but I did anyway. It is funny when people think of me as a reticent person. I mind my business, and I am also quite shy but not to the point that people can ride on my back to have a picnic. He always wanted me to know that good people do not argue or talk too much. Good people do have a giving heart, generous and kind. They are equally beautiful inside and out in every sense of the word, but they are principled too, and that is what our parents advise their children to become.

He would often speak to me about one beautiful woman in Kaolack, Senegal. Her name was Coura Thiaw (Chaw). Coura was a beautiful woman, trendy and well appreciated by her community especially the men. Hmmm! Yes, the men enjoyed her beauty very much. Beauty is not everything and those lines come from men, but they never settle for anything that is not beautiful. Correct me if I am wrong. That is what it is. Men say one thing and change to another like the weather. Anyway, my father spoke to me so much about Coura Thiaw who was my mother and her peers' idol. They all loved her ways. She was a 'Bon Vivant' that every woman wanted to look up to as this unmatched image in her community. I remember asking my mother about Coura. She had a beautiful picture of her on our wall. She was ever so beautiful, very traditional looking with unique and stylish hairdos that every woman wanted to have especially during festive seasons. She said to me in wollof 'Kii moiy Coura Thiaw'. Even her hairstyle was called Coura Thiaw. Her tie and dye clothes were also called Coura Thiaw. Everything she had ever worn was called Coura Thiaw. Men talk about things they appreciate, and women do what their husbands appreciate about the people they talk about to make them appreciative of them. Did you hear that? One thing I do know is that my Papa appreciated my mother very well because she was his 'LoLo', the queen of his heart. She was everything that a woman should be. She was very poised, and you can see how she managed to be the woman that she was.

Every child knows about this iconic lady because our grandmothers spoke to us about her so much, her name cannot be removed from the history books of Saloum especially Kaolack. She was a woman of good characters according to the stories I have heard about her. My grandmother was a close friend of hers. She passed away though by the time I went to live with her in Senegal. But her name was always mentioned, and I guess she was the last icon they had in their community. The new era began with all these talks about Nightclubs, and the Koledera sound elders hated so much. They never looked forward to Saturdays because there was music everywhere and all I heard was my grandmother going like "They sounou Djamano" talking down on our modern ways. She went on explaining everything they did, how they lived. I must say, based on what she told me, these women were very civilised, very supportive to one another. They even helped each other set up their businesses. She showed me so many things they copied from this beautiful Coura Thiaw that everybody wanted to see wearing her garments.

Women of her time copied her hairstyle, her boubou designs and everything she did relating to beauty even the way she had her 'Fouddann' done which is Henna but designed differently on the toe and fingernails, inside the hand and on the back. It was the same she covered her feet with the Senegalese henna, the 'Fouddann'. They had it done differently, and that completed their outfits just like how we use nail extensions. Grandma did bore me with the talks on Coura when I thought I escaped Papa's lecture on how he praised my mother. "Jongoma Nii lay mell -Nii Coura Thiaw."

Our parents talked to us about highly influential people for us to look up to them and listen to their stories. I think is a constant traveller, Papa wanted me to go out there and learn from the best, and not do anyhow or follow anyone but to be myself. He wanted me to be inspired by good people, that is why he was always keen to tell me stories about all those people from community messengers to community leaders. To him, a reasonable person is someone with integrity, and that success is not just about how much money you have in the bank. It is about goodness you have within, the good manners and decent etiquettes you possess that can win you more than what money can buy.

My grandmother as well did the same thing for me. I looked at all the women she was friends with, and even the men who look up to her named many children after her in Kaolack. It has made me realised that she was a strong woman, respected by both men and women. This gender equality and equity issue is not a new thing, and I wonder why there is too much of a fuss around it now. Women can continue rallying to defend the status quo, but men must learn to buckle up and let us deal with our issues of concern. They can begin with the understanding that it is not all about the glass ceiling. There is more to the movement than that.

Knowing your worth can be a life changer, which I always say to my son. He used to think that he did not need to bother me when I asked too many questions. I hear myself asking him to tell his version and not go yes, yes, yes. I was not raised that way to go on saying yes when I have some critical things to say or when I had to defend myself. If you allow yourself to think that your parents raised you to be everyone's comfortable ride and no fees, you will live raw and die raw, not to talk of starving, being weak and everything in the book for the world is not kind to people that see beauty alone in everything.

Every person is born beautiful. That is what I heard my father say to me and that beauty does fade the same way the henna fades away. I am going to tell you of your worth as my children. He did want us to know that we can ask him anything, contribute to discussions because we are important too. He did emphasise that we did not need to agree with everything people say to us.

All our parents, especially African parents do tell us how to fend for ourselves from wee-age. I know that for sure. You will not be lauded by how you look alone. Beauty alone cannot help you be the best version of you. It is the last thing people think of when they see you. It adds to your being, but it is not vital since it is something you can afford if you become successful in looking after yourself.

I reminisce on these points now that I am a grown woman, fighting my issues and trying to make my contribution in society and in every way possible to make this world a better place as they say. Everybody's contribution matters. Mine, I know does matter as well. I do not take anybody else's effort for granted for unity is all we need to be there for one another. It is true that we always need someone to tell us how beautiful we are but having inner beauty is more important than anything else. With that, you can develop the passion for helping others shine. Passion for what you do is a great asset to possess. Understanding the powerful effects that it can have is equally important because people almost confuse passion, the love of what you have with power on others and it has some adverse effects too.

CHAPTER SEVEN
The Thirst

I am going to go a little bit spiritual here, and since I read both the Quran, the Bible and the Tora, I think I can give a gist of what has made me feel the readiness in me to venture on the myriad of journeys from which I think I can learn. In (Matthew 5:6) we are guided to understand that Shaytaan will attempt to offer us whatever we hunger for, whether it be money, power, sex, or prestige. But the Prophet Eyssa a said, "Blessed are those who hunger and thirst for righteousness…Whatever you do in life, who you are, where you are from and how young or old you are do matter a lot. But, the importance lies in the impact your existence shows. Doing good is the only thing that can save you from calamities and unfortunate events or any misfortune. It is a belief that we have all grown to understand. Who are we to say that this deed is what is good or bad? All boils down to acts that will follow you to your grave. Don't we all need the light? We sure do.

Let the character and outlook on life be right/ confident and of course be of inspiration. Be amongst the many people who just want to wake up every morning and absorb all the goodness that is around them. I make a habit of wishing well to whoever is standing next to me searching for something to become successful so that they can always remember that all I ever wanted for them was a success. When people succeed, they will not have time to say vile things to you or do you harm. They will not have time to yap about useless things. Successful people do not have time for so many things that Satan lure idle minded people to get themselves succumbed to all sorts. Have the thirst to step on the ladder that can take you to the direction your heart desires to go. Stay hungry for 'goodism', the significant expression Dr Maya Angelo used to describe everything that is good that comes out of Africa. Stay hungry for good things and never feel the need to keep the thirst that can become satanic.

We've all had our fair share of hard life. One starts seeing vicissitude in multiple facets when there is a chance. Life goes on, and we must understand that it is nowhere to being stagnated. When we are overwhelmed with challenges, we think that life has not been kind to us and we begin to contradict our beliefs. We often misinterpret things without noticing it. We must be amongst those people who will always feel the need to be assured that there is so much goodness in this world to share and that hope is flourishing in everything we touch or even in every challenge we face.

Personally, I interpret challenges as a guide to find what is best for me. I do not want to force anyone to be that person that I always ask myself to be, but I am influenced by these same positive ways of thinking, and that is healing.

Isn't this the silhouette's speech or little voice? Of course, it is. In my dreams, I interpret everything as the silhouette of what is to be and anyone I admire and aspire to be. By visualising a defined profile in a person that once touched your heart through learning about them will do it for you. I imagine apart from my mother, the grandmothers I knew who have raised beautiful people; my late father's mother Mayae whom I had the pleasure to live with briefly when I visited her in Fatick. Mayae was an epitome of a beautiful Serere Linguere. She had many children. All of them women except my late father. She had long curly hair, very fluffy and a pointed nose. She was a special lady. I used to wonder why she had those looks. Perhaps it is because it was old age. I am not ageist, but I had noticed that she was different, and her traits were remarkable.

Understanding her was a hard nut to crack for me. But I loved her from the depths of my heart. She is one of the people I think of and says wow, I wish I knew her very well. Was she like that when she was younger than the old age, she was when I met her? Interpreting everything in reverse when I was present even the time I went to bed too was always opposing to what it was.

The love that I had for Mayae was immense, but I always thought that she was unhappy with me because my Papa left home for the Gambia and she needed her only son to be around her. The granddaughter often got the bad mouthing, and that was me the innocent one. Mayae was something else. She called me names in Serere that even my late father after getting upset about it started enjoying it. To Mayae, I was 'Ndettarraan' meaning 'Deew Saangaam' in Wolof, that one without a name or perhaps 'Somebody'. I was not Somebody. I had a name and beautiful names in fact. I always felt like a stranger in her home because I was different from the other grandchildren. She gave me not even second-class treatment but rock bottom treatment. I giggle when I think of it now, but it was not funny then. I used to feel sad about the way she treated and bad mouthed me in the beginning. It was not my fault that Papa left to go and live in The Gambia.

Like many of his old friends did, he left home leaving all his belongings and siblings behind with Mayae my grandmother. She considered only those that were with her as her grandchildren. To Mayae, her daughters' children were the right grandchildren because they were always around her doing the 'Mameyaa,' the grandmother-grand-children banter with her. The bond that we always see happen between grandparents and their grandchildren was missing between us, and I craved for it. You could investigate my eyes that I was lost and had no clue how to muscle into her life. Bwoy! She might have been those children grandmother, and the mamaya was easy for them. But for me, my attempts were always chaotic. Don't laugh. It feels like coming into a new country, and you want to start speaking like them without knowing what is typical for them and what not. My relationship with Mayae was not all that in the beginning. I did not understand her badinage i.e., the wit that comes with the grandmother-granddaughter relationship. Anything that was said seemed like hatred towards me. That is how I used to see things. But, Mayae was enjoying it because she knew that there was no way she was going to wage hatred against her son's daughter. She had no reason to. After all, she was a people's person, and she was a role model, and hate was not what she had in her for anyone. That is how I felt, and I thought that she never liked us. She did not ask about my siblings, nor my father. She did not know us much to acquaint with us, and we did not know her well. That's what distance does, and it can create hostility. Very powerful rifts.

She was a great woman though, but my father's children missed out on her generosity, kindness, and love. I wanted to know her better, but it took time for us to bond eventually. I missed out on the kind of relationship she had with her other grandchildren. But that missing bond, I had it with my maternal grandmother Aminatta. Although I lived with her, she was always busy in politics. My constant search for the silhouette was an inconvenience. But every time she was around, I felt her presence, her love and it felt good because I was her chosen grandchild. So, Mayae did not count for a moment until Aminatta was away again. Did that ever make me sad? Of course, it did, and I always talked about it with my mother. With mom, nothing was that much of a nuisance. She always told me to deal with it and that I should understand that people have busy lives and that I should concentrate more on my learning. She had forgotten that I was still a child because nine years was too young an age to be dealing with complex issues. You will understand that it is fragile period and that a child's psyche can easily get damaged before they reach puberty. I needed the attention that I always had when I am with her, Papa and my siblings.

Strangers, which I mischievously called my families in Senegal at that time, did not have to give me all the attention that I needed but I wanted more and demanded because they agreed to have me, and they could have said no. I do not know details of their agreements between them and my parents, but they needed to take care of me. I sometimes wondered about the level of my mother's strength. But I listened to her carefully, and I began to consider what they gave to me, and that granted me the freedom to be and I endured whatever got thrown at me. It is courage topped with firm belief.

Nowadays, that kind is not easy to find in our generation. I am sure that many women of her age were like that too. I can still hear our elders laugh at the things we did not like. It is baffling. We are not iron made, besides we are living in different times. Aren't we lucky?

Pending on grandmother Mayae, my presence I know did remind her of the void she felt when her only son, my late father, left for a foreign land. Before going to the Gambia, Papa travelled to Angola, Gabon and many other countries. Guinea Bissau and Casamance were his favourite destinations. He never ceased to search for his roots and the many links to his family. I became the traveller that he was. That was when I was younger. When everyone expected to see me home in the Gambia in June, and I was nowhere near they could find me, they send a search party to come gets me from wherever I was. Sometimes mom travelled to get me, but I always wanted to stay to quench my thirst. I was recognised with my big hair and adequately protected. My young uncles liked me, and they looked after me very well. I was always on the go with them in search of my identity. Papa was like that too. Sometimes, age does not have to limit. Don't let age define you. At nine I went away from home. By eleven years, I could travel from Senegal to Barra. By fourteen I was able to trot from city to city on my own. It makes me laugh when I try to think of how Papa and even my grandmother used to tell me the kind of face I should give when I do not want people to approach me. My son laughs at me when I try to talk him into that. It did work for me although I do not do it anymore. I do not have to. There weren't any places Papa did not visit to find his relatives and the people he held dear to his heart.

He once told me about how his great-grandfather ended up in Gabou Kansala, Guinea Bissau and returning with young warriors. Some of his cousins bear the Manneh/Sanneh and Dione/John surnames. The latter was the surname of the first King of Sine out of the 57th. What a great kingdom Sine was. His name was Mansa Wally Dione, but he was ne Manneh. Mansa means King and the Serere could not pronounce it well. So, they called him Meyssa Wally Dione. He told me a whole lot about his travels, enough for me to write a book about. That was a highly knowledgeable man with so much wisdom in him. I would have written a lot and kept it if I were interested in writing then, but I was just a kid and my interests were about my marks in school for every semester and not story writing for the sake of it. If I knew that sixty-three (63) years decreed for him, I would have sat down and recorded everything he told me. I procrastinated so much in my life, and the thought of the word scares me.

Gratitude

As young children, we wanted presents and small pocket money to enjoy the whole summer holiday. All I was interested in was having enough information to write my school projects. As you know, young people do have a mind of their own. Patience was not something I called one of my best virtues like any other young person. That's why I do not nag my son that much because I know that one day, he will do as I did to be on top of his game earlier than we did in our generation. Praise the Lord! So far, he is doing good, and his interest is far beyond what I had expected. Praise be to God the Almighty.

There were so many things I needed to do, know that that I did not do or know. I had to do my best to fit in with the people that I loved so much. If you know my father's and my mother's family, you will love everything about them.

That is what I used to tell my classmates when I complained that I was finding difficult to feel part of the family. Especially grandmother Mayae who was not happy about her renegade son as my naughty cousins tease their uncle. I was not yet born when Papa left Senegal, but I had to live under that her shade of minor displeasures. Hmmm! I was amongst those she did not know and was not inclined to love us. It always made me feel sad because I did not understand nor spoke Serere and every time she spoke, I thought she was talking about me. "Nyaaw Njortah" that is utter insecurity. Deep inside, I felt her love, though, but she did not know how to show it to me for fear of her other grandchildren being upset. I called them little rascals. Grandmother feared them. I can laugh about that now, but I did not find it funny, seeing them tease my grandmother like she was a little girl chasing them around nonstop. It was not funny at all.

I forced her to feel that I was, in fact, the princess she did not know but she was her favourite child's daughter. Her son, my father, was the love of her life which made me the real breed of the Faye Clan. How I used to taunt her about Grandpa Waaggaan who was long gone. May his soul rest in perfect peace. He was the principal LouLanne for bringing us the one we loved and cherished. I argued with her about not liking me. Whenever I said that she went 'Sababba Jegga Korro,' I can only interpret that as the big words that come out of this girl's mouth. That'll do.

How could she not like me? I embarked on a mission. That mission was to make grandmother adore me by force, to accept and regard me as one of her grandchildren who loved her very much. That's how I badged into Mayae's world. I learned to speak Serere too. To my Papa, my relationship with his mother Mayae was a film. I entertained him with all the words Mayae used to say to me, and I called her all kinds too. He used to like my response when he asked about his mother. ' Huh! That woman, Papa' I always said that, and it was hilarious to him. But I loved her so much I became addicted to her vile words and everyone knew that. Loving her did not stop her from saying negative things about me which were entertaining. She called me all the names under the sun, but I did not care. We had to fight first before we became 'Tandems' good buddies. Even when I said hello or Njokanjal Mayae, she would insult me in Serere for saying it wrong with an accent of my own. Can you imagine that? I said it with flair, and she did not like it. I was naughty and deserved all her taunts. On top of that, she wanted me to say it her way and even the way I called her. Mayae did not want me to call her Mameboye. She wanted me to say 'Maam'ess' meaning my grandmother. She was the dictator I did not know existed. She threw all the words she could not say to her son to me. I was her punch bag. Huh!

I laughed at her when she complained about my lack of understanding of Serere, the native language. Learning to speak Serere made her happy. I guess she needed me to be initiated into the Faye clan too because she heard about my regular visits to my mom's town and village; Saassaara, Bilori and Gandiaye, and not to her home. Jealousy has been around for too long. I loved it when she prayed for me because she said it in Serere and I could understand was that she was asking 'Rogg Saine' for protection on my behalf with a lot of 'Yaassamm'ah Rogga...' May God grant you...peace and longevity. I am known for asking for prayers wherever I went. I guess it is because it made me feel safe because I was away from home. She did not hesitate to pray for me every time I asked her. Her words still ringing in my ears "May Allah beautify you, and she adds "You will be set for success too, " As for me, success then was leading in class and being the one with the highest percentage. That was enough for me. Whenever I did well in school, I ran to her to let her know that I had good marks which she did not understand. I had to tell her "maa djell peh" I am first in my class or I had more marks than my peers which she did not understand anyway. But she was always happy that 'Ndjumma' was doing well and that Papa LouLanne will be pleased.

Bonds

I eventually became so close to Mayae, but she was always jealous when I briefly come to Fatick to say that I was not staying long because I needed to go to Bilori and Saassaara my favourite destinations. I was treated like a princess, and everybody tried their best to make me happy from breakfast to dinner, I had all my requests ready for me to indulge in. My great uncles were in big businesses which meant that they never lacked anything.

In the beginning, what she hated most was the fact that I did not attempt to try to speak the Serere language with her or anybody else in the family. The only words that the young cousins of mine taught me were swearing words. That is very common and natural when learning a new language. I was cautious and did not repeat any of the words the boys taught me in front of Mayae. It was always so easy for her to pick up a stick and chase me around. Sometimes people found standing at the gate waiting for someone to walk in so that I could go inside the compound. I almost thought that my grandmother Mayae was not with it. She was an old woman.

My father planted a big fruit tree in the front yard. People always passed by to pick them up. The fruit is called 'Xhewerr' and tastes like red grapes. She still sat there, under the tree teasing children. The things that old age can do to people is hilarious.

The boys taught me naughty Serere words. It was very ill-disciplined of them, but I used, some to tease her and she did not want us to call her names. She hated it, and all her other grandkids knew how to make her angry. She would bad mouth me, and you could feel the waves of Mindis and the breeze combined whenever she addressed a topic about my father. I always hear LouL'anne, LouL'anne, LouL'anne nonstop without understanding one word about what she was saying. Three decades later, Grandma was still not happy that Papa left Senegal for the Gambia. He had a good life there and could have stayed and raised his children there but decided to do what no one has never done in the family. Was that my business? No, it was not but it became mine for wanting to be part of the family.

Anyway, I was this naughty granddaughter who retaliated, and I did the 'Pellor' with her whenever she was brought her claws out. I could not take her jibes anymore. Every word she said, I responded with ten. In the end, my aunties began enjoying our multiple 'pello' sessions. My tete a tete with Mayae was the best of title tattle moment. The little I knew then in Serere eventually made her feel so happy, and she was always thrilled to tell me stories about Maam Waaggaan, Wassyla Faye and the rest. She knew my mother's family very well because they are all related to the Diouf and Faye clans. They are from the same kingdom. Today, if the kingdom is to be revived, the Grand Djaraff will have the last words and that day is highly anticipated. Our lineage extends to Dakar and Saint Louis, Ndarr where you find so many people with the surname Paye that is the same as Faye. In a way, there is the Lebou blood in us.

Some people cannot speak a single, full sentence in Serere to start comparing me with them. Yes, I boast about it even though it is said that is ungodly to boast. But I do, a little just to give myself a tap on the back. I can talk a whole paragraph long in Serere without fretting. I knew a little about the many names she called me, the name such as

Ndetarr and Ndetarraan' did it for me. I said, of course, I am a Ndetarr. You only call those you don't know what kind of name. But she assured me that I had never been a Ndetarraan in my father's own home. That was just a saying, but no one saw me as a Ndetarr. She assured me that I was her beautiful granddaughter who liked hanging with boys, and she was going to change that. She was old school. She wanted to make a ten-year-old girl become a lady. Don't you think that it was too soon for a girl my age then to be imbued with continuous etiquette training? It was not. I feel great being around these two powerful women; grandmother Aminatta Diouf and grandmother Mayae Joquel Diouf.

A brief recollection of how papa felt when I first told him. It was the day I went to report Grandma Mayae to him. She told me when I saw her again that she knew what I did. I told my father everything she said to me and her name, calling "Mann nga demm calaameh tchi sa baay"? She said. We had a funny relationship, but we loved each other. I will never forget the day I said to my father what grandmother used to call me. Oh, the frown on his face! I can still see with my eyes closed. I became free of her taunts. Don't you agree that I should have done that sooner than later? I think so.

But when he told me what it meant, I just laughed. Of course, I am 'Dew sangaam' to her. She was 'deew sangaam' to me too. I never knew her Papa, Mayae never laughed with me at the beginning which was hilarious. I used to sit next to her craving for the nana and granddaughter relationship, but she just stared at me most of the time. She knew how to intimidate me, that woman. I smile when I think of that, but it was my thirst and I wanted it to end up nice for that acquaintance was the icebreaker. I did not give up, and that is natural to me. I pursuit her until I got what I wanted because there is something I forgot to mention. Papa told me to have his mom as my best friend and that she was a lovely lady. She was once upon a time, Maam Waaggaan Faye's Coura Thiaw too indeed. Often, I heard her go…Choh! Sababb'a Jegga Korro' That was her usual sigh. She spoke deep Serere and would often say something in Serere that I did not even try to understand.

I paid small attention to my parents' discussion. Both mom and dad spoke Serere. It was impossible for me to think that I can ever express myself in Serere, but I have tried to talk to Serere, and I am so proud of myself now for grasping it. I am so much into my Chossaan and Aada (Tradition and culture) now. They will love it, and that is what I intend to do to finally find all my silhouettes. It is our language code, but we can share in the other tomes to follow.

In most times, I sit alone in deep thoughts. In my little corner, I mumbled. I always said that I wanted to be left alone to think. 'Laissez Moi tout tranquil.' You will leave me to be 'old woman.' I was not talking to her. I was talking to my silhouette. As I had mentioned to Papa, my cousin Seye pronounced Saye was and still is the best cousins we can ever have. He is LouLanne's heir. He loved him very much. We were interconnected so remarkably to the point that the rest of the family did not matter to me. Seye was one of the people I looked up to, my tandem even though he still refers to me as 'Jinneh' for being too much. It is funny that he still does and calls me 'Toubbenn' bi (the convert) But that is what cousins do. They tease each other. I always followed him everywhere he went like a herder and his sheep.

My soldier, my gallant father raised me to grow up and become a catalyst. I think he loved me for that. I once said to him that I felt like a twenty-year-old at my age. He always made me laugh. He asked me if I have ever been twenty. I was only 13 when I said those lines, and he was right, I had no clue how it felt then to be twenty, but I imagined that and felt the need to say it. You learn with these wise people, and that is how it should be with us and our offspring. I was given this leeway to fit in comfortably, learn and not fear people because they are my parents or elders. Respect is what they imposed on us, and I enjoyed that part which has given me the endurance that I have now.

Growing up knowing strong people especially women like Mayae, a woman who had Maida's touch, Aminatta Diouf who was this fierce and bold woman can add a lot to a child's upbringing. I enjoy nothing more than the virtues I have known them for and all I have heard about them. I am mesmerised by that, and it feels like perfumes with an everlasting smell that even a hundredth times wash will not make it go away. How I feel about these women will take me a long way. They are sharp reminders for me to hold on to and the lines to use when I need to walk away from anything that has a tendency of tarnishing my image or gives me lousy reputation before anyone. Grandmother Aminatta was respected by her male counterparts who were in politics because of the respect she gave them. They had no other choice but to reciprocate that. She earned it. She spoke and spoke louder when she needed to but also listened well when she needed to. I wish both were not old when I met them.

The spirit of these great women remains my cocoon. I want to assure the world of that. Did I inherit some of that Maida's touch? I do not know yet, but only time will tell if I have a bit of them in me. I know my father did and mother took the traits of her mother that I did not know but I could a lot of Aminatta Diouf in her.

In my silent and humble voice, I ask my Creator to connect me with the imaginary silhouette that I grow up thinking that I have had. Connectedness with the people who will always pray for me I have ever asked for in the kindest plea. It has helped me walk my track correctly. Pray for those who are in trouble, pray for leaders, elders and the society. Never forget that the good you wish for others does find its way to you. Make your heart as pure as a piece of clean white cloth. It isn't an easy task because no one is perfect, but it is not far-fetched either. It is not difficult to attain. It means being kind to yourself, and it comes with constant practice. All the things that are good for the soul that I need require a lot of practice. The ones I envy are those who can forget and move on smoothly without making too much noise? I hope to achieve that level even in times of difficulties. It is the only spiritual level that can help one attain that stage. It is called a sage. It is hard to achieve. So, in my father's household, we ask for the Lord of humanity to bless us with everything that leads to His mercy, with a calibre of people who can show us the way. We make our choices to live better when we stop worrying. The decision we make determines the end of our worries in our minds.

That is what I have always said to my son. I love you for the blessings and that because the entire universe conspired to help me find you and you are my blessing, my silhouette, my miracle that I treasure. I need not say more…

The same way I see the metaphorical life that I have had from the time I started noticing my journey and all the things in it; challenges, hardship, goodness, bondages, and obstacles that made me think of putting things together. This silhouette, in the form of a voice and the guidance scripted, has helped me start the mapping out. In this map, I incorporate everything that is to be produced to link the past with the present and wait for the future to unfold. I would not have thought of it in a better way but to relate my experience with the fictional story of a woman I could have been. That is Mossaan. A young woman who takes the time to be kind. She is beautiful. Anyone who finds it crucial to take the time to be kind, as they say, is gorgeous.

Many a time, folks would find it essential to say to me that I go the extra mile and you must change that. Where is that extra mile? I often ask. Don't you think that what is for others cannot be prevented? My beliefs guide me. That is how I see things. Hearing people say, "You always go the extra mile to please everyone" does not bother me anymore. But it makes me question their level of understanding of the spiritual world and doubting their beliefs but who am I to do that? What bothers me is what is it in it that is so wrong for me not to do. My responses always defer to what again many would think of my nature. I do have so many answers to that. It is a disposition; I cannot change because I was born with it and I am quite happy with it. I am thankful that, so many people have worked for me for me to be the way that I am from a very young age.

It is crucial to know that in life, the more you love your decisions, the less you need others to show that they love them. You need not depend on people to like your choices to do what is right for society. If what you do is not enough, you wouldn't have been chosen to do them. The universe, again, sends us precisely what we are ready for at the right time. Sometimes, it comes at a time when we feel we are not qualified, but it is often the contrary. It is the right time. We needed it, and complying does help ease the process.

The mind does not return to its original scopes once stretched by a new idea. That is a fact. It is always easy to get stuck in one position without finding the need to move on to something not bigger but better. I do not believe in the saying of bigger and better things because the level of humility in me does not and will never allow me to think that way. Everything we do is the best when we embark on changing our habits.

How vital is it to resist the urge to speak your mind in every situation? Humble yourself and do not put pressure on others or expect others to be like you. That is what I am always reminded of, and I like the fact that I am not derailing. Your destiny is not a part of your body you can efface or say you want to alter. You are not in charge of that area. It is not a part that can undergo surgery, be revamped, be filtered or be retouched. How I see things may differ from someone else's views. It is undeniable that the pace of understanding is so much and even more full to share. Life, from how I see it, is about learning from which we master most of the many curves if not all. At least a few should be understood. I believe in adding a bit of value to my surrounding in my small ways based on the people I emulate because I am a person, who takes a lot of learning. Never feel the pressure of changing who you are. With the rest, they either learn to deal with the way you are or not, and if you believe in what you represent, that is good for society. I learn to deal with hearing it one time too many, the ways in our habits that need to change. It is all I have that is good for me, I add with a peal of laughter. What will I be doing if I do not give it my all? I am not planning to change sometime soon because, it is again, one of the outlines I am searching. It might be what suits my personality. I would say judge me. Go ahead and judge me for my small mistakes, even when I am refusing to stop. I use the lines that are favourable to me. I never doubted that it is a gracious act, and since I can accommodate everyone in my little heart, I take it as a gift from above. I am grateful to my Creator, and I will never cease to be on my knees and ask for more favours.

It wouldn't be great to say that we would love to see more acts of kindness in every person we meet in our lifetime. I do yearn for that to happen.

This space of ours, where we live temporarily, is vast, and each one of us needs the security to feel safe in it. We can find the latter through good deeds first and supplications. These two acts are core to what we need to do here. I pray that we live to see our blessings unfold before us even though as believers, we are told and assured that what we receive here cannot match what we are to find after leaving this world. My mother made me laugh one time when we are discussing prayers, good deeds and all. She said that it does not mean taking what belongs to your sisters and give it away to people. I used to give out my stuff and even my sisters' belongings. I believed in giving, and anything that was around me that I did not need had to go. She also reminded me that being prayerful alone cannot guarantee you the best if your heart is not clean. So, I asked how does one know that their heart is clean? She said to me that I could know by doing good and being honest with myself for no one can know you better than yourself. You cannot fool anyone but yourself if you pretend to be what you are not. However, asking for forgiveness often can help you find yourself and start doing good by starting from within. The blessings we seek for shall be found for we ask to be surrounded with good people in our lives and to live in environments where we can feel safe, where we can confidently look at someone and feel the need to have them as our confidante and make them a shoulder on which to cry. I am quite aware of what it means to be helpful to others. As I have already mentioned, the number of favours that was rendered to me throughout my life when I had to live in other people's homes cannot be repaid. My parents remind of that. Anyone who has ever been good to me left a mark on me, and that has moulded me to also add to what they taught me as a young child. Anything could have happened to me. I am not saying that I did not go through challenges and situations that I wish to talk about but, out of hundred percent, seventy percent of my life living without my parents were great. I will be doing everything in my power to work for humanity, and I have so many good people to look up to and if need be, make a replica of their version.

Consequently, to my knowledge and to finalise, there is nothing wrong with going the extra mile if what you do is out of the goodness of your heart. Do I try to figure out what the excess mile would be? Can people stretch their muscles that much? It does not exist in my vocabulary for one can only do what is in their power.

I know it is abstract but, I need a feel for it so that I can understand it better. Until then, I am lauding whatever attribute I am blessed with and rejoicing from the goodness that I feel for everyone around me.

Where do you find solace? As you read, you find yourself gauging your level of understanding. I find comfort in seeing people happy. It yields security and safety nets that you cannot find anywhere else but within a circle of good people with good intentions and less malicious words to throw at anyone and anything they see. It is like moving away or passing through the lion's den to find yourself settled in the rabbit's cage. Wouldn't you have preferred rubbing shoulders with the friendliest or a harmless lot? Oh yes, I do. We all do. That is why I can put extra effort to please myself and live longer by making someone have me in their kind thoughts, and I add them to my good books. Those you are sympathetic to can make mistakes and say the ugliest things to you, but they can never harm you. I always say this to myself that understanding this can keep me steadfast and it will help me have a forgiving heart.

Don't you often wake up and tell yourself that you are on a mission? I do that daily, and it makes the difference in my thoughts more explicit. Besides, everyone should be on a mission because that is what we are sent down here to be.

It comes with a lot of opportunities to grab but never ignore the challenges that come with it.

The world needs as many missionaries as possible. Mother Theresa was, Dr Maya Angelo was, and in Africa, we had the likes of Yassine Boubou, Fawadda Wele, Mame Diarra Bousso and many more of our great women were, including our very own grandmothers and mothers. We know it or not, they were inspirational, and we need not look any further to get inspired. I do what it takes to gauge myself, to discover my ability to do things appropriately. Implementing my thoughts is what I do daily just to be able to impact the lives of people looking up to me which is a template of what I am experiencing with people that I emulate. As I jokingly say to myself when I am overwhelmed with negative thoughts, and I feel helpless. I use these lines such as this asking my positive mind to throttle my contrary ideas, and I do it often to stay sane.

I start this with my child who thinks the world of me. The challenges of raising children are enormous. However, if we think of how we were once, we cannot go on losing hope. All that we need is to take it one step at a time. As much as we want everything to be a hunky dory, they will never be. But, good always comes out of the grand wishes for success. That is how God works.

 As I have frequently mentioned in every line I say or write; wherever I am, I make it a habit of waking up every day with a zing on my feet to connect with everyone in a very positive manner. Inspirational is an understatement. I am elated to grab this world by the horn and sling it towards those who wish to walk the journey with me, for each to catch a hook and move on with it. The lessons and blessings are to be shared without any of us yearning for the more or lesser significant share of the pie. We remain positive in what we do, and while doing that, we practice the equality amongst us and make this world our oyster.

I know that it sounds like a chronicle, but it is not. It is what inspires me to write Mossaan. The two stories; my adolescence years and what I have learned when growing up has helped me reminisce Mossaan. They have got a link for if it weren't for my childhood experience and my countless of journeys, this would not have existed. It was the only story I grew up to know from the age of Ten. That is enough memories not to skip before engaging in anything. I kept it for too long, and I think that sharing it is way overdue. What do you think? What did I think of before embarking on a journey that I believe has helped me carve this one with utter contentment?

Mossaan's story is linked to my views, experience, the many wants, my desire to entertain, share, learn, grow, develop and contribute with the little I can. The importance of diarising events is manifested here significantly. Engaging the audience to be part of it is my target. Writing this with my urge to speak about my journey has given me a new lease of life, connecting me with the so much adored protagonist like I knew her more than I know myself and everyone involved in it.

Correspondingly, the imaginary friend that everyone closed to me knew about in my family when I was growing up. I had this little friend, an imaginary goat-friend which my son laughs about every time I speak to him about it. It was a goat that I used to see everywhere I went especially after dark. I reminisce often telling this imaginary story of a goat, I had a name for which I would not divulge, and I know that you wish to know. All I can say is that like any other ordinary child; it was my imaginary guardian and friend.

Every child has an imaginary friend. Mine was very special to the point that it protected me when it was dark. I always addressed him as a person and forever treated him as a buddy I did not have. I ever exceptionally referred to him and said, "I can see you standing right there." I did that quite often. One day my late Papa said to me "What if he responded and said, "I can see you too" "What would you say then?" From that day on, I stopped calling out his name and pretended not to have seen him again. It was always there. I can share the name but in acronyms. It is B.A. Simply that and not more. It always makes me laugh when I think of it or tell people about B.A.

My silhouettes are in numbers. Remembering each one gives me great pleasure. So, does this story of Mossaan. It reminds me of my young cousins in the villages I visited such as Saassaara and Bilori and towns like Fatick and Gandiaye and even few friends I grew up in the Gambia.

Written almost a decade ago, I express to you an astonishing beauty and ask what next and how do you want us to go on with the story? What did I omit? What would be fanciable? How do we approach it? What would you like to have that you could not have? The things you ask yourself when you attempt to present stories that can inspire or perhaps be lessons for anybody that indulges in reading it.

Storytelling is an imaginary world of its own. My imagination is beyond fiction, a fantasy or a fable, that is why it has taken this tactical approach. It feels good to connect to the story. The twist is the secret of a delightful tale such as this one with so much nuance. These are the first lines I drew when starting the script that depicts the life of a beautiful young woman. She is the most ambitious amongst her peers. We need not make her living/life extravagant for now, but one filled with challenges and solutions just like our own lives.

Do I know Mossaan?

Do I know what she is.?

Do I want her to be me?

Do I want to be someone that I know? But that would be wrong and illicit because it is only an imaginary story with a bit of reality that addresses the way of life for the youths of today especially young women. It is every young woman's story. Who is Mossaan? I asked again. Then the ideas started flowing. The love I had and still have for my late mother and the way I saw her with her people gave me an idea of where I am going to take this story. I feel like I knew Mossaan. She was fondly called Moss.

Mossaan's inspiration is Marianne Semou Djimmit and all the other characters in the book. Jokel Mindis and Marie Ndebb Diouf, of course, I do know them, for they accompany me everywhere I went. I take their company with delight and live with them just like how I managed from inception more than what my imaginary friend, who has disappeared now for mystique reasons not known to me, has done. These characters are amongst my many silhouettes. They are the shadows and inspirational petite charms that I have always craved for, and I speak to them and sometimes in my imaginary world and bubble. They never fail to answer back to give me directives that I unquestionably take on board. These characters are here to communicate to me at the same time guide me. They can watch and applaud when I say something useful. They correct me, disagree or argue with me. But they also laugh when I do or write silly things because they are part of the collective noggins that differ when I forcefully and wrongfully describe each of them to be something they are not and hide the good things they've done when they are supposed to be cheered. Now, do not worry why stories go the way they go. It does not matter how fanciable you wish a tale to be; it is always easy for them to go wrong when you try to add something you have not experienced or seen happen to someone. It is one of the main reasons why Mossaan's story is written the way it is.

I first had them as my imaginary friends/companions, then my storytellers and the ink in my pen. The same inked pen directs me towards achieving my goal of this project. They are in my life throughout. I go to sleep chatting with them in my imaginary world that I nicknamed my fizz. If this is not exciting, I do not know what is and what will be. Because I saw a little of myself in the primary person, even though I have never gone through arranged marriages nor lived permanently in remote areas for long, but the many events she went through. These incidents are not new to every young woman living in Africa. Society begins putting pressure on women from the time they are born and throughout their adolescence.

In Africa, our guardians tell us that the beauty of a woman is in her marital status, meaning being Mrs X, Y, Z. I know this calls for a debate, but it is true. The Mrs Somebody syndrome has become a predicament for every woman. In the west, they tell us that we must be thin and beautiful to be successful. That is when we reach the level that Mossaan is yearning to be. The struggle is in various stages. Because of young women like Mossaan, we all want to do more for society. Fiction is an imagination and description of events, and I do imagine life in different facets. I am not saying that I am not the lucky one to have gone through that, but my empathy allows me to speak about what women go through especially the girl child growing up in Africa. As an African woman, I grew up in an environment where a lot happens culturally and traditionally. Some of us are lucky to have had parents who were happy to go with the flow of modern times. My father was one of those parents. He was pro-education and never questioned himself about what he was doing about his daughters' education, fundamental to higher, but he also understood that it was not everyone.

Father always made sure that education for his children was his priority and his provisions were never gone unnoticed especially for me. I recall him addressing as hiss Tina Turner because of my love for big hair. I was as they fondly said when talking about me that I was a handful. He made me feel very special, praised me endlessly and provided all that I needed. The loveliest of memories I have had of him, was when he proudly introduced me to his friends. "Meet my daughter NennJallo." She is my Tina Turner. I always had big hair, which everyone I grew up knew me of. On top of that, I enjoyed dressing well as a little French Madame and looked very 'coquette.' A friend of mine, I would love to mention here, Fatou Kouyateh always shared her good stuff. She was very generous. Bless her. Faru as I fondly call her is such a kind-hearted woman I know. She is someone I have known from childhood. Deep in my heart, I call her my distinguished friend and one of the savviest and sassiest ladies. Her humility hides all the beautiful traits she has. She is smart and loving. All that is enough for someone to be deemed as a person of God. You see, it is a kindness that rewards kindness.

I will never forget the great people that I grew up knowing and meeting. With Fatou Sira, you can go to her house and take whatever you want, and she will still be laughing. She started her businesses at a very young age, and she shared everything in her possession with her friends. I was still going to school in Senegal when she already had a successful trading business. Coming home and seeing her was always a delight and what I looked forward to every year. She made sure I enjoyed my three months holiday when she was around on all numerous trips to Europe. We enjoyed going to the cinema, and there we were incessantly singing songs we heard from the Indian movies we watched. I loved those moments. Love and care are all the things I knew, and I will always encourage my child to be as loving as possible.

Papa was like that, and my mother was everyone's darling. He always introduced me to people calling me the most beautiful and famous names of individuals such as Tina Turner, Dina Ross and his little Coura Thiaw. He always added that I was just like my mother who had a beautiful heart. I bet if Papa were still around, I would have had him call me by these new influential people's names too. He was ever so proud of seeing people achieve great things. He was proud of me for the love I had for education, and I think that is how I won his heart and his trust. With him, it was less of a problem if I grew up and I did not know how to cook. It was a bit over the top, but I stayed in that joy and never wanted to let him down, nor my level in my subjects go down. I always came home with satisfactory results, and I still said, anything that made Papa happy, I would do.

Whatever Papa wanted, NennJallo would deliver 'Dounyou bolleh' we won't be seen fighting over learning. Papa always reminded me that he is not like those fathers who think that a girl's education ends up in her husband's kitchen. After all, learning was all that I loved doing apart from dressing nicely and asking for money to buy beautiful dresses from him. I was always ready to deliver. Summertime was a huge moment, a homecoming for me. He often came to pick me up from the garage to take me home. His car was always packed at the PWD garage after work. He did the same after picking me up. We usually walk the street to the house, meeting everyone on the way. Everyone knew when I was coming home and by the time we reached home, all my friends would be there waiting for me. They informed them of when I am expected, and it was always a great moment.

Having lived in Senegal for so long, I got used to the Wolof accent. I spoke Wolof with this charming accent of theirs. Though in Senegal and the Gambia we speak the same language, the Wolof in Senegal sounds different. They have a distinct accent due to the touch of French, and it is English for us in The Gambia. I was always called the 'Seneh' by the boys because of that. I often heard them say

"Kii Seneh la" It was fun - I smile whenever I remember the many incidents in Bakau where I was born. Bakau is one of the most beautiful towns in The Gambia.

A lady called Mbaa Suttay Jaiteh admired me so much, she never denied herself a good chat with me whenever she saw me coming. Every time I passed by her house, she would deliberately stop me to speak to me about anything; from serious to futile topics. She introduced me to her younger sister who was from their village, somewhere in Badibou. Little did I know was that she loved the fact that, as young as I was, I greeted people, our elders, by their surnames. I learned that from my grandmother. She always emphasised on hearing me welcome people in that manner. All I knew was that she wanted me to stay with her to be one thing to remember and make my parents proud that she taught me well and instilled some goodness in me while living in Senegal with her.

Our elders in the Gambia loved that about me though they found it very unusual, awkward, funny because I was still a child. I curtsied when I greeted people; I pronounced people's surnames when I stopped to greet them. I always do. It does not take away anything treasure out of my personality. As for Mbaa Suttay, I was an old soul, a character she could not understand, old-fashioned act as I have heard her say. Yes, I was a mature person far beyond my age, a reincarnated soul indeed. She does not see people do that anymore; she noted especially people of my generation. Not very often though.

Mbaa Suttay thought I was a polite girl and said that to everyone. Mbaa Suttay told her sister and everyone in their compound that I greeted people by their surnames. I saw that from my mother and my grandmother as well. She loved it when I said 'Mbaa Suttay' and I added…Jaiteh'. Mind you, I laugh too when I think of how I was, and I know I added a bit of mischief because I wanted my friends/peers to be less polite than I was. She liked that about me very much. It was funny, I bet, but I did not care much because it was good a quality to have. My friends laughed too and called me 'Gogg' (feisty). It does good to be different. It makes life interesting. I was also mature for my age that is what everyone knew and said about me. Yes, I knew, but growing up fast was the only choice that I had. At nine throughout my adolescence into my early adulthood, I was away from home for my secondary education. I had to be astute, vigilant, watchful as Papa always asked me to be. 'Baayeel sa xhell ci kunneh.' Don't give anyone the chance to do anything inappropriate to you. Be careful and look after yourself. He used those lines year in, year out to the point that I always repeated the same words before he said them and sometimes we were in synch when we said the words. He cared so much, and Mom used to tell me how he always felt sorrowful as he sent me away at the end of every end of summer holidays. It was our song and parting anthem. We had to say these words every time I was to go back for another academic year. Parting with my parents and siblings were always awkward moments, but the tears never guaranteed me extra days. Papa was very kind but too strict about my education. I thank them for the push.

I often laughed when my friends teased me about being an old soul. It did not bother me. I jokingly told them that is why I was the elders' favourite. I always laughed about it and shrugged it off. Mbaa Suttay wanted her sister to hear me say this. She had to call me to come back pretending that she wanted me to tell my mom something like she was sending her greetings. Smiling, we greeted each other, and I bet she was eager to hear the Jaiteh. I should have kept it to myself. But I did not. I effortlessly gave them what they wanted to hear. It was the sound of me saying, Mbaa Sutteh, Jaiteh that did it for her. Both laughed, and she said. "Paap Babou la Senekaal dingo Lemm nyingti. Aa hadama yaa ta baakeh" meaning, that is Papa Babou's Senegalese daughter in Mandinka. She is very people oriented.

My father also started understanding the nuance and the reasons why people always tried to differentiate me from my sisters. It was only about identification nothing less. It was the only way they could describe me as we found out. It was OK for they meant well. Nothing relating to discrimination of any sort. It became reasonable to us, as sisters, when people wanted to talk about us. My late father easily knew who to ask when something happened, and that people wanted to say that it concerned me. Yes, it was me they referred to, and I was his NennJallo, his Senegalese daughter, and the 'Senkalingka dingo.' Yes, the Senegalese daughter was me. The one with the big hair was me. The one who was always with the Paris Match and Hello Magazines. They just singled me out and gave attributes that when I remember them today, made me smile.

I beam at the kind words and the fact that my existence impacted my surrounding all for the love of people and learning that I had. Papa was always proud to call me his daughter and my siblings knew that too. With all of me and my flaws, I could shine and enjoy my childhood. The people that allowed me to have the best of youth that has given me the opportunity to be here today are called my A-Team. Nothing compares to the love between siblings. They are my strength and number one fans, although my son claims the position and it is his, but my siblings can own it whenever he is not looking.

I thank God that we were all kind towards one another. There was no grain of jealousy between us when we were growing up, and today they are the people I run go to whenever I am challenged. There is still none to date because we believe in living the kind of life, both our parents had wanted for us even when they are no more. The experience they wanted for us does not depend on wealth or material. It is solely in the harmony and peace that every human being asks to live happily.

Mama Diouf and Papa LouL'anne were the backbones of the dream team I crave having. It is the team that taught us how to say, 'I am thankful for my pains and struggles moreover with my blessings.' They were the team that many of their friends adored. Those two never argued nor fought each other. All I ever wished for was an extraordinary, fun loving man for a husband and a gallant father to my children like him. Dreams do not cost much that is why everyone can afford it.

I prayed about that when I was younger. Papa was a principled man, very humble, modest and hardworking and trustworthy. Mother's blessings were beyond the limits. She was a blessing for having that kind of an intelligent gentleman in her life. He raised my mother's siblings and did everything for them. She never complained about how much Papa had or did not have. She is the role model every child could wish for. It gives me immense pleasure to talk about him in that manner and about the beautiful people I knew growing up. Their moral values society tend to be gradually losing its grip on, remain laudable. What they instilled in me is more than diamond and gold. It is my treasure for life. Something that I will always refer to when I need to smile because I know that I can still hope for the better even with empty pockets. It includes the virtues and the myriad of life lessons that can only fortify me. Being prayerful is one of them and key to everything I do nowadays. Mbaa Suttay was one of those people I can never erase from my mind. I am not related to her, but her love for me was noticeable. Whenever she called me, I knew she wanted to hear what I was to say. I knew she wanted to indirectly introduce me to people she had spoken to about me. I always smiled about the fact that they found my way of greeting very old fashioned but charming. It was the environment I was living in, and you know how young people absorb things so quickly.

Kaolack is in Saloum, and most of its population speaks the wollof like no other. It sounds pleasant to me as I have tried to talk about the way it is expressed. However, I only manage well with the greetings, and that does it for me. It is called 'woloffal Faana-Faana', the wollof that people from the Saloum region speak. Luckily for me, I did not talk too much about it because I did understand most of the words and never wanted to be humiliated by asking what they were saying. That is how shy I used to be.

My mother was always entertained by my imitation of the wollof. Granny Aminatta Diouf's best friend and husband Mam Ngagne were all Saloum-Saloum 'Fanaa-Fanaa'. They spoke the most beautiful Wolof accent. My father also had a mentee called 'Doboss' who was very well known in Bakau. He entertained us with his jokes in that same accent. I had to ask him once when I heard him speak Wolof with the accent I knew as any young person is keen to do because I was used to hearing the accent he jokingly belted out. He too imitated his people. What I like most about those days is the fact that there were no animosities between tribes and our childhood was not tarnished with all the different issues that we witness now in our society. We enjoyed the 'Kalanteh', the banter and teasing each other of all kinds. I blame it on time and evolution and politics. But it is instead the lack of awareness and understanding that there are some issues and values that we do have to touch or change. Once we try to do otherwise, we fail big time.

My traits were also my benchmark. The character reference people could give on my behalf without hesitation. Polite which I was not sure of. An old soul, yes, I was. Not bad at all given that I was always busy wanting to be present in everything. I bet my sisters were jealous of hearing people say how poised or polite I was because it is not what they experienced with me. I can laugh about that mischief from me. I was always pulling their leg. If I was not arguing with KharDjata, or fighting with Marie or Fatou, I was doing something that mom would be complaining about or not doing chores I was assigned to do. My oldest sister used to nag me a lot. I think she thought that she was my mother. She did not let me breathe one second. Fatou was always in my case, monitoring my every move. Isn't it lovely to have everyone looking out for you? I had teachers, mentors, and guardians in the family. When Papa was not around or mom, everyone looked after me. They still feel the need to look out for me.

It warms my heart to hear them say the good things they say about me. Even if they are saying it to make me feel good, they are doing a great job of that. I tell you why. It is because I want to remain the way they perceive and avoid doing anything that will make me feel that I am derailing. I was their kind sister, the kind, and adorable young lady everyone like but I was naughty too. Some call it mischief. I replied in the same tone when Mbaa Suttay's nephews asked me where I lived. I replied and said 'Senekal' for Senegal, the same way their aunty pronounced it. I said it that way naughtily but in a friendly manner.

I got that every time I saw a group of elders. I guess they enjoyed hearing a tiny person like me speak like an old woman because our generation of young people always think that that style of greeting is not for us. Well, I was so used to it, I annoyed my sisters. I could not care less. I will greet you and even bow if you let me. I got that habit from my grandmother Aminatta Diouf. She was also the one we called MamBoye Amina. She desired poise, class, and ethics in every child she raised. I was the last and youngest to have passed through her gates as she fondly said it and she expected nothing from me but to be successful in my education. That's all she needed to see me achieve.

I was there to learn and prohibited to do anything that would bring shame to her household. I was the favourite great-niece, she was not my mother's mom, but the youngest of her sisters. When my grandmother passed away, she was there to look after my mother's affairs. She took care of my mother and her siblings until my father decided to take over.

The politician she was made her my ShaSha Fierce. Very rigid, but I got away with little things now and then. Well, I was the youngest, and I had a special place in her heart. That spot was dedicated for me to occupy. It was the area reserved for the LouL'anne breed. There was not a spare zone in her big heart for someone else. It made my older cousins go green-eyed, and I grin every time I teased them and said that they are making their faces look as if they have accidentally chewed on lemon seeds. They always went, here she goes again laughing hysterically.

Lucky me, is what I always said to myself. If that fierce woman, as they called her, had a soft spot in her heart for me, then I was the luckiest young lady in the world. I had no plans of losing that place. I clung to it and never did what she did not want me to do. All she wanted was to see me coming home with satisfactory results to show to my father.

Grandmother's home was a hub for all her brothers' children. She had a prominent place, and her doors were open to every one of the children from the vast Joof family where she belonged. Those gates in her two homes in Sam and Thioffack in Kaolack will never be forgotten. I remember everything learned from there. Both Sam and Thioffack are located, behind Medina Mame Baye Niasse county in Kaolack. So much was learned from there. I cannot thank her enough for the things she had done for me. I wish she here so that I can introduce my only child to her as she fondly said to me that my son when I have one would be taken to Senegal to hear my story and everything I used to do or say. May she continue to Rest In Perfect Peace.

Grieving is a moving river as I always say. There are four people that I had in my life that I can never forget. I am grateful to my Allah for blessing me with the like of them. What they have instilled in me is beyond what I ever imagined. I always ask for strength in their memories. Their words fortify me and that I believe that is the reason why I do not give, and I have a firm conviction to accept my fate, come rain or shine.

I shed tears every time I hear of someone passing because it reminds me of the same pain I went through when I lost them. Losing a dear one is very painful. Especially losing people who would cry with you and help you find your feet again. You cannot have that in friendship today. Death is a myth, and I am one of those people who believe that I will meet the people I love again when I join them in the Gardens of HEAVEN.

I still remember the lines she taught me, and my parents always said the same things to me. They were cultured and adhered too much to tradition and beliefs, but still thought of us, and instead of being rigid, they were reasonable with us. I remember asking my mother about how to dress when I go to Diakhao, Gandiaye, Saassaara, Bilori. I was worried that they would think that she did not teach her children good manners. She replied that no one is forcing me to be what I am not. It is up to me to learn and see what I can take from whatever I come across that is good. We come from a very traditional family. Both my parents have this deep 'Chossaan' in their families. I am knowledgeable about them, and I am proud of that given that I was born outside the traditional environment and as many of our relatives say, living far away from it all in a way is our safety and of course the peace of mind we enjoy today.

No matter under what circumstances you were raised, emerging triumphant is what they expect to see you do. You must learn to think of yourself positively because it is your life. She said that to me mainly because she wanted me to believe that no matter what she does for me when I am in the classroom to learn, it must be me versus my future. That is the grandmother's talk. I had to have that in mind and the belief in making things fall into the right place. I bagged that and lived with it. I still do, and I am happy that those values are here to stay with me forever.

Coming home to the Gambia was always like a pilgrimage for me, I reiterate because she made it happen for me and never wanted me to go home feeling nervous that I did not do well at school. I always looked forward to it and all the great things that awaited me. Everybody welcomed me with open arms. They pampered me, and I felt on top of the world. I could always see the positive vibes on my parents' faces expressing happiness etc. What I had noticed was that everyone liked my Senegalese Wolof accent. Many of them teased me a lot though, but it was fun. Some called me 'Grand' as that is how Gambians addressed Senegalese people. Even my sisters and my only brother did tease me about that accent and the fusion of all sorts and the French language in it. I always felt the difference when we communicated. Some of them deliberately asked me futile questions just to hear me speak. I felt the love and admiration coming from every corner.

When a child is loved, they grow up to enjoy what the world offers plus everything around them. It is how I want my silhouette to grow up to become. Humility is the best approach to life and this is one of the basic principles we live by.

Going back to Senegal had always been an emotional moment for me. For my parents and my siblings, they never take their minds off me particularly my mother. It was when I had my child that I began to understand what bond is and what it really means. They were always worried about me being so young, how I was living, what I was up to and all sorts. I have had some tough times as every young person. My fair share did not fail to greet me as I have always said to my family. But it was part of growing up and going through the paths I had to pass through. As Papa reminded me that, life is a circle full of traces of breadcrumbs that you must find and follow. Make sure that you stop at every point if required and continue the journey, but never give up when you face obstacles. Another friend called those barriers the stumbles and stones on which to step onto and consider them being part of your dance. Never stop yearning for better days and keep dancing because it is your dance.

Life is a voyage and sometimes the days seem longer than a century to us especially when we are overwhelmed with troubling issues. In this second decade of the twenty-first century, everything we do has and will have a sagaciousness of Deja Vue in it. That very sense of repetition in action, when I felt under the weather, reminded me of a journey that had no end to it. I often felt depressed, but only for days because of the change that I always anticipated. I never looked forward to night time because it meant going to sleep at night without hearing the laughter of my parents and sisters. It was always awkward. But, I had to brace up and cry for at least a day or two until I got myself back into the system. The journey was a scheme. I still make every ride to be exact. Nothing can change that about how I feel in every situation.

CHAPTER EIGHT
Evasion

Defaulting is quite an inevitable thing. It might sound too brief a statement, but that is what it is when it comes to women and decision-making, political participation and le Droit de Vivre meaning the right of living. We do have a lot to learn from and to adhere to the sacred commands. These are not new areas of our society to look at, and that is for sure. We would not be enjoying our freedom today, as a people, had it not been the efforts that the ones before us made and what they have put in place for us to enjoy at least a little even though we are always complaining about one thing or the other. Things would have been different for fathers like mine who had to rescue his daughters and did what was right coming from very traditional families. Liberty for women should not be questionable. Nevertheless, freedom is defined as self-determination, and it should not be denied to any living soul. It is universal, and it is not a western concept, so is feminism. Our mothers and the ones before them that I would like to address here as 'foremothers' worked so hard in very harsh condition for countless years, to give us better upbringing. They did not just sit there and take any orders from our great uncles or great aunts without negotiating. The partnership that existed between them had worked extremely fine and existed for a very long time and well before we were born. So, my argument has always been, the motive that is behind all the noise about women and feminism especially when African women want to make a point about something in our society today. Why do men of the modern world feel the need to stigmatise women's quest for total freedom and accept what the system and movement requires? There must be reasons why women are denied equal pay and accused feminists of going against norms that weren't there in the first place.

I have seen in the village circles how some elders stood for women. In fact, negotiation is all they did their entire life for women to continue to be influential in their communities just like the way they looked after the villages when men were out in the field working and even before that, fighting to gain their kingdoms and all. These are the days that we need to keep reminding people that vie for regression rather than progression of the women folks, for the sake of denying them their rights.

The ones before us did marry well. The strong women before us did their bit, and they did it their way. They had the perfect understanding with their spouses and leaders of their communities compared to us today. How they lived their lives is commendable. It was not real feminism you see people write in books or talk about in conferences as some claim today, but it was feminism with a difference and even more powerful because the men then sought counsel from them. It is said that when you are aware of what you are fighting for and do your best in the process, no one can deny you your dues. There must be something we are doing in our generation that is not gelling well with what is required. That is what I always tell myself and even discuss with friends. This topic is still worthy of hot debate. Women not only loved the causes they fought for but did it with all their might and enjoyed winning without all the trouble that can meet them along the way. They genuinely valued their lives and wanted everyone to see them, as essential and as equal. So, feminism today should not be a contrast to what it was. In fact, all women crave having the zeal these women before our generation of women had.

The feminism as our mothers disagree is not western culture. Most of the time when we ask, they tell us that the concept in Africa is about loving yourself as a woman and asking for your dues. It is not detrimental to say no to what you feel is not going to yield positive results. Feminism should not be coated with fear. It is a state of mind and that freedom committed to it. I must keep reiterating on that. As my boss always said to me…" There is nothing wrong in repeating yourself and reiterating on one point especially when you want people to hear you" It also takes me to her particular line. "Do they hear you when you cry" Many women do, but their voices are not loud enough to be heard because they give up quickly. Until the feminism idea is fully understood, nothing we do quietly is going to be tangible. We must make some noise and loudly. That way we can address so many issues not just inequality but what will give us the ability to do what we must do? Yes, I am referring to all of us. We can tell our own stories.

African history, especially of the great women, needs to be rewritten broadly. The word feminism can and will never be a borrowed word for us women who have seen and heard so much about how strong women led their husbands and partners to win their wars and arguments between states, conflicts and debates. As many would like to accuse us, we have not become feminists because of the education that we have or living in the West. We had known the western way of life well before we travelled. Colonisers came with their culture and left it with us. They were the first ones to visit us as I have always said, we learned a great deal from them and they too did the same thing. They came to us first, and I think that we must remember that every time we want to address the issue of Feminism vs Western Influence.

Let us think of the times before Independence and other things before playing the blame game. I thought I should mention this furthermore since this part of my favourite tome is addressing my motivation, experiences of growing up in Africa, my pro-feminism father, my prospects, my inspiration and desires in life. "Man commences cutting his wisdom teeth the first time he bites off more than he can chew". That is what they say. But one must bear in mind that a mistake is merely another way of doing things right the next time around. You learn to do things right by vying for honesty, accepting to have encounters with dishonesty or deceitfulness when you shy away from the truth, acquainting with people who believe in the fact and live by it. You will encounter straightforwardness, greed, mischief, trust, loyalty, civilisation, contentment, jealousy, envy and everything you hate or love in this life. It is part of what makes a right way of living what it is. It is also a choice to make the best out of it.

When they ask you the nature of wisdom - you can say to yourself that, it is PACE - Adopt the pace of life as the secret is patience. If you are naturally patient and a true believer, you will not go wrong often no matter how difficult things seem to be at times. Feminism can never be tricky for us to embrace as African women. It has always been with us, and we must not allow the touch of a new culture to tarnish the way we used to think of it.

Almost every rational thinking, planning, manoeuvring, conceptualising - all of them have their reverses, but there is a need to balance them. How well you adjust everything you deal with in your life determines the kind of person you are. You cannot avoid the question for people want to know everything but give them what they need to know. The answer you give should always relate to what you need to do to emerge triumphantly in every way possible. There is wisdom in you that will manifest itself when you start differentiating what you can or cannot chew. We have been taught to avoid denying ourselves the chance to expect the unexpected. Believe in predestination but cocoon yourself with the best in you. That is the savoir-faire sphere you must hang on to. It is enough to have it all but, having it and tackling every issue that presents its challenges is the answer.

Our readiness to challenge anyone who accuses women of knowing feminism after they have travelled is what should be on the agenda. It is in a way a very negative thing to say to women, especially African women who are trying to do justice to this world and for all that it is worth. Finding the right spot is dejectedly an ongoing issue for us, and it diminishes the power of all the work our forefathers and 'foremothers' have done for women of all generations. We have learned from the ones before us, and the learning continues just like a race. It is achievable and possible with the gentlemen who think the world of us and celebrate us completely.

We cannot achieve what we wish for without a vision, and that comes with a lot of positivity. We are free to display our needs in the vitrine for all to see and turn our back to negativity. I have always been told that if you look at your life as a vitrine and only aim to put up beautiful things, people will just commence seeing what is desirable to look at and add no value nor give power to what we have. The work starts with us. Always know that what you are about to do is going to be lauded by people who are watching. Never expect anyone to watch. Let it only be unintentional. Since then, I never looked back and allowed the things that people say affect me that much when I fight for women's rights and for negativity to cloud my judgment. I embrace harmony and positivity in every sense of the word.

You know how you can sometimes talk to people about something that you go through and they make it their dinner table topic. That is how the small-minded people operate and newsmongers. However, you must bear in mind that it is not a choice to never let it be too obvious that you will still rise above any grouses that pull you down.

My analysis, of it, using the light bulb, gives me the peace of mind that I always needed. Think of the light bulb and its brightening effects. The enlightenment is not just the brightest of lights ever. We are taught to believe that we must understand that it is not what we think that we can put the finger on for the switch to do its job.

I would add that this bright light that you feel is invisible. Always feel that light that brightens your inner being. With that, you can start to make sense of everything around you and become invincible. Your imagination can allow you to find it touchable like an object you can use to eliminate anything that is a hindrance.

However, it is irrefutably conforming with what the minority would say about the whole feminism notion or ideology. Feminists are out to grab everything that was here and enhance it. Unlike the powerful man with his mundane ways, who also wants to be seen owing all the emblem of money and power, the big homes, beautiful cars, money, and farms.

Women used to stay behind to raise their children, look after the homes during the wars of the late 1800s in Africa. They are known to bear the brunt and were utilised for vengeance, and all sorts and that did not matter to them. They still rose up to the tests against all the odds and did what they had to do to protect whatever they were left with and start again. Blasphemies are the only things that women did not take pride in. A million women rising that we hear today is something old borrowed to enhance whatever the movement has to offer. It is not new if you learn the stories of the women of Walo et al. They rise in numbers today because of what inspired them and that it the power of unity.

Women have become more protective of their homes, husbands or partners, offspring and remain supportive of their communities. It is enough to attest to the work that African women did then and what is today seen as the work of perfect feminism. What is the difference? Time alone is the difference. Nothing beats time.

Feminism begins with the voice and having 'le Droit de Vivre' These are the tremendous traditional values that were here once. The emblem words were never invented to fully explain the peaceful aura that encompasses us when we are undeniably in communion with the minds of the same thoughts. It does not matter how far away we are when thoughts are alike. It is the same when disciplines are carbon copies and that intention is good. When you do good regardless of who people portray you to be, what they think of you, how they see you in character, good will always be what the most humanly will be remembered of you. We do learn to gain knowledge, but we pray to have wisdom too for learning without understanding is futile. There is no doubt that the many anecdotes our elders, peers, and people we interact and acquaint with tell us do have an impact on us. It matters not how many times you find yourself in a dug-up hole by tripping on it fortuitously. To attain a certain level of insight, one should embrace anything linked to be in accord with and to have patience ingrained in their heart.

A man was once asked, "What do you gain by regularly praying to your Creator?" The main answer he gave was a bit scary but true. It was scary for those who did not have the patience to listen from the first lines he uttered. He answered and said. "I gain 'Nothing" causing everyone to gush about his answer. He spoke from the heart. He then continued. What he added to it showed how he used his wisdom to clearly, explicitly and indirectly equip those that asked him with the knowledge they never had. He then said, "What I lost is anger, ego, greed, depression, envy, insecurity and fear of death." That is what I gain. My I AM concept has bagged this one too since it makes sense to know that it is always about materials or wealth that defines answered prayers to many of us. It is the way we also fight our fights to make a point which is wrong. We can win by understanding the matter first before starting to deal with it. What I have learned about what we women want is that the change we talk about is not how we behave. It is about how we can make everyone especially the opposite gender to know that we should get back or claim back what was there before. The freedom of women is sacred and has always been there.

Sometimes the answer to our prayer is not for this Duniya/World. It is not gaining but losing what we do not need, forgetting what gives us pain. The ultimate gain is missing what is bad for us that does not make us look useful before the One Who created us. Being in the know is excellent but understanding what you know is more celebrated. It tends to hold more authorities.

Life is like a sandbox which many of us fail to realise. We should also remember that it is not and should not be an expedition to the destination or the grave with an intention to arrive safely in a fashionable way and an attractive well-preserved body. If you are in this life of blush, ditch it, but preserve some of the goodness it offers because it feels good to have it rosy. The wise man or woman would say "Dream about, but not foolishly". That is what I learn from close people that I look up to without hesitation. One of the things I think of all the time. I am mindful of all of that.

Consciousness looks like an unmitigated good. It helps you avoid obsessions then stay inside the norms. It also helps you succeed in whatever you lay your eyes and heart. You will live a long life. Confidently, as the saying goes, the more conscientious you are, the better. What we women want is the consciousness and tarnishing it is impossible. You can never succeed in trying to reroute the notion of feminism. It is too late. It is about self-love, and that is a universal trait. Everyone needs a bag of love and Feminism Equal Love of Humanity. You cannot paint it with a stained brush. That brush shall never be in existence.

CHAPTER NINE
Spurs

Branches of life are the twigs we need to put together to reach the levels we seek. On each phase, we are required to do what we must do. That involves each level of its blessings and lessons. As I researched for and listened to many diverse stories, African and Western stories, I came across one of the best I will never forget. It amazes at the same time inspires the most amongst many of them. It is about a brave Bissau Guinean, an African woman called Titina Silla. Tracing my roots to Kaabou or Gabou Kansala in Guinea Bissau, it gives me immense pleasure to mention her name. It is not that I am related to her, but as a woman, I can relate to her.

The story of the women of Walo in Senegal follows. It is about the women of Walo - famously known as Talataiye Nderr. The heroic deeds of these women and many others caught my attention too from way back. I always use it as a reference to every topic I want to engage in about bravery of African women. When it is about inspiring my community peers, the use of such stories of these women plays a significant part. These same stories give us hope because they are encouraging. We cannot do what they did because our time is entirely different to theirs even with all the resources that we have now. What we have is the learnedness, and we cannot ignore the use of their strategies if we can. These generations of women were smart, courageous and fearless. Fear did not dissuade them from acting virtuously. They were simply brave. At times, I ask if women of those days were that courageous. I am on a mission to discover each one of them and their times. That includes their stories, their vision and contribution towards society. I envisage great discoveries to add to what they furnished me with to share and to use as my inspiration just like the way Mossaan is illustrated in the book.

These women did whatever they could do to end the many challenges they faced during their time. There were other exceptional stories worth sharing, and history can only tell us what we do not know and clarify what we think we knew but with trivial facts.

We can only find out that much based on what we have got from our research works. It cannot change our lives for us if we do not wish to improve as a people. What we can do with the information we gather is up to us. But, it is important to be resourceful; read, document stories chronologically so that our offspring, heirs, and heiresses can someday share like what we are doing now.

We are aware of the many events because we have knowledgeable people sharing with us. We count ourselves lucky that we are fortunate in a way that our elders were and are not lazy to tell us what they know about their families and the society they lived in. I am not the savviest when it comes to history, but I love learning about various times. It is thrilling to know how much similarities we can find in this modern day.

There isn't any significant nuance between the suffragettes and the women of 'Talataiye Nderr'. They fought the same causes that women are fighting for today but every generation with their own. However, to have a cause to fight for means you disagree with some of the issues that are causing society's malfunction. The word emancipation is what is used to describe liberation and every woman wants to be that boundless. By stage, we try to gauge where we stand as if it is a ladder we are climbing on step by step. Women who do everything to support their communities are my inspiration. The latter comprises of their children, how to raise them well and cater to their needs sometimes singlehandedly without complains.

I am encouraged by women who go out and work in the fields without thinking that what they are doing is a man's work. I do get inspired by the woman who knows her worth. The woman who knows that she does not have to have all the degrees in the world to feel liberated. I remember learning about the many stripes women are born with especially the African woman. I have finally concluded that for the African woman, the lines should be three. Being born black, being born a woman and being unbound. Do you know why? It is because, from the commencement, we were trained to believe that we were taken to hold the fort no matter under what circumstances. We also must remember that with the storm comes tranquility. Nothing ugly fashioned against our goodwill shall prosper. I have always believed in that. My independent mind has exposed me to the fact that if I do not believe in myself, nobody will.

Travelling during the academic year is all I did, and I spent three out of twelve months with my parents and siblings. It is a laughable matter now, and that is what I know how to do it myself. When my siblings tease me that I grew up on my own, they hear me agreeing to that. Yes, I practically did grow up on my own. In a way, it has taught me a lot because I had to grow up fast. The only negative thing I found in that is that it made me shy, but that was in the beginning. I was painfully shy especially when I had to be amongst people I never met before meeting them for the first time. The people I had to live with had etiquettes that I never knew existed; their mannerism was over the top, and the French everyone spoke made me feel so intimidated. However, my age saved me the trouble because they felt the need to teach me a lot. I was welcomed and accommodated as my grandmother did for them. I was often away from the two people that brought me into this world. Even with that, I had all the care and love that I needed. Alhamdullilah! I hold fun memories of these beautiful and well-mannered people, of my father, and my lovely and serene mother who always made sure I had the best things to take with me every academic year.

But what I cherish most is the person that I have become because I find strength in knowing what has moulded me. It is a treasure that I wish to keep forever. No capacity of difficulties, rejection or pain shall lead me to self-destruction because that will be insulting to those that had helped me grow as a person. It has added the 'sagesse' or sage gained from my wise guardians, and I have become more spiritual than ever. Never mind the knowledge gained from learning. Nothing is a mirage if you refuse to consider them as such.

There were times when things were terrible, and I thought about my other siblings. I was not the only child, but I felt that I was given everything and cocooned as if they were helping prepare for what I will face tomorrow. I was made to believe that I am here to discover and to lead.

I began to think of not just me but for all of us. I was more in for how to live a worthy life, and it was a wakeup call for me to begin getting involved and help my parents to support myself financially. I used the money and created my small business of materials I sold to my wealthy peers who always looked forward to my return from holidays.

That business did help me double the money Papa and Mama gave to me. The thought of economic empowerment that I always talk about comes with luck. I used to think that I am more of a philanthropist than a businesswoman lately until I started thinking of how I did it when I was only fourteen. I promised Mom that I was going to do my best not to lack anything and that I would use the money they gave me wisely. What she did not know was that I knew how to gain a lot of profit from it. I usually looked at her, and I felt emotional for her hardworking nature. She did everything for us especially the times when Papa was not working due to so many things that I wish to keep for a later memoir. Life is a journey that only the patient can walk without too many mistakes. Some stories are better left untold. With my father's it is more of spiritual and traditional issues that every man of his generation from his lineage had to undergo.

Although I am not exactly the woman in this story, I see myself in her because of how ambitious she is and what she wants out of life. Every woman you know wakes up to rise and shine, to make a difference in society. Mossaan is a doer, an empathetic person, a link between people to people and someone we can all read about and find a fraction of her in us. It is of immense importance to take positive approaches on any matter when we need to get inspired. I repeatedly say to myself that there is a Mossaan a "Belle Djigguenn" in each one of us.

My journey began in The Gambia, West Africa where I was born. I became a Radio Presenter a year after my return. At an early age with only with only a Sixth form qualification and hardly undergone any training courses, I was battling with the lack of skills that could help me make ends meet. A brief customer service work experience gotten for me by my late cousin Sainabou Sarr exposed me to the working world. After that, I stumbled on one of the best leading men in the broadcasting world. His name was George Christenson, the master saviour whom we can never repay for his noble deeds. I had no training on journalism/broadcasting, but he believed in me and gave me a chance to give it a shot as he said it because my voice was something he thought was what he needed to hear on the radio. His wife agreed, and the rest was history. I believed that it was not just a trial but the beginning of what my career path would take.

A few years later, I travelled to the United Kingdom after a short trip to Sweden where I did not think was right for me. My humble beginning in Scotland was an opener to me, and I began to fathom out what would be best for me to do. I decided to pursue my studies in London as a trained journalist and broadcaster, a field I knew a lot of but had no qualifications in but a good four years of work experience at Radio One FM owned by the late George Christenson.

Broadcasting/Journalism was the only field I knew and engaging in it has had an impact in my life. It has opened realms of opportunities for me. I was selected and chosen amongst a group of affluent migrant women where I volunteered as Database Administrator with a dear sister, my buddy, Bossibaa or Bouttross Ndey Jobarteh. It is a Pan-African organisation that was created by some African women to support migrants and refugees, especially women. It is one of the top agencies with an ECOSOC Status under the United Nations' banner.

The founders are pan-African women/feminists, educationists, and development workers, highly educated and significant contributors to the continent and the world at large. These women started their work and funded it themselves by coming together every Saturday to sell things and support women in need in the community. They worked under those circumstances before they had a breakthrough and started getting funding from Camden Council. Ndey and I joined AMwA when Bisi Adeleye Fayemi was the Exec. Director, she was very supportive of all the beautiful women like Nana and Gloria Ogunbadejo whom I see as my Sister. Later we got acquainted with all the board members who have become our families. Years after that, the organisation continued growing, and I was still a novice trying to understand what these women were fighting to achieve. I remember when some of the women shunned me for saying the wrong things and that I am a liberal feminist.

I had no idea that I was supposed to be amongst the gang of feminists who spoke a jargon that I did not understand. It was a rigid wall to crack. But, I concentrated on what I wanted and continued my education was that green light that kept flickering right before me, but I refused to look attentively. After I had gone to Uni, I started to feel good.

The journey of learning began, and I was still meeting the inexperienced staff of AMwA. One of the most admirable women I will never forget is today my adopted Igbo mother, Mary Kanu. She is kind, witty and prayerful. Gloria is now a reverend, and that warms my heart knowing that after all the things that we do to find our position in society, we can still get time to show gratitude to our Creator the Almighty God.

Meeting these affluent women after I had finished my journalism and broadcasting training was a good start for me. I was a newly qualified journalist, and I had big plans to try and get a better command of the English language. Having French as my first language was a challenge, but it did not stop me. Like any other international student, being trapped by ambitions was my dilemma, and it was the first article I wrote and sent it to the Gambia for publishing on the Observer Newspaper. That is what we have experienced and living to date. We were trapped by ambitions, and now that we have reached where we needed to be, the rearing of our offspring caught up with us which is also another blessing. We are never fully satisfied with our achievements. So, we keep going with greater vision.

We keep learning and making a grab of every opportunity that comes our way. But that is life. It was not easy trying to make it in a foreign territory far away from where are from and outside a culture that we know. I am that I got the push from these women especially my friend Ndey whom I fondly call Bossibaa or Bouttross. We got that name from the late PanAfricanist Dr Taju Deen Abdul Rahman who was our mentor, friend and colleague at the Africa Research and Information Bureau. Zaya Yebbo is another great guy who taught us a lot and shared so much of his intelligence with us. You can imagine having these experienced people showing you what they know. Ndey's name was challenging for them to pronounce. They always called her Edey, and they decided to call us Bouttross-Bouttross because we were regularly together, and the pronunciation of our names was similar. I had a hunch that they wanted to formulate something like Ying and Yang. That is my guess anyway. But, these guys introduced us to AMwA because they had always worked in partnership with the African community. They called us that Bouttross-Bouttross just for fun.

It is true, we worked as volunteers, but the opportunities were countless which made me feel so lucky, and I often asked myself 'Why me? Why us? Nevertheless, I embraced those opportunities as part of my journey. Nothing would have changed that. I am a believer, and that was for me to enjoy but be grateful for too.

Later, I joined this team of women migrants in Media in film studies. It was a course designed specifically to support women who were already in the media in their respective countries and wishing to continue their journey to qualify and work in a place they now call home. It was not a course for me to just adapt. It was a fresh start because filming was not within my remits then. Although I did not do many productions works as an amateur when I was on my broadcasting and journalism course, writing became part of me to produce the team's production. This brief story about the beginning of my career in the United Kingdom reminds me of what I had to go through; the desires, the challenges or limitations but the achievements I cannot evade. It is considered with gratitude even with the problems; I praise the Lord for the path, the opportunities and the lessons that have become my blessings.

During this period, I consulted many women before becoming a fully-fledged filmmaker in a world and market with overqualified and topped filmmakers who are already highly connected and in the know of where the funds are to make their productions; big or small. When everyone sat down and waited for their big break in filmmaking, I tried to explore other avenues. Coaching and mentoring younger women and starters in areas where I became a professional and an expert.

 I enjoy writing and learning, but I also revisit the multiple paths I have walked in and remembering my late parents always gives me this oomph that I can never have even if I had taken dozens of cans of Red Bulls. Those wings are not going to be called routine or being straightforward. They are sacred. They give me an irreplaceable quantity of energy.

Meeting people from all walks of life has been my wish and my forte in making friends facilitated my learning although I have vowed to continue educating myself about distinct cultures. I get to talk about mine and my experience growing up in Africa. Living in the west has not changed me a bit. I am still this traditional loving girl, a person who enjoys preserving my cultural and traditional values. That is the only reason why I can write a story about anything related to my African heritage. It gives me an immense pleasure talking about an African Woman and giving talks about the many myths, the challenges, the obstacles, and the hurdles. The exciting fairy tale, stories about Africa melt my heart. The African Woman with her many stripes is everything worthy of addressing. What I have noticed is that people do not pay much attention because they know little, but once you encourage them, they become interested. One can learn a lot from these stories. Even though I like to talk about the many negative things about the misfortunes, the beautiful things to celebrate are still within. It is that culture we talk about which we love to disagree on some vis a vis the layers we hate to enjoy, but that is part of us.

Presenting Mossaan to the world makes me feel proud because it is one story that every young woman will relate. It is a complete unabridged story that depicts the life of a typical African girl/young adult who has grown into a young woman. She is a woman who has got plans, inspirations, and ambitions for a better future. Her expectations were very high in a community that provided little to her. What inspires her was the many peers of hers who have travelled to the cities to work, but as house helps for most of them, only a few of them had been to the towns for further education. It was the only job for her level of education.

While dreaming of a better future, Mossaan's exceptional

character became more and more impressive to the inhabitants of the village. Everybody wanted to see her happy. She was not very content, but her daily routine in the village kept her busy.

Written with enormous affection and gratitude to the members and supporters of my work with the emancipation of African women, the girl child, mentoring and coaching are areas that have enabled me to become passionate about sharing my thoughts. I do this pointing at the contribution towards a society that every woman should think of, subsidizing towards what is encouraging to our youths especially young women and girls and not forgetting grassroots women. Getting inspired by what will be a life-changing journey should be the message and one that should also be to help spread it and share it where it needs to be shared freely beyond bounds. I call it a mission on a niche 'Aspire to Inspire.' People who know me well understand where I am heading with this catchphrase that I use in everything I do.

One cannot elaborate on this story without a mention of those who signify a great deal to us. These are the people that form what I call family. The ones who are so dear to us; our loved ones who have helped in making this dream a reality with the support of The Lord of Mankind, our Creator. As mentioned in the movement and campaign for women and emancipation of change makers, Mossaan's fictional story is a perfect fit. It is a story that each one of us can say is familiar with because it is how they raise us in

Africa with few exceptions. It is a way of life that the African society indoctrinates women. It is not an extreme, although many agonies and perils fill up the journey. It is not to be confused with slavery. All we can do together is see it as a story worthy of embracing for her strength is not inattentive, and her determination to bring change into her own life before she could do anything for her environment is not futile.

Mossaan is worthy of mimicry because her characteristics as a young woman are the combination of a dream of every parent for their daughters. Nevertheless, it was a heck of a ride. Beautiful things are capped with thorns. Growing and playing are what children should do; they should be having fun too. It is the primary part of a child's life. Did we have a proper childhood? There is a big question mark for many of us, but nothing we go through associates us with what our sisters who are not allowed to live their life go through.

The world is our realm and can become a better place with all of us working in partnership to live harmoniously. As the saying goes, we are not stopping at understanding that we are human beings. We are 'human-becoming.'

CHAPTER TEN
Child Bride

Your belief that you do not have what it takes will keep you from doing what is necessary to get what it takes. I came across family members, not immediate families, and people I befriended who surprisingly do tend to give me a tough time when I want to become, moving away from the regular human-being to human-becoming. Only a few understand that we are here in this world to not have our hands folded and not do much or try to do something.

We are weaved in with people we may love but disagree vehemently with, concerning their values, beliefs and actions. Building a healthy relationship is not easy. It is the healthy family life that our parents made us realise that it is worth inculcating in our homes. We must understand where we end, and others begin and protect our values and beliefs while being flexible enough to allow others to feel what they feel. It is all a beautiful experience, but one that does not come cheap.

As some of my artists' friends would say when I ask why they want to keep pushing me to work on areas I do not feel comfortable working. As jovial as I can be, I cannot imagine myself working as an actress doing things I cannot do. My friend Agnieszka always said to me that the reason why they are pushing me in that profession is that they know I can. Expressing that they will still make sure they get me the part where I fit in. I might not understand their wish, but they say that they must get me to the "toppermost of the poppermost." Just like the relationship the pop manager has with his or her Singer/Artist. They usually work their socks off to have them on top of the charts.

While it takes a lot of time, energy, effort, a lot of pondering, marshalling of thoughts and in-depth consultations to draft something as massive as this big story, the girl child in Africa and her uncontrollable quandaries although a lot of efforts has been made to deal with them. It did not take me long to gauge its reach. It did not also take me long to know what is next. I do not wonder why, and I do not question if people will start wondering why to necessitate this kind of approach.

I know that you will say that she has lived it. Yes, I have lived this experience just like any other young woman growing up in a patriarchal society in Africa, in a community whereby, you are listened to if you are a woman, but it is your words against the rest.

Accepting the norm is the best way to show respect to elders.

There are many ways to tackle matters, and we all know that one cannot test gold without fire. Growing up in a society that shows and tells you that your words are just simple words does not do much for a girl's confidence. It still exists today even when you are highly educated. That is the reason why I disagree a lot with people when they stigmatise educated women. Education is not a ticket to full emancipation because, in our culture, you must be under control, but respect is fundamental to everything we do in life. It is only senseless men who disrespect women, but our culture does not dictate that. That is an insult to a society that has moulded us and those before us. Taking women for granted is an abuse of their human rights.

My first-hand experience, to be precise and concise, was how and when I witnessed seeing young women being married off at an early age. While I was enjoying my childhood, some young girls were living a life that was beyond comprehension. There is remarkably some significant number of brides who are still children in the world. When their peers are in school and playing, their parents are busy making money on them causing them to suffer all kinds of ailments. Some of these young children are today affected by health problems or traumatised by what they encounter daily in their marital homes. A young body cannot take such thing. This practice is still going on in our society today. Today, we keep talking about freedom for women forgetting these young women who need the world's attention to end their ordeal and bring the perpetrators to book.

What I have learned is that marrying off young women puts them in grave danger. These young maidens who have not even reached the right age to be called maidens or get married are preys to these insensible men who dare to call them their wives. They have a choice to reject any proposals coming from the parents of these young brides even when they are offered to marry them. It is only fair for them to find people in their age group or marriable women who are not as young as fifteen not to talk of twelve.

Most of these girls end up having fistula disease caused by a torn uterus they endure when giving birth. This condition kills its victims slowly.

I witnessed my late father defend the rights of a young child bride in the Gambia. Poverty is a crime, and we must work together to tackle these issues that warrant parents use their daughters as a money-making mechanism. Papa did not know this little girl from Adam, but he had to do what he did to make a point and to also teach the husband that what he did or allowed to happen was unjust. I won't go as far as calling it an abomination, but it is disgusting to the core. It is burdensome. My father felt disturbed by it and could not help it He had to say something because he had young children at home including me. I was with him, and that alone has given me an idea of what would he have done if he had the authority or power to have that man caged for violating a minor's human rights.

That act of his made me feel so proud of him, and I smile each time it crosses my mind.

I still talk about the story of him when he confronted a man who was boastful about his child bride. The young bride was of similar age to my father's last born at the time. I understand why it affected him so much. He talked about it nonstop.

It does not matter how much one wants to protect every child; there will always be few who cannot have you think that you have the right to control what they do with their life. The young girl had a family, and they chose to treat her the way they did. No one can argue that, but children need safeguarding, and Jainabou amongst many young brides was amongst these victims of injustice. What happened to her was inhumane.

Thankfully, my father was not one of those people who saw injustice and kept quiet about it. That was his character. Something happened that I will never forget about the local shopkeeper's young bride and the scuffles between him and my father. The girl was as young as my baby sister Marietou and witnessing what happened that day was an experience I can never forget, and I still talk about it proudly. It was a callous act, and I get teary eyes every time I think of Jainabou.

Our great men and women continue to fight for the eradication of harmful and heartless practices our leading men and women cannot do alone without the accord between the people and the governments in place.

While influential women and men are doing their bit, so many young children's situation is worsened by the crimes committed on them. Often, you see men on the defensive when it comes to cases such as this. It is the responsibility of our elders to oversee the welfare of our vulnerable young adults and children. The expression 'Sauve Gardez' did not exist in vain. It is to safeguard anything that is precious. I must add one thing that my father told me, and I shall continue to live with that forever. Thousands of people fear that if they are over certain age, they will have to start over again and will lose everything if they shift or modify their career or lifestyle and or situation. I believe in destiny, and I always go like, whatever happens to me would be my fate. I am not scared of anything that should happen to me. Who am I not to accept what is intended for me? I see myself empathising with people like that little girl Jainabou whom we met in the shop and wished she had the choice and a father that I had. The same opportunity I wanted for Mossaan.

On a hot afternoon, there I was walking home with my father, and as usual, he loved buying us afternoon snacks and all the sweet goodies for us with lots of breadsticks or French bread loaves to give out to children in the streets to take home. We stopped by the corner shop, and a little girl was sitting in the corner of the room behind the shop counter. She was all smiles and looked mature for her age. My father and I walked into the shop, and this young girl, aged 12, greeted us with a beautiful smile. I remember asking her if she was alright. The dark circle around her eyes were visible, but she seemed well. We walked in, and Papa asked her where her uncle was because that was all you could think of if you are not aware of what was going on. The little girl smiled. She hardly understood Wolof, the language we speak. She is Pullo Fouta or Fulani from Guinea Conakry in West Africa. The shopkeeper heard my father's voice and walked into the shop from the bedroom attached to it. With pride, he responded that she was not his niece but his beautiful young wife. Can you imagine that? She was only twelve years old. Out of shock, I heard my father saying words I do not wish to repeat, but I was shocked too. I was practically staring at the beautiful little girl. I had my eyes on her. God knows what I was thinking. I said in my head, and it was disgusting. I was thinking about the unthinkable. Jainabou's radiant beauty and innocence make me teary every time I speak about her. I was also embarrassed and did not have a word for Mamad Salieu, the shopkeeper. What a shameless man, I thought. With all the beautiful women in the world especially in his native country of Conakry, he could not find anyone but that baby for a wife? It is as if being offered a chicken for dinner and you choose the 'Poussin' the new-born chick. Huh! That was disgusting to me. Even when I think of it now, it sends me to cloud unknown. I just wanted revenge for the little girl.

My father was not the typical scary dad to me. He taught me how to tell him politely what I felt and when he was wrong about something. He gave me the authority over anything he said or did though it was rare to have something to say to a man who was very principled. However, he was very fair and always said that he was not as perfect as many would think. But, his temperament that day was a sight I had never seen. Indeed, a day I will always remember. It was as if World War III was about to commence. I had never seen my father in that kind of rage. The pride that the shopkeeper showed suddenly dwindled and those grins immediately became gloomy like Orbit was about to hit. What baffled me most was the fact that Papa was not pleased with what the man told him. I guessed and thought he was thinking about his children. I did not understand him then, but now I do for we continuously hear about the child bride, violation or rape of vulnerable young girls and women all around the world. Africa and Asia are at the centre of it.

Many people deny their daughters the opportunity to be children, to get a good or complete education because it is a waste of finances. To those who do not have much, they feel that giving their daughters in early marriages will enrich them. I had the chance to see it first-hand and my father's stance as a reference. I still remember very well the name of the shopkeeper. Everyone called him 'Mamad Salieu' Borrom Bitikk, the shopkeeper with the pretty young wife. I can never forget him because that same little 12-year-old girl died when giving birth by the time she was thirteen. It was apparently her first born. I always wondered why, even though she was his wife, they did not keep her for him until she at least reached sixteen, the almost normal age.

I blamed the community elders of Guinean women of the town. They should have discussed this and made it clear to him that she was to be kept in a family home until she reached the age. She was too young to be a wife or to be giving birth. Traditionally, men could marry a very young girl but for her to be kept for them until they turn at least 16 or 17 years of age. Mamad Salieu was not smart enough. From his grin, I knew he was not with it. I was and still am glad that my father did give him a good telling off. It makes me feel good that he did. Poor Mamad Salieu, I bet he saw my Papa as a killjoy.

These two 'kals' never spoke to each other again after that incident. Their friendship ended that day. Mamad Salieu always liked my father's jokes. Both spoke French; they joked about President Senghore and Saikou Toure when they used to send insults to each other through the airwaves. Yes, I knew all about that because Papa told me a lot about the rifts between Zeng and Touré. Senghore used to call Saikou Toure 'Guutuut' a bird that makes too much noise. That is how they used to chat. Mamad Salieu was a nice young man in his late thirties, but my father did not discriminate him because of his age. Papa told him off, and I felt bad that he was not to do that to him. I thought he was meddling in somebody else's businesses. But, any man with the right senses would have done the same. He even went to the point of asking my father if he gave him money to pay the bride price. It is seriously the kind of things that happen in Africa especially in remote areas where these types of acts still occur.

Jainabou, I later heard, gave birth, and her baby was stillborn. She too could not make it due to the complications she encountered. She died also. Many young girls get Fistula from it, but her case I can say was worst.

She did not enjoy motherhood because she was a young soul, and I think that it was unfair for her people to do that to her. Mamad Salieu was just a man who wanted to satisfy his urge. He had money to pay for his twelve-year-old bride. There was no law in place to protect Jainabou.

I kept saying to myself how right he was when he said that nobody paid for his bride. But no one asked how wrong her parents were for giving this poor little out for charity just like that. Her life was not important to them. That is why they did that to her. The girl was a victim of circumstances, and that was unfair for her to go through what she had endured. Due to extreme poverty, many parents give their daughters away in marriage for the bride price they ask is usually used as a source of income or business start-ups or to finance their sons' education.

The sums families ask for bride price depends on what they think the potential groom has. But through the myriad of research I have conducted, some parents ask for a lot and men tend to cater for that amount for their big day which can also be the Dooms Day if the bride is a child. Many men had to spend many years planning for that bride price. It is a favourite thing in a marriage.

My late mother and I were chatting about the incident, and I told her that seeing my father in that kind of rage for something that did not concern him was incomprehensible to me. I was angry that he meddled in and I recalled telling Papa that he was wrong and that this was not within his responsibility. "It is the shopkeeper's life, and you do not have to tell him anything. Let's go, Papa." He just smiled at me on our way back to the house. I was vexed seeing him argue outside our home. I did not like what the shopkeeper said to him either because he was my father. Although he did not say any rude or derogatory words, talking back to my father was a no-go area.

Mamad Salieu, the shopkeeper, had so much admiration for my father before the incident, which made me feel sad. I did not like that part at all, when he talked back to him, but then, that is what happens when you fight for a cause. You cannot say that people will agree with you comfortably. Mamad Salieu respected my father very much. He greeted him with his hat off. It is a sign of respect, but that little argument destroyed the high esteem he held for Papa. C'est la vie. Knowing my Papa, he would do it again for he hated injustice. That was what I disliked the most.

Even at home, I was always protective of Papa. I never wanted anyone to say something negative about him when he told one of my sisters off. As far as I was concerned,

Papa was always right. His love for family was remarkable and enough for him to wear the best family man crown. Even though my mother disagreed with what Papa did, she did not complain much in front of me, but she had few word with Papa. I admired the relationship they had. She would kindly tell him her piece of mind and got on with her thing. He listened to her as well. I overheard him saying to her "You should have seen the frail little girl's face and that man's stupid grin like a lost soul" It was heartbreaking. She was such a young girl. I think what Papa hated most was the grin on Mamad Salieu's face. I add a bit of salt to it when I narrate the story to my sisters to make them laugh. I say it in the Fulani-Wolof accent. Heh! He was jolly. He was expecting a round of applause from my father. Sadly, he got a good telling off and Papa got him too. They had their little tittle-tattle there and poor Jainabou sat there smiling. Her innocence spoke volume.

We should count ourselves lucky I told my sisters. We did not have to go through all that. I know that even if we had nothing but sand to eat, our parents would not dare give us away that young.

My Mama and Papa were two very close siblings. There was always laughter when Papa was around. Hearing him in a rage was not taken lightly by me. Mom was outraged hearing that Papa lashed out at Mamad Salieu. It was not his life and conducts. It was somebody else's life and could be sorted out by those closest to them. She said that it did not concern him but, if I were in his shoes, having five daughters to protect, I would have done the same. She was so right about that. Mama Diouf, my mother was always supportive of Papa because of his stance and the fact that he wanted his daughters to become what he wished for them, to grow up and make their own decisions in life. It was necessary for him to give us a chance to grow, learn and develop. The words she said continue echoing. "It is his life, it did not concern Papa, but in a way, he was right." The life of a young pretty, innocent, young child bride perished just like that. It left me shocked, and I am still in awe even though it happened a long time ago.

I became more exposed to family, cultural, traditional issues as I grew up, certain things began to make sense to me. Issues that women grapple with began to be of interest and many a time; we heard women fighting against one thing or the other. To say that I was lucky not to have had this kind of experience is an understatement. I began to be over-protective of young women just the way my father was. It was normal for my mom to have reacted the way she did. But knowing my father's stance then gives me more power and the flair to keep fighting for this noble cause. Women must be protected to have a choice, a voice to be able to decide when it comes to what happens to them and their daughters and nieces. The mother of Jainabou, the young bride, could have stopped her young daughter from whoever gave her away in marriage. She was too young to be given away to a man who was almost twice her age or even more. Mamad Salieu did not look well himself. He was always walking nonchalantly. But she had no choice. I did not know her, but I am sure, as they usually do, she could have been amongst the bridal party that brought the girl to meet her husband all the way from Guinea Conakry.

The Fulani people usually have some week-long exciting bridal ceremonies. I have had the chance to visit few brides during their weddings. They always served excellent food. The whole week long, people come in with gifts and nicely cooked meals from their homes and all. What I liked most was their serving time of the 'Teddungal' (white couscous and yoghurt). It was my favourite. I wanted it so far sometimes I asked my mother to get me some from the women that sold it. Bajen C. Faye, a very dear sister to my father in Banjul also sold Dang akk Soww in Banjul market. She adored my father so much, 'Loul' or Prince of Sine in Serere was the names she called him. Bajen Codou used to tease us a lot because we did not speak Serere. I often heard her say "Barkaa Darru" meaning the useless lot. That is what you get when you come from an affluent clan who respect tradition and have no clue about who you are. Your people will address you anyhow, and you cannot do anything about it. That was the price we paid.

No matter how much you try, learning a language when you are older is not easy. But we have our lingua. I am speaking the vernacular and vehicular Serere which is better than nothing. Any word to give me a Laissez-passer is welcome. I am sure she would have felt so proud of me flaunting it in my way if she was still here with us. Every time I saw Papa with the white container, I knew it was my yobbal which is the gift from Bajen Codou. That is how we called her. It was her delicious food 'Dang akk Soww' that even Papa liked. He never ate anything that was not cooked by my mom but Bajen Faye's Dang akk Soww (Couscous and sour cream and sugar), he loved very much. She was his sister, not blood relations but Papa always believed that the real Faye surname comes from one branch. If you are a real Faye, then you are from the same lineage of Salmon.

My mother understood the issues women went through so early. At the age of seventeen (17), she was already married and lost her biological mother. She was left to raise her brothers, and my father took responsibility for all of them. The challenge that women face is countless, according to my mother. She was a smart woman, very poised, hardworking and very caring. She was one woman who would do anything to make sure that her children and people around her do not complain about an were OK.

I am hoping that I will do justice to my only child's upbringing just like she and my father did for us. I will do, and I vouch for doing under different circumstances. She clarified things to me when I complained about Papa's involvement in another man's life. She said something to me that I will never forget "NennJallo," as she fondly called me, "if you were a man with young daughters, you'd have acted the same way." She kept on repeating that to me the same way I keep bringing it up repeatedly.

I am not a man, but today I can openly and proudly say that my journey has given me so many opportunities; a voice that I can use to help young people, women, empower myself and help others. I can use this view of mine to advocate and campaign for myself, fight against any injustices done on me and women in the world mainly African women.

Child marriages, the abuse of human rights, education are areas that are core in society and once tackled adequately; our community will change completely. It is encouraging to live in a family that is against it. I know if my father were still alive, I would not be grappling with so many issues I am facing today in this modern society. We can never lose hope. I am doing things the way he would have wanted me to do. Stand strong. Be firm and put God first for He is the Seer and Knower of all things. If you are not wrong, just go on and follow your heart. I do my work and anything that affects my mental and physical health. I have become a fighter and fighter I shall remain until the end of time.

I am proudly going to start voicing out somethings I never thought I could do throughout in my lifetime. Something I want to say I am proud of is my involvement in the literary world where my pen will be used to draft anything that is a hindrance to me. I am taking this route where I want to channel my thoughts. How will things pan out? I do not know but what I am sure of is the fact that I love writing and I have got many stories to write about life including mine if space allows me to pin it down with the many titles in the pipeline. I am enjoying penning this one first of many geared towards educating, reminding people of their heritage, activating thoughts, opening thoughts that will be of help to our society.

I wish to share my views with the rest of the world and continue taking part in the fights for women's rights and education, involvement and for the empowerment of the girl child. It is imperative. Many families do not still invest in their daughters, young women to go for higher education because they think they can be their source of riches by marrying them off to a wealthy man. That is what is wrong with society. However, there is a better side to things we are witnessing today. I must say, I have seen more parents spending a lot of money for their daughters to get the kind of education they need. We are moving forward slowly, and I believe that we can get there should we continue with the advocacy work and tackle issues that are hindering our progress.

The right for education for all and the eradication of harmful practices are on the wall for all to notice. The chosen path to edification holds the key to African women's voice and empowerment. It is about life improvement and welfare. Women take part in decision-making processes at all levels. I also believe that our elders who are so rigid when it comes to changing the way they see the girl child, or the woman have now started giving credit to women. It is a considerable improvement.

Mossaan's story encompasses a lot but still a slice of what women go through. Gladly for her, it is about eliminating everything that does not promote advancement about our culture and the traditions we love. It is about making a leeway to societal norms and abolishing that which encourages abnormalities and things that do not add value to both genders. The different avenues sacred to guide us shall never fail us as a society. We must keep our exploration going.

Being a woman does not mean that every burden must be added to the stripes already on us. We always need to accept what society must offer us on a plate, but we also must work together to exterminate what is wrong in our communities today. The thing with us is that we do not put a borderline to what we should omit and whatever we need to keep celebrating ourselves. It is what to add to my inspiration. As a woman, I would like to promote everything that gives us the excitement and urge to tackle our matters well and by ourselves. We owe it to nobody but to ourselves to reject whatever there is that does not prove favourable to us.

It touches on the environment, education, conduciveness, diversity, Droit de Vivre, Savoir-faire, empowerment, emancipation, aspirations, inspirations, personal well-being and developmental aspects of society regardless of our geographical situation. Having a giving heart not forgetting the knack for doing good is the icing on the cake with this plight of ours. "Djoundjeu doyna borrom xhel" as they say.

It means nothing more than what the guiding principles teach us. Many issues do not need an explicit explanation. Some acts are enough for us to draw a line. The reason the story starts with mine and a journey I so eager to tell is because there is an immense nuance between what we fight for and the one that is so simple but filled with challenges Mossaan undergoes.

CHAPTER ELEVEN
Revolving

Mounting – Rising has become the daily code and quote for every girl especially young Africans. What do we call freedom in an African milieu? How do we African women think of liberating ourselves without the acquisition of formal education? Do we need anything like a 'rend fort'? Like a pad to save us from breaking when we fall? To explain this is not as astonishing as we may think. It is essential to look at things in a positive mode constantly.

My intentions on this story are nothing more than trying to achieve positive outcomes from which people will have at least few areas they can identify themselves with especially young women living with parents, guardians and so on. There is no such thing as success without failure. You make faux pas before getting things right and in order.

These may sound like legitimate reasons to stay stuck always. But in the finality, is that anything that keeps us from taking proactive measures to at least explore and try on a new, more rewarding direction is an excuse. In working with so many people especially women who have transformed their lives facing all odds, it is visible and apparent that when we make decisions beyond all doubt that we deserve to be happier.

Our quest for change comes with a lot that I do not wish to call challenges but issues we can tackle moderately. We see them as part of our race because some of the things the world presents to us are considered as an asininity to an extent especially when we fold our hands and do nothing when we can.

We are equal. As the great wise men and women say. "We were all humans until race disconnected us, religion separated us, politics divided us and wealth that every person seems to be fascinated with classified us". I also want to remind myself that stories have taught me and so many others about the wills, dos and don'ts of society. Learning to gain support and giving support to one another, also working on a progressive community give relevance on our common issues and not us individually. Both young and older women yearn for change and discoveries in a society that embraces change and competes for metaphor.

Our stories must be told for change to happen just like in any other community. What is our story? We must ask ourselves this very often. Should we or must we ask someone else to write or tell our stories? It would be incomplete for every man to his or her account. You can only write yours the way you would want it, and with honesty, it comes out inspiring, exciting and enticing. The fact that we are all made of flesh and bone is enough for us to see one another as equals, no differences of any sort. It is whether we as a people can willingly put aside our pride and feeling of self-importance and accept the fact that we are all the same, the same human that comes from our Creator. However, self-love is the only thing that will allow us to display appreciation for others. You cannot love others when you dislike everything about yourself. That is impossible.

Many a time, we helplessly witness horrible things, incidents happening around the globe and we wonder why after making so much noise we end up keeping quiet. We are overwhelmed with so many problems that we need to tackle, said a devoted activist I met some months ago. But we must not give up. We cannot wait to become experts to start doing something. It is the same way with our stories. We must tell them as much as we can; in every language and method.

After all, we are in the second decade of the Twenty-First Century. We have enslaved our thoughts enough. We have not failed to have ourselves and one another restrained and sometimes with those of the same race, the same tribe, the same colour, the same gender since the dawn of time. We are capable of great beauty and the darkest of deeds. Through our stories, we can learn how to be better and how as a people we can learn together to tackle anything we may face. It is where the turning point kicks in.

We are not supposed to think that some people have a higher value than others. Nothing should separate us from being united. We are all humans. The same way I can tell my story or write a story that I am familiar with is the same way you can write or rewrite every bit I write here. The twist is between what is in the wisdom from the knowledge we share. Experience is nothing without understanding. They come as a package.

I love to acquaint myself with people of exceptional wisdom the same way I like that earthy smell that is in the first rain that hit the ground. The wise woman in my grandmother always told me in Wolof language "Loiy daww beh daanu?" If they don't chase you when you walk, keep walking. There is no point in being in haste. Keep walking calmly and keep trying to find your stride and the right lane. We all have our passage to walk on. To some, it is a sandy path. Others already have theirs paved with all sorts. But, that does not mean that you must think that you deserve goodness more than anybody else. Always be thankful for even the turning points that you do not desire. Better days still follow. Yes, they will come when you know what the best thing for you to do is.

The struggle for women has always been about full liberation. No matter how much we think we are, the challenges remind us of the labels that come with being a daughter, a sister, a mother and everything our gender speaks about us. Even though the burden is on us, the onus should not be on us to believe that we can take in everything thrown at us. We believe in the notion that the people whose first instinct is to smile when you make eye contact with them are some of Earth's most significant, hidden and most valuable treasure. We are the gift of humanity. We must take pride in that and be thankful for everything that we are as humans.

Does that make any sense vis a vis our quest for self-emancipation? Is emancipation about accepting anything? Or is it about bearing the brunt? My brief answer has always been not the end because there is no result to this question around the word that most people fail to describe adequately without attaching a stigma to it and a movement formed by women. If it is not OK to give a tangible answer, then it is not the end. We must continue to find the space in which the freedom we seek is present without changing as the weather does. Everything will come to the table at the right moment on any issue that needs attention. All that is required is a thorough analysis and coming up with answers that address societal norms. There is no need for unfounded answers or radicalism.

There is a coated and multifaceted question many of our male counterparts ask us when we say that we are emancipated women, or we wish to become liberated from the bolted chains. What is the link between us African women and society? Liberation does not come cheap. It has never been cheap and will never be no matter how empowered we become if we relent in promoting parity. The memorable story incorporates every aspect of societal norms. The valiant sentences our learned sisters used are always 'It is not like before when we do not have a say in anything for fear of being ostracised.' Other things such as 'I am an emancipated woman, and I know my rights' or even 'I can do what men can do as a woman.' Women are not asking for liberation to fight against men. It is women against a system that is altered, and I would like us to revert to how our great grandmothers lived with their partners then. It is the modern times that has changed the good things that were here before us.

In many countries, especially in East Africa, women do go through hardships when their husbands die and leave them with young children to look after. Most of those women do not have the right to their husbands' wealth or properties. Families of their husbands claim the wealth in times of death, and the wife and children often chased out of their compound that is supposed to be their inheritance. That is an example of what happens to women in some parts of Africa. Feminists are not making noise for trivial issues such as equality that most men think that it is the only thing that matter to women. It is the right to have a voice and to be allowed to live in peace without having to deal with issues that are solely infringing their human rights.

The rights and freedom women fight for is far beyond the chores at home or salaries the media tends to focus on every day. In fact, gentlemen proudly run errands at home, do shopping and look after their children. That is not the fight, and we must remember that it is necessary to fight what is relevant.

The apparatus is not about gauging our strength compared

to men. It is not about being able to do what men can do. It is just about living a life that is worth living, about being a contributor, an influencer and taking part in everything that concerns the welfare of families. What is wrong with emerging as the respectable and as a perfect partner/husband? We owe it to society, to do our quota as citizens of the world. We need to be engaged in every aspect of our lives so that no one tells our stories. It is also, about living a better but simple life free from worries.

We must address these issues in ways that are inspiring and influencing without breaking the laws and trust. It is about time we walk on a path that gives positive lessons to learn from and blessings to receive in return because, I am talking to the guys here, if you support another woman's quest, you are unknowingly saving her life and many others without guilt.

We often mean to suggest that the mind of an African daughter is underdeveloped and untouched when it comes to thoughts and that society has a way of manipulating every girl that is under their family's care. Put together effortlessly; the story showcases the life a young girl lives, the pros and cons and the norms that society has set out for her. The girl child lives by directives. Full stop!

To think like this is to think of societal norms and what disobedience has in store for any young woman. Rebellion could become a song your unborn children could hear, and that is an abomination in many cultures. To feel like this is to think of what her natural self, charisma, character imposes. We are not going to take the non-purified approach to present Mossaan to the world. We are obliged to portray her as a trailblazer for what she must go through before achieving her goals. If she is not yet before you, all you should do is follow her, get to know her, support her, laud her and put yourself in her shoes if you are a woman, not just an African girl.

CHAPTER TWELVE
Exploration

If you a daughter of the soil, or of the continent of Africa, I want you to know that her journey is yours too. Follow her voyage without judging but be the shadow that follows her every step of the way. It might be a door opener for you to know your kingdom too. I like to call the environment from which I come from a (realm) where we are always in search of total independence, asking our Creator in our prayers for a rewrite of our future, but that is not guaranteed. We often ask, and wait, and we do the same when we do not like something about our characters.

The anecdote of the WEAVER is a must add here to remind us of how life goes. For the weaver to complete a mission, the proper and adequate use of the bundle of threads and a right weaving tool become a must-have. Every professional pianist needs a page-turner. We cannot go on without thinking about that. 'Le Tisserand et sa Navette' The Weaver and his weaving tool. It is a tale that I always use. Wherever we are guided to go is where we must be heading towards and wherever we may find ourselves is where we should have been. We do have our paths to follow. We must accept them as they transpire, but we are still to keep on going and doing what is right for us they should all see it as an affordable feeling. You can only deny it to yourself by choosing not to, but no one can.

I desired for the story to be a traditionally charged, culturally oriented script and naturally inspiring. Consequently, it is not just an ordinary tale either. It is a contrast between a real character and a fictional character. The essence of it is to gauge what modern time entails. It is about learning and endless tests and soul-searching.

Living in a contemporary time does not mean that things that used to happen should be eradicated it entirely. It is a uniquely charged method in which exist the rules that enhance the mindset and the understanding of the world around us.

I have been living in the West for almost twenty-two years. As an African Woman, I have not forgotten one bit about my upbringing. I feel proud talking about the environment in which I grew up. There is so much I can remember and feel proud that I keep. The countless traditional, family, cultural values instilled in me make me smile and I question myself. I can never make this happen for my own children. I can offer a lot, but things get diluted as time goes. These are issues that I often revisit to gauge how I am doing conferring to the requirements society asks for from each one of us. My sisters and brothers from the same background understand what I mean.

To share what our culture entails means that we want you to realise that surprises come in waves and no amount of knowledge can prepare you for anything. We live, but we are also forced to learn daily. In fact, it has rendered me proud for I only see and visualise the positive side in everything I lay my eyes on and how it makes me feel to have grown into the woman that I am today with my own family to look after regardless of the many challenges I may face should I wish to do the same in instilling the core values I was raised to have. It is not as easy as a transferral of skills between the skills advisor and a mentee.

These very societal values have also aided me to become the person I am with the knack of becoming a full-fledged emancipated woman. I encourage women empowerment, and I am all about giving women the power to excel and the girl child to gain confidence and believe in herself. Empowering women and girls is where my forte is and even giving men with lower self-esteem the voice to say yes; women have the same right we have got. I would do anything left for me to be an all-rounder principally because I am pro development for all.

People would think that I am talking down on the culture that I have known when I address women issue. Contrary to that, I want the world to know that our problem is about how they African women are accused of copying from the women in West about what feminism is. I can never, it is a point of pride for me to be able to share what I know of our great-grandmothers because they knew freedom and had a voice. The reason why ours is difficult to show is that we lack the unity they had in leadership.

I know this could instigate debates, but I am willing to bring out all the notes to the table.

My liberal parents raised me to understand that I am nobody without these traditions, the culture and the clan where I belong. Respect for tradition is something they often emphasised on. Contrary to what few would say, I will never talk down about my rich culture. As the saying goes in Wolof "To insult any generation is to insult the wills of God." No one should talk down on the blessings bestowed upon us. There is a reasoning behind every tale, and this one is one that encourages debates for the sake of evolution and change does not happen overnight. That's my view. There are also many ways one can inspire change. "Sallaan na Guenna gaawa djoy waayeh bounou ka laalul du joyy" - as a way of feeding the neuron with newness that the world talks about daily. If you prefer to be dormant, that is how you shall remain.

"While Ahab sulked, and fumed on his bed, Jezebel taunted him and ridiculed him for his weakness, then proceeded to have the innocent Naboth framed and stoned to death. Naboth's sons also stoned to death, so there would be no heirs, and the land would revert to the possession of the king. Such a single-minded determination to have one's way, no matter who got damaged in the process, is a characteristic of the Jezebel spirit." A system that misleads does not have a place in society. The way feminists are being framed is far from what it is. Anything valuable to us should be treasured. Somewhere along the line, nothing can stop naysayers from getting a go at what is supposed to be good for everyone. They will stop at anything to get the final say. We must preserve what belongs to us. Our traditional and cultural values are no interference with what we want our world to be. For some, the fact that women formed movements to liberate themselves is a burden, and it should not be. It is a perception that needs to be settling. The women I learned from are nowhere near being anti-men or compete against men. From my grandmothers to the modern women I saw growing up, and even at work, these women demand nothing more than a space to showcase what they have got for solidarity amongst women to be the anthem all women can sing along and together.

CHAPTER THIRTEEN
Altruism

The kind of attention we give to people could be the same that people can reciprocate to you, and we all know that this is the rarest and purest form of generosity. It is something that anyone can relate. The issue with holding high expectations is that they occur frequently based on your natural strengths and perspective on what is the right or wrong way to do something. It is a Self-Sacrifice - It is not just about Le Savoir-Faire or Droit de Vivre.

It is vital to possess the type of virtues everyone in society desires, but it matters considerably to understand the world around us and its myriad of paths that desire a proper and realistic touch. This is purposely about the light of goodness that is needed and the best in people. Many of us are confusing the nuance that exists between the reality and the make believe that the expression communicates to us. How it is perceived and what it entails are two different things but very easy to gauge.

A spiritual guide of mine always said to me that he is in for women liberation because the religion we belong does not deny women their rights to be. However, his question was still about how we got to start thinking that we want to be equal to men according to his understanding of issues around women and emancipation de la femme. Now we do not ask where did we get the idea that women used to be considered inferiors to men? Our daily quests say it all. If it weren't for the dynamic women that stood up, the trend today would not have been benchmarked. The thought of us women treated as inferior is alone insulting to us. He had said. You will love what he will have to say about women. He continued. "Women have a bigger share of the pie that society has ever offered. We are blind to see it but the power that women had is nothing compared to what we think we can achieve despite the numerous movements we have in place. He mentioned the women soldiers of Islam etc.... and all the strong women of every religion. He also asked, "Why would you women want to be equal to men?" "Men will not be complete without you. You cannot start comparing all the things you can do, to ditch them and embark on a quest to get what men already have. Take a breather and gauge all the things that you do that men cannot do". That was enough to encourage us to take a pit stop. But the matter is beyond that.

It is about lifting the glass ceiling. Many of us do misinterpret the expression and I think a lot about it must be addressed so that we can become more knowledgeable. Mossaan's ambitions to leave the village for the city is solely for her to be able to make ends meet, to become economically empowered and that is what men do too. People migrate to find work and that is simply what she dreamed of. But she was under a rigid guardianship that she did not dare leave without becoming the talk of the village mainly because she is a maiden who has not yet found a suitor. Here she presented her predicament.

My spiritual guide was right about women and their rights which did not come with the stripes we were born to know. We are Africans, and we are women. Independence did not come as a readymade coupon to use and go for a nice movie watch or a moonlight party. We had to start the work from inception. Women before us did the hard work and it is an ongoing quest.

Feminism and emancipation go hand in hand. In fact, in Islam, women are not forced to take their husbands' surname. That is one of the most interesting findings that allow women to vie for what is right and adopt it. It is, therefore, the mental liberation we claim for, and that is already in us. It comes with wisdom. Without it, we are not going to mentally attain the level that we want.

Today, I came across a different interpretation of the word itself from all the things I have learned, the journey I have walked on so far, and I can't get enough on researching about diverse groups and what people say about it. My liberation might differ from yours, but the protagonist in this book's ideology is one that we can comply with and see where she ends up. As a traditionally raised young woman, the idea can be different or goes both ways. One should gain combined knowledge and wisdom to race for a total state of achievement concerning complete deliverance; spiritually, ideologically, psychologically and physically.

I hope the story is going to give you the oomph that it has given me. I write with the aim to entertain you and like a storyteller. That is my torch. One can never have enough of light to gauge otherwise to a material with a substance that can be resourceful to you. The feeling of being part of high up-to-the-minute forms is the way for me. If you are a stranger to the African culture and tradition, reading this story will support you in your learning about our patriarchal society. Mossaan even though everyone liked her, she did not lead an exceptional life. She was an exceptional young woman who knew what she wanted, listened and did all she had to do to remain in every body's good books. She was a vulnerable young woman who did not have a choice but to obey her parents and elders of the village. With grace combined, limitations were never absent. Life remains filled with challenges.

Mossaan woke up daily with good intentions to serve everyone around her. With all that, she was not termed as a home help but the princess that she was. What she constantly did was so noble of her. People appreciated her, and all her friends followed her footsteps. They all benefited from having a beautiful human being like her for a friend. She was truly a God sent and her job was to rescue every person with whom she crosses the path. We often saw her display a meticulousness in her leadership skill, doing everything without complaining. Her quiet and polite demeanour was priceless. She possessed all the good qualities of a leader and worked very hard to maintain the good relationship they all had. The mystery that surrounded Mossaan comes from her strength, her aura, beauty both inside and out. To say that she is entitled to all the good treatment she receives in the village is an understatement because she proves herself time and time again that though she was young, they have a unifier and a leader in her. She needed to be trusted to go out and follow her dream. The beautiful name given to her from birth illustrates everything that she is today. Mossaan means she is a beauty. Puzzlingly, children to live up to the names they are given from the day they are born. That is why it is necessary to choose well when naming your child after someone or anything. I often see people name their children after all the beautiful names of the stars and others. What is important to know is the meaning of the names given to them and the intentions. Some people do name their children after the Moon/Luna, Sky and it melts my heart to hear that and I bet they know why they do. That should not be my worry, but it is something that draws my attention a lot.

My late mother always said that she believed in what her people used to tell her about namesakes. Children do tend to live up to the character of the person they are named after. Therefore, we have so many great women's names that have been chosen. Every woman wants to name their children after great men and women. It is all good and dandy and I like it when I can look at a person and see everything in them that I read about those great, wonderful and exceptional people of our society.

She constantly said that we should be mindful of whom we want our children to emulate.

Culturally, we are made to think that the names we give to our children reflect the personalities of the people we name them after. It is essential to give them significant and meaningful names. that fit their personality. Mossaan was beautiful in every sense of the word. Chosen to be the beautiful one, she lived up to the attributes of what beauty is all about. Grace is nothing less than what is in exquisiteness. Mossaan was that kind of a person. What was right about her was the way she displayed her strong personality traits on top of that, she had the ability to compartmentalising everything that troubled her.

Mental Liberty - Mossaan had that and more. She was able to speak up but at the same respected her values, her family and elders of the village who spoke highly of her. Deep in her thoughts, she knew that they had her best interest at heart but what she needed was to go out of the village like other young women in the neighbouring villages.

As a young child in Africa, I was the confident one who openly asked many questions about the way many people would behave as if they own you. In Kaolack, I saw my late friend Kine suffer at the hands of her Baye Faal Uncle or he claimed to be one. He was always angry that we were going to school and hated the way we dressed and walking home in groups with all our friends, both male and friends chatting our way home and stopping by the junction at the

Buvettes to buy our goute (goutay). I used to think that he was mad. He was so controlling even his niece's friends could be caned for committing little mistakes, for example, entering the compound without greeting him. He insisted that people kneeled when greeting him. He was not my Mbaa Suttay that I respected. He did not have that from me because he is one of those men who oppressed vulnerable people.

When he was ready to beat the hell out of Kine, even us the friends weren't spared the wrath of this and his old and ugly girdle made of hard and worn out leather. I would have added any other name if I could for that ugly looking belt. It did not matter how much we pleaded with him not to hurt her. However, my grandmother's visit to his house, after I had reported him, made him leave his mom's home not for good but at least for a long time. He thought that he had the right to beat up every young person in his neighbourhood because he pretended to be a pious man, or even called himself a Baye. He had no remorse. He beat up anybody who visited/entered their compound until the day he laid his belt on my back claiming that it was not done on purpose. It was not that bad. But because I hated the idea that he was preying on my orphaned friend who had nowhere to go. I had to be a drama queen that day. I run home to The Grande Dame, my Nana who did not take it lightly. She took off like a Phoenix with two strong men to go and see this mad guy calling himself Kine's uncle. Everyone complained about how he used to torment people. Kine finally had her peace in their home because he was ordered to leave or else. He only had to return after few months. He became our friend calling us 'chiip-chiip' mocking us, showing us his ugly brown girdle he called a belt. He called me Toubab because he said that I did not want to understand the culture I was raised in and that it is normal for uncles to show their nieces the way otherwise they will derail. I was baffled that he thoughts that our culture dictates that kind of nonsense and that uncles have the right beat on their nieces. What we did was normal. From school, you walk home with your friends. I did not know that he feared my grandmother until that day. I guess it was about respect, but I would have liked to know the reason. I was so upset with him, I rolled my eyes at him everytime I met him at the entrance. People warned me that he would repeat what he did, but I threatened of reporting him to my Grandma La Grande Dame. I was so proud of her and how she saved me from these guys' nonsensical behaviours. I always wanted her to return home soonest whenever she went away on her political tours.

Women do have the right to their lives but the mindset of these illiterate uncles like Gaas is troubling. I used to see Kine with marks all over her body and nobody dared to tell her uncle that he was wrong for beating her up for doing absolutely nothing. He used to observe and monitor what we wore to school. In the end, I did not bother greeting him nor passing by their home because I could not deal with his trouble. He was not the only one and I felt sorry for these young women going through this kind of abuse.

So many African men enjoy abusing women and I have always said that they are not gallant enough to deal with issues like gentlemen and lack the ability to hold decent debates with people especially the opposite sex.

CHAPTER FOURTEEN
SHIELD

Our society was not built to guarantee us eternal protection. Things change, and even people do change a lot. I am not condoning the denial of freedom on us, but I think a lot of the western influence in the lives of our youths today. Just like how we say that feminism is not something we learned when we travelled and that we were not exposed to the western culture here. Young people especially back home are more in touch with the society of the west more than us living in Europe, USA, Australia. That's because they have ample time and with a bit of money one can buy anything. They watch television programmes that inform them of a lot nowadays. Here in the west, we do not have enough time. As migrants, we work our socks off to make ends meet. They have moved away from being caged to a semi-independence that even their parents tell them how to be free in a society like ours.

You can quickly be labelled as 'Nyaaka Kilifa' meaning derailed or lost. It is disrespectful, and it can have you labelled an outcast. What I loved and still love about our elders is that they do not force you to obey them especially the coolest and modern elders. They will just wash their hands off your business and let you be. It is scary not to have Kilifa/Guardian. However, when you need them to intervene in your business, that is when they will tell all the things that you did wrong. 'Nitt dey amm Kilifa.' They will always remind you of respecting your elders and making them your rock. It does not matter how old you get or how educated you to become the decisions older male siblings; relations make about you cannot be entirely exterminated. In some tribes, women cannot travel abroad without the permission of their brothers. It was worrying to me the first time I heard it from some Ethiopian friends with whom I attended a conference. I do not know how realistic that is because I have never been to their country nor talked about it with anyone.

I am pleased with the way my father raised me and how lucky I am to be able to tell the many stories about women, what they go through and what society dictates that we do not do much about to change our situation. We cannot be caged. It is the man who has all these rules and wants us to adhere to them. It is good that we consult our Creator in everything we do for the many predicaments we encounter cannot be ignored nor subscribe to without raising our voice.

There will always be a germ that will keep growing in your lifetime. A person without strong background is nobody. This intense experience is the concept utilised to show the responsibility people have on you and everything tradition and culture demands. Keeping these values is safe. When someone has taken their time to ask for your hand in marriage, it is a whole project the family of your future groom/husband undertakes to know your roots. The family members you did not listen to will be the same people that your prospective groom's family will consult. They ask not because they want to the branches of the tree you fall from but to know what step to take towards asking your hand in marriage. Eloping to marry someone is not something that is encouraged in our culture. So, as much as we would like to be free and be our bosses, we must consider the good things that our culture and tradition dictate.

Our paternal aunties would say when men come to ask for your hand in marriage and find you well grounded, groomed and surrounded with loved ones, they will feel safe to bring you into their family homes. The extended families or future extended families will feel honoured for meeting someone with a strong background; poor or rich. It doesn't matter. These great Kilifas or elders are the same people responsible for the bride price. In many families, the bride price is not a big deal for some families just offer an amount, jewellery, homes, cars and anything they feel they can give. That is, of course, the husband's decision but the sisters of the groom who are called 'Njekkehs' often make it their job to work on all the nice to have gifts for their future wives/brides. When they love you, and they know that their 'Chamenj' brother can afford it, they will move mountains for you.

In Africa, when you are married, you don't just marry your husband. You are married to the whole family. It is normal, and traditionally, your extended family has taken over. In some cases, we find too many difficulties. But that is how it goes. You are a new member and that you come in with different traits. Adapting is a choice but a critical decision.

Some men do not feel the need to ask or give more than the 'Nyennent akk transsu' the amount presented to tie the knot. If parents communicate that they are not asking for a bride price 'Meyy bou Njekkeu' for their daughters, they will feel happy to keep their cash to themselves. That said, it is rare to find a woman of our generation who does not want 'Meyy bou njeukkeu.' I don't blame them. Times are hard. Even when or if you work, there is no guarantee that you will keep your job forever. The world has become irrefutably tricky.

Everything seems different. The bride price is, to many families and young women, future bride, a sum that could be used as a start-up fund or to support the bride and groom to build a life together. It is the little wealth that contributes towards buying the goods needed for the home etcetera.

In our Serere families, asking for bride price is not a priority. Most of the time, you get more than what you want if you demanded it. Ah, how generous some people can be. I must say, for some reasons, we do not often ask for bride price. It is not obligatory to ask for a bride price. I am one of those lucky ones with parents that never wanted it for us; My father was different. He had his unique ways worthy of emulation. I would have copied his style including this. But, I do not have a daughter, and I know that I have the task of making myself ready for my child, Bijou, my Jewel. Anything for his future, I ask Allah to grant us the ability to provide for our children. I ask Him to guide him to the path that pleases Him.

Papa was pro-education and wanted us to get it. It did not matter what level. All he wanted was for us to be in learning. He made sure that we went to school. Amongst my siblings, I proved that I could not be anywhere else but on the benches of the classrooms doing my thing. It happened to the point that I was labelled, the bookworm and never found the need to do other things. My abilities became limited. I understood early that the school benches alone could not give you the knowledge and wisdom that you need. The world is full of wickedness, and nothing black and white can prepare you to deal with it. I could not do anything but reading, writing and speaking. I attempt to change that with my son. I ask him to help with chores, and he happily does. I even teach him how to greet elders in the Yoruba way. I admire the way young people greet their elders, and he does not bother doing it especially when he wants his pocket money from me. That is quite an achievement.

I do get bored, but when I gauge my level of understanding of what goes on around me but, I feel the completeness in me as well. I only went to school, I say to many, to be able to read and write. It is an essential thing to me. It is what people are supposed to do. Learning is a right that everyone is entitled to do. But wouldn't it have been a mistake if I didn't follow the versatility trend I see in everyone today? You know, in life, we all have our unusual ways of achieving something. Mine was not about learning to become someone's wife although etiquette was all I had inculcated in me by the women in my life.

CHAPTER FIFTEEN
Elevation

Like any other parent, my father showed me the way, and I am still able to visualise the look on his face every time I achieved something concerning my learning. It used to give me joy looking at his facial expression and his gesture or moves showing his appreciation that I gladly interpreted as 'that's my daughter.' I kept making him proud in my little ways. I thought I owed him that respect by listening to his directives and it made me feel happy that I had always wanted to please him. If anything, he was the only one I tried to please. Other than him, my mother. That is my Creator guiding me to be just like them.

Sometimes, I look up and gently tell him. "Papa, wherever you are, I hope you are smiling down on me because your smile is enough. It gives me a boost. I have not achieved much of what I wanted, but I thank my God for the journey. It is never enough when you know that the One you ask from has got so much to give. In gratitude, I pray for more daily by giving thanks. Am I wrong for doing that? No, I do not think so. The Lord of Mankind has got so much to offer, more prominent than the whole universe. That is my belief. I smile because of my ability to be thankful and where I am right now. I do not complain. I have stopped complaining but never will I stop showing my gratitude to my Creator for having had you in my life as the pusher. If I was the professional pianist, your presence as a page turner made you the Leader I have always yearned to have. You gave directives, and I followed. That is the kind of dream that I had that has transpired and poured into this story that cannot fail to encourage and inspire me more as I am prepared to be reading it daily.

Wherever I may find myself I know is where my Creator has decided that I would be. Whatever I may get from my little knowledge, I will utter my gratitude to the Almighty. It remains a motto I will be referring to until I leave this world and that is what I also teach my young son. Papa never surrendered when his children's future was concerned. Those who were for education were pushed to learn. Our neighbours, families, friends witnessed him try his best for his daughters, especially me. I never wanted him to see anyone else try to impress him. I always wanted to be the one to influence Papa. I knew what he was all about. He taught me so much and enough to go to school with and impressed my teachers. Not that they could not show me, but I have always loved to be a step ahead.

I remember asking him one day about who he was. Papa, I said. Who are you? The lovely grin on his face gave him away. Whenever I met our uncles, I would ask them what they knew about my father. However, I never tried too hard to know everything about him. He was a simple, ordinary guy who never wanted to answer any questions coming from his most quick-thinking daughter. I thought it was good to hear stories people told me about him. Therefore, asking was the only chain breaker. But Papa never budged. He wanted us to see him as the humble Papa that we had. It made life easy for him and us. If anything, the love I fell from him, he never allowed me to think anywhere beyond the great person, beautiful soul that he was. I never wanted to hear anything negative about him. As a child, you are always highly inquisitive. At times, I asked him questions just to put him on the spot. I remember asking him a ridiculous question. Why Gambia Papa I said. His response was "Why you NennJallo?" meaning why did I have a daughter who keeps on nagging me?

My mother always laughed that I was a nag, constantly in Papa's case. I wanted answers because I loved living in Senegal better. Things were so good, and I did not understand why to exchange that kind of life for the deprivation. I was obsessed with my father. People do get upset with their parents' decision, but for me, anything from Papa was good. His friendliness and the love he had for family and his overprotectiveness towards us melted my heart and gave me hope. I have always felt his love because I was not afraid to sit and chat with him like a friend. That is how I warmed up to him. He liked us to listen to him, and that is all I did to make him happy. He taught me the real pronunciation of the French language. Often, I looked at him, listened to him speak French, and I wondered what he was doing in the Gambia. He was just unique, and everyone would tell us especially his family in Senegal. I can vividly remember when my cousins frequently introduced me to our relatives. Every time we were out, we would stop by an aunt or an uncle's house. I can't express how that used to make me feel knowing that family is not only those whom you share the same parents. They were always saying 'O bee LouLanne O' meaning that's LouLanne's daughter. Yes, I was the official "O bee LouL'anne" I loved the name too. I won't say that my Father was the best, but no one was better than my father. That is something I can say out loud. Accuse me of being biased; I will surely accept it.

I remember hearing his friend tell him one day, which he was raising me to be a boy and that is wrong. Papa's reply was hilarious. She said. "Papa Babou, allow this girl to be a girl. I have never found her in the kitchen helping her mom or her sisters. She has everything done for her." Papa replied to her and said. "Lady Bann, Borr la. Bess dinna gnow, Dinna ko feyy". It is a loan. She will pay you all back one day. He made it his point of duty to trust. It is how optimistic he was. Today we talk about positivity more often. He was all that and beyond.

His constant directives did not do me any harm though I always had the heart to do what boys did. Many complained about the way I carried myself before leaving for Senegal. I was never shy to express myself to the extent that I saw myself as a boy which was my mother's concern. I always heard her say…" You think that it is favourable to transform this girl into a boy". What she meant, bless her, was that behaviour wise, I did not do chores that girls did. I was always doing other stuff; climbing trees, riding bikes, wearing only trousers, etc. She said it in a very positive tone, and she meant well. Mom was always smiling, making jokes, teasing us and grooming us to become her best friends. She teased me about my relationship with her when Papa left us. May his soul rest in perfect peace. We became friends when I did not see him anymore. I had no choice but transfer my love to her like I was at a trade fair. But Mom knew I loved her. What I did not like then was her effective training for me to learn to take care of my sibling so early. I was young too, and I needed to be a child. I only heard those lines from Papa, and I copied word by word. She reminded me of that everytime we spoke, and we all laughed about it. I used to call her on the phone to teach me how to make her special sauce and 'Thiebbou Djeunn'. I just did not like being her little helper in the kitchen. We all laughed about that. I did not regret it. She did not, and none has regretted making me healthy and instilling those qualities in me.

How I wish every girl in our society today have parents who are supportive. Mother was not the only one who articulated to Father that, she agreed with helping to teach us the essential things of life using education as a backup. She used to pay school fees for many children until she left us. Most of my charitable work derived from the humanitarian work she did for her community where she lived before she passed away. My mother has left her mark there. I thought we owe it to her to continue her work and make it formal. She used to remind me of her frustration whenever she asked Papa to tell me to do something. He would say to me and would leave it at that. When mom asked, he answered. "Njills, I have told her" in a jovial manner. Oh, bless him. He was my partner in crime. He laughed every time people say to him "Yaangui yarr sa mborr deh, sou maaggueh daan la" You are raising your wrestler. You will be the first to be defeated. She will grow up not following your orders. His answers were often concise and sweet. "She is my Boy-Girl" "Do you have any objections to that?" [smiles…] …It gives me great honour to remember him and talk about him smiling. They were my rock and the backbone of their families. I have always said to them that they loved their relatives so much it is still them versus us the children who deserve the first-class treatment. I laughed every time I saw my sisters run around like headless chickens to entertain our visitors from Senegal. They will cook, go to the markets, stores in Banjul to help them buy clothes and, their businesses. 'SissiYekko', that's me, always under my father's feet being a little madam claiming that I had so much project work to do. Caring for a parent even when they are no more is very important for a child. Let alone having them still around. Parents are who make us what we are. I learn from this anecdote that our parents are our bridge to paradise. We must not depreciate their memories. They are our raison de Vivre, the Ubuntu concept we cannot find anywhere. We are because they are.

CHAPTER SIXTEEN

Ambitions

was that behaviour wise, I did not do chores that girls did. I was always doing other stuff; climbing trees, riding bikes, wearing only trousers, etc. She said it in a very positive tone, and she meant well. Mom was always smiling, making jokes, teasing us and grooming us to become her best friends. She teased me about my relationship with her when Papa left us. May his soul rest in perfect peace. We became friends when I did not see him anymore. I had no choice but transfer my love to her like I was at a trade fair. But Mom knew I loved her. What I did not like then was her effective training for me to learn to take care of my sibling so early. I was young too, and I needed to be a child. I only heard those lines from Papa, and I copied word by word. She reminded me of that everytime we spoke, and we all laughed about it. I used to call her on the phone to teach me how to make her special sauce and 'Thiebbou Djeunn' also known as 'Jollof Rice'. I just did not like being her little helper in the kitchen. We all laughed about that. I did not regret it. She did not, and none has regretted making me healthy and instilling those qualities in me. How I wish every girl in our society today have parents who are supportive.

Mother was not the only one who articulated to Father that, she agreed with helping to teach us the essential things of life using education as a backup. She used to pay school fees for many children until she left us. Most of my charitable work derived from the humanitarian work she did for her community where she lived before she passed away. My mother has left her mark there. I thought we owe it to her to continue her work and make it formal.

She used to remind me of her frustration whenever she asked Papa to tell me to do something. He would say to me and would leave it at that. When mom asked, he answered. "Njills, I have told her" in a jovial manner. Oh, bless him. He was my partner in crime. He laughed every time people say to him "Yaangui yarr sa mborr deh, sou maaggueh daan la" You are raising your wrestler. You will be the first to be defeated. She will grow up not following your orders. His answers were often concise and sweet. "She is my Boy-Girl" "Do you have any objections to that?" [smiles…] …It gives me great honour to remember him and talk about him smiling. They were my rock and the backbone of their families. I have always said to them that they loved their relatives so much it is still them versus us the children who deserve the first-class treatment. I laughed every time I saw my sisters run around like headless chickens to entertain our visitors from Senegal. They will cook, go to the markets, stores in Banjul to help them buy clothes and, their businesses. 'SissiYekko', that's me, always under my father's feet being a little madam claiming that I had so much project work to do. Caring for a parent even when they are no more is very important for a child. Let alone having them still around. Parents are who make us what we are. I learn from this anecdote that our parents are our bridge to paradise. We must not depreciate their memories. They are our raison de Vivre and the Ubuntu concept we cannot find anywhere but with them.

Being born in a situation where distance alone can deter her from achieving her goal due to the small range, Mossaan did not have to travel far for her to meet her role model. The model she saw in Marianne Semou Djimmit, having her good friends and family, give her a lot of purposes. No need to be selfish or stingy about her kindness. Mossaan knows what kind of a role model, she will be because she had always aspired to be a good and a useful Samaritan to the people of her native village of Saassaara. She is one woman who captured everyone's heart.

Writing the story of Mossaan is not the beginning, but the first message that hopefully goes beyond our terrain to encourage others to contribute whatever, wherever, whenever they can. I intend to make this happen and be more proactive for it to be the launch of several exciting series, write-ups that will aid people; non-Africans, non-Senegalese, non-Gambians for them to get the feel of what it means to grow up in Africa. Moreover, I want to highlight the challenges that come with wanting to be liberated within an environment where the people in it do not quickly want to be told about freedom especially when you are a girl still under your parents'/guardians' roof. It is also important to remind you that even when you are over the age of childbearing, you can only leave your parents' home when/if you are married. The African tradition does not allow a woman to leave the house unmarried, though things have changed a lot lately. Thanks to the West for giving us the opportunity to live freely. Does our society agree with the influence of the west? It is another big one linked to the many questions parents try to comprehend. They may not show paranoia, but the worry that makes one look ungrateful to what the world gives us every day. That is the opportunity to move around, do a lot and most of all learn about other cultures the world over.

Moving from one place to another and locally alone can give you so much knowledge, not to talk of going beyond frontiers where you can find out what was never known to you. It is the same as men giving women the chance to express themselves in a world where the male gender dominates anyway. When three village girls embark on a journey that they know not of the fruits it will yield, gallivanting (in their little world) the tiny streets of Saassaara they will only end up finding what they did not expect. These three young women ended up meeting their role model, their idol returning home from the Big Apple.

There were older girls in the village who have also travelled to work in the nearby cities. Very few of them went to Europe. Marianne Semou Djimmit is one of those sisters who has been living in the west for a decade since she got married. Knowing how it is in Europe, it is not always easy to travel back home without proper documents. After ten good years, Marianne made her way back home. She is everything the girls wanted and her visit, we have seen, changed the whole narrative.

The return of Marianne Semou Djimmit from New York has made their lives swerve gloriously off course. They lived their own lives before they met her, but it has caused so much interruption vis a vis their routine. It is about finding the balance between continuing with what is already known to them and finding out about new things.

It did not take them long to decide what their lives would be should they also seek for better lives outside the long and one-way traffic of their native village. However, it is Mossaan the most beautiful as they happily call her, who will be leading the way because she has always associated city life with wealth because she wanted to become economically empowered, I repeat. It is in her soul.

I knew that writing this, part one of this sequel was not going to be an easy task. It is a whole lot of regiment But, I took the ride in my stride and never looked back from inception. It is a gentle and absolute ride, but to my surprise, it has done me well. I am now able to say that I can with the right material and ingredient to add to it. I have become more devoted, willing and eager to keep on going with my new-found love of putting things together which is the pleasure of writing. I have had my doubts and anxieties. I also have in my mind all the people that love stories, writing, helping, scripting, creating, and all that is part of educating others, inspiring others and mentoring. All the above have played a massive role in making it happen.

Ordinarily, they remind us that the eyes are the mirror of the soul. I am an avid admirer of Tim Fargo who referred to what we dream to become like a piece of cajoling, conceptual tool in the form of a collection of words that warm the heart. "When there is silence, give your voice. When there is darkness, shine your light. Whenever there is desperation know that hope will topple it."

DREAMS - Reveries have a way of inspiring us. We are always on a quest for our inner beauty, inner calmness, inner peace, and solace to come out. Luckily for us, we can never lose sight of them because we do mean it when we say that we believe in our inner ability. We are in charge. What we have no control over is our predestination. However, we are aware of the Divine presence that is to be measured through our breath and everything we do from the time we wake up in the morning to the time we go to sleep at night.

Let's remember that it is a man's world. For many people, it means women have little to contribute towards this space called planet earth. That is so not the case. It is true that we do have a long way to go and I would say this because I believe it. I am sure the great feminists will disagree with me, but we must face it, there is a need for us to continue to work or dream together and not make our dream the mirage that most men say that it is what we have and not a tangible movement that can make any change happen.

My childhood story is the cradle of this tome and part of the sequel that will solely address the life of the powerless. I have learned that fiction always relates to something that we have felt that some of the attributes are of those that I know of friends, childhood friends I have met. I often refer to the saying that "Every professional pianist has a page-turner." Interconnected with this young African woman, we can all see ourselves in this story and gauge the way our elders are so hell bend with the unique method of raising the female child.

They have undoubtedly equipped us with all the right virtues. For older women, they tell us about our strength and where it lies and all. They always say that the power of a woman lies in the kind of man you attract. We relate with Mossaan who our imaginary twin is. I am a firm believer that no one was born to suffer or to be vulnerable, and it is true that no one comes into this world with a silverware in their mouth, but we equally did not arrive into this world to suffer too. We must heed to the idea that equality does discriminate as strange as it may sound, we are also taught to believe that women have always had the power to rule and to win.

Many astute men think that our fight for liberation is modern and has had an impact on the way we have governed over anything; the kingdoms, regions and even the way we organise ourselves culturally. I listened to a talk by a well-known scholar, a leading man in African. He spoke about issues that women are grappling and on so many matters praising the female folk like no other. I must say that it was a first for me. That talk was an eye-opener for me, and since then I have never bothered on fighting for liberation. I fight for the causes that affect women all around the world but personally, I do believe that I have always been a free human being because The Almighty had made me and allowed me to wander outside the cage that many people would like to place women.

We have always been opened to thinking and adding value to society. Mara went on to say that women are given the privilege to take care of every business concerning their communities, and why would you want to start fighting for parity that will make all that you have done be regarded as futile and reduce your status? In the beginning, I thought that he was only saying that to make women who were at the gathering feel good about themselves, but he meant every word he said and quoting from the Holy Book. People also shared many real stories referring to influential women historically. It was a topic he had mastered for everything he said came from the heart.

Our great kings respected their Queens and gave them enormous responsibilities of their kingdoms. Today, all of that has changed, and nobody should blame women for seeing things differently and let us be and continue our quest or revindication for a just society. The vision of life needs to be implanted in us even though we have diverse ways of explaining what our desires are. That explains why we are different in looks, mannerism, etiquettes, aura, grace, attitude, and mentality. I consider the perspectives, and I have mapped out the ideas for each section in several ways. I like to explore this in the future. With who? I am not sure, but possibly with you the bibliophiles as potential partners. Your words are as famous as my pen.

CHAPTER SEVENTEEN
Realisation

Evolution - It is a good thing to have dreams. Dreaming is the best thing one can do to live in hope. I am not sure about you but that is all I do. I do not see anything as random happenings. What I find interesting about a dream is that it can be discharged to the core. It is settling because it helps you create a compartment in your mind, a hub in your heart that you want to be in touch with daily. It also gives you a push without limitation. I would like to be encouraged to keep on exploiting every compartment so that each one of my dreams can be peacefully grasped and grabbed. This is what I tell my son. Fund your idea. It can nurture anything you feel can yield a positive outcome.

I have never doubted the power of my dreams. In fact, listening to people talk about their visions encourages me and gives me the boost that I need. Pressing forward is what we sing about, but some of us do tend to give up easily which is not promising even though they do have their reasons for forfeiting whatever they had going on. Somethings cannot be achieved without a sharp mind. So, I nurture the spirit first and I do that by telling myself that I can do it and I say that repeatedly. I have always said that I owe it to myself to believe that it is not foolish to dream big. Whose business is it going to be if you have small dreams? It is the same as having big ideas because you are the only one who knows what you want out of your goals.

Dreams can do a lot for you and to you. What dreams do to you is that you are always pushing yourself, persevering until you feel you have put your finger on the things that you so desperately needed to achieve. Most of the young women I have known growing up are power grabbers. They are active women who cling on to the smallest opportunity to hold on, and they do because they believe in themselves. Who would blame them? I like to be associated with people who do not ask me why and how are you going to make it?

We live in a world where we are forced to do whatever it takes to succeed. Another reminder here, being successful is not about the amount of money you have in the bank. I thought I should clarify that before proceeding. We are successful when we understand what challenges are and how we can deal with all our predicaments. It does not matter how big we dream for our children and for even those who are not yet born, challenges of society alone can distract you as a responsible person to be a step ahead and plan adequately. It is funny that we sometimes forget Who the Big Planner is. Nevertheless, we know that in our dreams we present our prayers and our hopes for a better life. That is how I interpret any idea that I have. I rely on them to understand what my next step is going to be, and I pray about it.

I used to talk about why I wanted to have an education not just because I was young and that it was all I had to do. I tried to follow my dreams and to achieve my goals and amongst them was learning how to drive. I used to nag my father to teach me how to drive. He started teaching me how to when I was only fourteen. During that time, a lot about my character showed up.

The impatience in me that everybody thought was related to my teen years and hormonal imbalance. I did not understand it then, but I do now, and that encourages me to work with young people. How they dealt with it is the approach I am prepared to take with my child and any other child I work with now and shortly. I have said that we had a special bond. I gave up quickly after many trials and even when he said, we will do it again tomorrow, I did not believe that I could do it. I was a perfectionist that I did not need to be because I was still a child who was trying to find her space. In a way, that delayed me on so many fronts. I was a challenge, and that is what everyone said. I was demanding because that is what they believed in not knowing that I was the way that I was because the right people in my life were working on my personality. There is a need for us to understand that young people always go with what their seniors teach them. It takes them a long way. Here I am reminiscing so many events that happened over three decades ago.

I regularly complained that I was not hard to work with when everyone thought so. I was born ready and always wished to do the job correctly. I was always like - Let's get down with the get down. Anything I wanted had to get done for me without a fuss. How can I grow up outside what I have known? I cannot. All I knew was grace. What we had was enough to serve an army of people because of the blessings. Barakah/blessing is what feeds our souls.

In this era of Social Media and everything we familiarise ourselves with, the image has become the first mess we have to deal with. It is a significant issue we grapple with especially us, women and the same things have transpired to our children. Every girl wants to live it big as they say. Some terms are too scary for me to use. I wonder where humility has gone. We often hear about "Living life to the fullest," and we all know what it means even when the peak is not what it seems.

Seeing pictures of supermodels, celebrities, public figures and media personalities, wanting to be like them has become the norm for every girl and even boys growing up in the west and Africa. But, we should not put anyone on the fence and blame them for what is happening in our society today.

Working at Radio One FM in the Gambia, we used to think that we were the best thing since Audrey Hepburn and that we were the celebrities of the Gambia. We were many young women working at the most listened to Radio at that time. The Radio Station belonged to one of the most generous people in the country. Honestly, George was a blessing to our nation. The man encouraged us to celebrate what we had and most of all ourselves for what we had achieved at that age. He called us the chosen ones. He was indeed right about that because he made us believe that we are going to do great things. We were the little people with good radio voices. That exposure was enough to mould anybody especially young women like us. Everybody knew us, and the location was the hottest and the best 'Frequence Magique.'

People got used to our young, sweet voices; some will come all the way to visit us out of curiosity. It was all dandy. An opportunity of a lifetime, we had. Yes, and the owner of the Radio Station did his all to give us the best training and made us household names. Our clothes, perfumes, we did not have to buy them except if we needed to have too many or to give out to our siblings or friends.

Many of our local tailors also made beautiful dresses for us without asking for a penny from us. All they wanted was a mention of their names on air. That was enough. It was their free advertisement, and we got told off for giving free adverts to them. Time was very crucial, and because some many company owners were stingy about their number of slots and the timings, George did not take a chance with us allowing giving them the opportunity to complain and demand free time as compensation. They were smart because it brought them a lot of clientele. I remember being told off one time when we dedicated too many requests, George called them 'your free advertisement slots' are too many. Your tailors and shop owners should start paying. Our boss was brilliant to detect that we were up to no good. George always knew when we were on our games. We had enjoyed his banter and those perks that we would not have had elsewhere. There was only one George Christenson. To say that we did enjoy our time with him is an understatement. Who wouldn't have? What I have noticed is the brief moments in life that can be life-changing. We must be paying a little bit of attention to the different cul de sacs of life that we meet along the way. They are critical, and they can make or break you. I often go online to look at the last messages he sent me and my responses. Every time he saw a post that made him happy about us, or I would say about me, he quickly threw in uplifting messages. That is what a kind person does. I call those little gestures the cul de sac. I can always take a tour around the moments I am proud of and remember the goodness shared and about the fights that were solely for the betterment of everyone who had worked under the banner of what he had created for the youths of the nation.

Society tends to make us what we become; what we are not and what we wish to become. It can also destroy us when we do not comply. Besides, we must not make this unquestionable double whammy our worry because we cannot do without this system and its multiple facets? I got that from my Tata Nanette Aada Bassine. Bless her! She once said to me that she was watching me and that I will grow into a beautiful young woman she always wished for in her prayers. Her final words were always about how I should not complain even when I face challenges. They are part of life she said, but I should understand that I will ever get back whatever people take away from me. she was referring to is the way that I was with everyone. I have always said thank you to people and showed my gratitude. She thought that I was too naïve to allow myself to believe that people can never harm those who do good for them. She advised me to have a strong faith because with that at least I will be able to pick myself up and move forward. I cannot change the way that I am. But, it does not matter what people think they do that can harm me, I will still rise, and my principles will always be there to have me bolted and grounded for I can deal with whatever that is thrown at me in a most civilised manner. I cannot be seen talking too much about anything nor anyone.

She addressed society as a female boss. "Society is a female with her crews that she can manipulate as she likes because of her powers" Tata Aada Bassine was an astute woman whom I adored so much. She was very coquette, civilised. She owned a private Etiquette School in Dakar. I was a regular visitor to her house because my School Blaise Diagne was not far from her at Point E. She usually sent her Chauffeur to come for me so that I could join her for her usual afternoon tea with her 'Grandes Dames' friends. That woman was too much. I always have a smile on my face when I think of her. I can still imagine her ruling her tribe. The world to her is her shindig. She can dance anytime she feels like it for she believes that only those without a vision can sit back and unwind. Tata was prayerful and very alert. None of her friends was the way she was, but she did not see the difference in anything they had compared to her wealth. Even though the woman was wealthy, you can never see her show off. She treated them equally with a lot of respect as well. They loved her for that. The wealth she had did not make her feel superior. These are the kind of women I grew up to know and make them my role models. I jokingly called Tata Aada Bassine and my Mom child collectors who are known for accepting to bring people into our homes. There was never a dull moment in Tata Aada Bassine's house. It was always full of people from their brothers or cousins in the villages. You will always find two or three people coming to live with her from her native village of Saassaara. She did not mind doing it because she had a lot of money. My mother did not care much because she believed that she could share the little she had with anyone that came to live with her.

I used to look at these Diouf women and I smiled knowing that they did not have a drop of wickedness in them. My late mother always made me feel so proud of her giving and accommodating heart. I wish I were as good as she was. Tata Aada Bassine and Mom always talked about her firstborn Tessanou or Sanou. I heard her frequently say things like; my daughter would have lived longer to do this and that. She missed her so badly, and I believe that she would have been happier had she lived longer. Tessanou I heard was a beautiful little girl. She died mysteriously, but I still add her name to my listed siblings every time people ask me how children do my parents have. They remain in our hearts even though we have never met her and Papa Demba. She could have been our rock, but I would like to believe that they know that we are doing fine. Hearing the names of our eldest siblings was enough for us to feel that they were our shield.

What I always thought was that since I was the dreamer of the house, I will grow up fast and look after everyone. Mom wanted a responsible daughter who could help. Parents never stop worrying about their children, even when you turn one hundred years old. Tessanou the firstborn is not here, but Mom had made one of her daughters to be the woman she was. We have her whole being in Khadijatou even though Fatou is the older. We all run to her whenever with all our problems and she never hesitates to do her best for us. Mother would have been proud of her. She looks after everybody, raises everybody's child and runs everyone's business errands. I call her the manager of life, a Godparent, a guardian in every sense of the word. She is a real great-granddaughter of Wassyla Faye, a true Guelawaar. My siblings are all I have got.

I had it tough after my father's demise. I did what I had to do too. It is a day I can never feel brave enough to address without feeling emotional. Fast forwarding to why we need to have dreams, but we need the patience to allow time to help us understand it. Women can turn anything into treasured substance. Every woman has this brightening light in them. If you ask me how I portray the woman in me, I would tell you that I see myself as the crescent moon, which symbolises the beginning of the arrival of light, guidance and divine mercy. Come on! Say those lines to yourself too and smile. You can even laugh louder. Nothing shall break you or stop you from saying those beautiful lines to yourself. The fact that the crescent moon is a reminder that my religion is a symbol of peace, adequately understood by its best servants, is a gift and favour from Almighty the Creator.

Women are dear to society. We are the epitome of Excellence and Beauty. Precisely everything you can find in Mossaan. That is what every man would love to have and see excel because she rises to serve her community that she loves. She does not want to hear anyone label her a 'Go-Getter' because she has a dream.

We can never escape our destiny. No matter how hard a journey, we should accept what comes with it, and we should also know that it is one fated for us to walk on. Mossaan embraced changed when it was the only option she had. We can be that Mossaan too. The best thing we can do is to accompany her through and walk with her on her journey with one sole purpose; to learn all about her, the stories she shares with her friends including us. If the niche she wants to find is challenging, we can learn how to come out triumphant, because she wins when we become winners too.

Mossaan saw many of her elder sisters, peers, cousins left the village or gone abroad to join their partners and that has had an impact in her life. The fact that she remained in Saassaara without a suitor was a bit embarrassing to her. But she thought she could keep herself busy by showing her interest to go to the cities to work, but no one was keen to show her the green light. But he supportive nature makes her feel that she can do even better should she leave to go to the city. Her ambitions aren't too much to ask. As she always mentioned. She wants to leave the village to go where she could go for a better life. Not everyone can go to the town, as ordered by the elders. But she refuses to compromise her wishes. She wants to do more for her community and herself.

As usual, every journey we embark on begins with one single step. There is a thing called stage from birth - one scene at a time. You become a toddler then pass through adolescence, a teenager later adulthood. Whatever you do reflects what the end would be for you. Just like how our spiritual guides would say it to us. The life we live here is just like a dissertation we are writing. It begins with the chosen theme, then developed with different approaches to work on the body, and the final bit will become the recollection of why and how you managed to finish it and the content at work. Mossaan's chosen theme is the dream she wants to accomplish, and she has an idea of how to write it entirely but not without challenges. But she embraces every bit of it.

CHAPTER EIGHTEEN

The Lane

I light a fire in my soul whenever I hear a good story. Yes, I do light a fire in my soul. Knowledge is a promise, not that acquires power. Life presents us with plenty philosophies. If you want to change your way of thinking first, then take multiple actions to get there. Knowing that wisdom is not age can be your amulet. It comes from life lessons.

When you connect to the point of origin, you are uncovering the purpose and the promises you brought into this world. In another way, you are revealing yourself, reconnecting with your most authentic self.

Mossaan sees herself as the one who automatically becomes the force behind everyone. Although not arrogantly, it came to her naturally. Things do happen to us that we cannot explain. It is the same way with Mossaan. She knows that she is the one everyone talks about in the village. She jokingly tells her friends that even the old men in the village like her to bits. Don't underestimate this shy young lady. She also has her 'astuces' her 'femm', you know, the hidden secrets that she does not want people to know and see display often. Don't laugh, but that is how it is. Mossaan is more serious about what to do to make everyone happy. She goes the extra mile to support everyone, especially to those visiting or returning to the village after a long vacation from abroad. She never concedes to anything regarding chores and providing moral support to her friends and her young cousin and siblings. It does not bother her. She is the one whom everyone seeks knowledge from when they want to know about activities or affairs in the village. That part is a bit burdensome to her. However, she has always found the best way to approach issues.

Her over energetic personality is hidden. What surfaces most is her hands-on approach, her polite demeanour, attentiveness and her willingness to contribute and make sure that she does her quota.

Although she is only twenty-two years old, Mossaan is trusted enough to be the head of every delegation when they have a lot of work to do in their allotments/gardens. She assigns tasks to the women who trust her so much. Responsibilities come with maturity and not because of the age. They are executed perfectly with wisdom. Mossaan had all that it takes to rule her community, but she knew little about her strength. She is a passionate person, and that is incredibly powerful.

As an enthusiastic and driven person, she has high expectations for herself. She might not have had the privilege of living in the city which they all think is the best life, but the leader in her knows her worth in her respective community at that young age. What can save Mossaan from the dream she thinks is best. I have tried to take this approach, to guide and inform her that, at the risk of being counterculture, it is best to try and lower her expectations and indulge in what she has already got that has made her what she is. It is a community of people that gives her so much credit for all the genuine reasons. But, hey, we do not always see what is best for us until it is late.

Saassaara is a small village where most of the people are related. Mossaan feels that her very own people will eventually start looking at her and think that she is not ambitious and that she enjoys being that person they all see around forever. She feared to settle for less, and she started feeling that the place she loves so much might not be the ideal place that can give her what she wants to achieve for her village and her people. What they do not know is that she does not have a choice. Though she does not mind helping, it has become a routine for her, and many have started looking at her differently.

"Those blessed with so much do not know how to use it. Never underestimate the power of a solid idea. The fact that you have got dreams means that there are goals for you to tap into and that is very promising. I put my heart on anything I set my eyes. The only time you fail is by not attempting to try.

As the elders rightly quote this and they got it so right. "Those with bigger buttocks do not know how to sit"

These are some of the many reasons she wishes to pursue her dream and change her life for the better. For Mossaan, every opportunity that comes by will be for grab. She eventually waited and waited for a chance to come by for her to see how things pan out for her. She has never ceased in thinking and wishing for a life-changing moment. Her dreams of changing her life never stopped for she felt it is her right.

There is a lot she can do no matter how many routes she will be taking to get there with the help of Almighty God, but she must initiate her journey.

Her journey began with a lot to encounter in her early age but surrounded with only goodness which she believes is the reward of the person that she has been despite all that awaited her; things that will happen to her and what she lives for until her last moments on this earth.

The route to emancipation is never going to be a comfortable ride. Mossaan embarks on it despite the expectations with the high hopes and challenges that greeted her.

Before moving forward into the dialogue, I want to give you the feel of what this beautiful character is all about, and I hope that no one will blame me for not providing more details, I wish to keep, about the rest to avoid giving too much of a gist for now. We do not welcome imperfections, although they are part of us. But that is how we can omit those traits out of our lives. I am sure you agree with me.

For example, Mossaan's friends are so laid back, and she happens to be the perfect one, always punctual and respectful despite having so much on her plate. She is one of the most beautiful persons you would want to know, beautiful, inside and out as they say. From the outside, her life seems to be well framed, but in need to adjust people's expectations to show that the perfection they see on the outside does not reflect what is inside. Have you noticed that most of us are living the same way mentioned?

Today, the social media platforms have immediately become our mirrors and fighting tools, contrary to what they are designed to serve. I envy those who over commit themselves to multiple things that keep them away from the hubbub of these unnecessary banters that are only bound to cause disastrous endings and endless remarks coming from people that are not able to judge. Why can't we go back to the old days and bring out the imperfections in us that can be perfected by those who love and care about us?

How do we banish imperfections and what are they? You and I know that things came first before names. There is no room for entertainment for anything that transforms a character. Be in the know by frequently learning to appreciate good things most possibly and beautifully. Mossaan has a way of showing how supportive she is but she can also prove to everyone that she has no intentions of making people think that she is willing to change or postpone her life plan to accommodate somebody else's goals. People can easily misjudge you for being kind. Not that many can differentiate generous gesture and obligatory gesture. She continually reminds her friends and everyone around her that her characteristics are not for a switch. Always do your best to understand, and most of all include gratitude of life's irrationalities. And finally, then perhaps a capacity for closeness.

"There is nothing rarer, nor more beautiful than a woman being unapologetically herself; comfortable in her perfect imperfection. To me, that is the true essence of beauty."

It is easy to find someone who quickly thinks of the way they are at what they need to be? The need to cover up is not there. Many of us do try to show to the world what we are not. It takes time to try to fathom out how a person is, internally. Making that breakthrough is impossible. To be suitable is for one to ignore any weakness one may have while knowing his/her strength. Not many of us are good at covering up the blemishes that always surface. So, why not to try?

Mossaan is a young woman in her twenties. She is ambitious with little to start with when it comes to her educational background. With most essential attributes that have made her what she represents in the village, here are a few we will not fail to come across whenever we read an interesting piece of literature.

She is honest and polite to start amidst the beautiful

attributes to shower her. Her beautiful aura encompasses patience, care, kindness, loyalty, being helpful, pious, respectful, natural, traditional, humble and content, you name it. But, at the same time brilliant and curious, but never meddles into people's businesses.

What more can one ask for in a human being? Mossaan has faced so too many challenges in her life. How to transform her life has always been the avenue she often refuses to visit. Though very confident, she has a fear of knowing her fate because she is not sure what it is to discover. Everyone in the village wants a better life. It is not always about waking up and getting all, you need. It is not that simple in the community. The good thing is that Mossaan does not give up. She says a little about the avenues she wishes to take, but no one has bigger dreams than her. She keeps on going, and that can never stop her to be that person who gives in easily. She has gone through a lot in her existence; ridiculed for her lack of education, for her extreme support to everyone, going the extra mile to make everyone around her happy for every time her cousins returned home to the village from the city or abroad, the first person they ask for is Mossaan. Helping without a second thought is all she does because that is in her nature and never look for anything in return for the support she gives out to her peers, friends, family members.

From inception, Mossaan was a community builder as stated earlier. When you start believing in yourself and become sure of how you can impact your surrounding and change your life, nothing people say to ridicule you can make you change your mind. She is someone who believes in making things happen and creating a harmonious environment for all is what put that zing on her feet every day she wakes up. Precisely the kinds that world needs. Here again, it is what this book is telling the younger generation of women, to keep believing in themselves and contributing towards their development for life is a journey, not a practice run. Too many people in the village, Mossaan acts as their aide, showing them around to family members they have not met or other community members who are part of their families or cohabitants. But she is more than that. Mossaan is the gatekeeper, a responsibility that has come naturally to her. No one has forced her to be that person, and she does it without wanting anything in return. A lot awaited her for the journey that transformed her life, the same route is turbulent and led her into all sorts and so much before she settles and starts regaining control of her life.

The story begins with a lot of experiences she has never expected and has a lot to tell her children one day. As she has always said, every stumble she has made as part of the dance of life that she could not have mastered and avoided. Her grace and faith have guided her. Lessons that every human being should learn.

"Mossaan" The 'Beauty-filled' character that most talk about in the village where she lives and beyond. If it does not make it to the screens; big screen or small screen, this is how I would like the reader to view it. It is an approach to make you enjoy it and yearn for seeing it on a big screen. Nobody can argue with results. A smart person learns from their mistakes, but a wise person learns from the mistakes of others. It is what I share with my peers.

Be the author of your own story and never think of letting anyone write it for you. Write it the same way you are eager to finish the walk you have started, by doing that, remain in your lane.

As I venture out to introduce the kind of work and area that tickle my fancy, I briefly share the next steps and to demonstrate how thirsty I am to produce the myriad of stories of women that every girl should know. I am fascinated by the work of our women in ancient Africa and even the modern great women of Africa. We cannot talk about women without globalising their stories. It seems that women have a common struggle that is why I believe that talking about what I know best coming from Africa helps non-Africans to learn about us and make their comparisons. Feminism is not a European concept. It is a universal concept that depicts Self-Love of gender that we have not had a choice to say yes to or no. I would agree that feminism is about loving ourselves as women. That is why we have the right to dream big and embrace all possibilities we must explore.

CHAPTER NINETEEN
Longing

Living in the moment is something many of us find too challenging because we are often busy assessing our past and planning for the future and taking part in anything forgetting that we cannot keep pursuing what do not know. Make a dream worthy of first understanding what is it that you want in life or out of what you are seeking. Anticipate taking pride in being part of something that is set to help you grow, learn, excel and become an influence.

Walking your way to the finishing line is essential. It is for each of us. The finishing line is no one's belonging. If you want to make a mark, follow your instinct and make your wishes come true. Suddenly, a story came to mind; a severe but exciting topic lingers in the head of a writer if you want, an aspiring storyteller, filmmaker, the name pops in, ideas flowing, it is one that is undoubtedly going to be the beginning of a myriad of stories that follow. What happened next?

The power of nostalgia is in self-doubt. If I were to write a letter to myself, I would not know where to start. I get nostalgic about being fourteen. There are a lot of things about being fourteen that I do not miss. But that does not stop me from desiring the limitless dreams that I had. I miss the Naf-Naf designer clothes that I wore and having

Vanessa Paradis as our role model and star. I miss the magazine that I read. I miss the places I have been. I also miss the people that I had as friends. I even miss the best teachers that I had since primary to high school and the unflinching and untarnished optimism that I had.

Being nostalgic is awesome. But, when I think about the past, I feel kind of guilty about it. We have all had moments like that. Don't we? It is part of growing up and the experience we had. If you think about it, nostalgia has a lot of negative connotations about it which has caused many people to see it as a disease, labelled as a psychological disorder. In Wolof it is called 'Guellou & Fattelekkou', I think. It happens when you lose someone very dear to you.

Deep nostalgia happened to me three times in my life, and it was not pleasant at all. Through these three phases of my life, I encountered a lot of pain and did not know how to deal with it. The first time it happened was when I left home at nine to attend secondary school. The second time was when I lost my father who was my only and trusted close friend. Well apart from a mother who did not understand the pact I had with my father. I was angry at first because he was only sixty-three years old and we were too young. No one can erase that scar from my heart. The deepest again after almost twenty years, my mother left us also in a most sudden but peaceful way. How can death be peaceful? It can never be, but it is crucial to talk about how she did not go through any terrible illnesses or pain before she finally answered the call of our Creator. Death is amongst the painful moments that make people dislike nostalgia. Because it reminds us anything, it tells us. I heard about people answering the call of Allah – people who died suddenly. But my mother's death left me thinking about the things I should do to live just like the way she lived her life. She had the most peaceful last moments, and I thank Allah for giving us such a great woman for a mother.

I think fondly of the past, and I know that nostalgia is not a sickness. It is the moment we use to think of all the great and bad things that happened to us. It makes me remember my faux pas and the stints worth revisiting and repeating. Nostalgia can be an essential part of our life, and I do not understand why all the negative connotation about it. It is OK, to be nostalgic. That is what I eventually said to myself and remembered the good times I had with my family especially my parents. It is all OK, and I cannot go through it without thinking about the sad things. But that is fine. I switch to that mode to allow it to ground me and not let it weigh me down. We've all led meaningful lives that make us feel proud of ourselves. How can we empower ourselves living without shame? A journey is as good as its destination. It is our reinforcement, our spear to our bow and arrow. That is the trick. I understand why the negative connotations continue to be around it. Even though I cannot avoid being in that enclosure, I do not let it weigh me down. I hold on to everything that reminds me of who I am to hold on to things that tell me of who I choose to be, whatever I have decided to do with my life and why I would want to leap from 'human being to human becoming.' I already know that I belong to the best creations of Allah. That is enough for me to go on to search for what I choose to become. Nostalgia gives me winds in my sail. I do not go without uncertainty. The many unwinding roads in life have already hobnobbed with everything we go out to find, and I am ready to go and obtain the comfort that I need to take me a long way. I can only get that through everything that has made me who I am today to catapult me into the future with all my flaws.

Our promises, the kind we have been revealing in the pursuit of promises processes from the beginning. The areas as mentioned above are specific to each one of us. What do you discover about yourself? Wouldn't it be great to know? I have always said that what I find out is Peace. So, I am Peace. What are you? My 'I am' being what I inculcate in my path. Universal promises are excellent qualities that all souls have the potential to embody in their lifetime, and we are all bound for greatness because it belongs merely to our Creator. Even non-believers I would like to call believers who do not find the time to kneel and pray do understand that there is someone above who oversees our destiny.

We anticipate the kind of person presented before us. Her looks, her mind, her body, her soul to us, her looks, how her mind works, her attributes make her the piece of the puzzle. Of course, the story centres around her.

Somewhere in Africa, Saassaara.

Saassaara is a village of serenity, love, and gallantry adorned with so much traditional and cultural values; the history once captured our hearts when concluding where this beauty should be emerging. Mossaan was known as Moss in the village and Marianne Semou Djimmit known as MarSemou with two of Mossaan's friends, Jokel Mindis and Marie Ndebb. They pave the way to this fantastic and appetising story created not only for an educational reason but at the same time entertaining and intriguing.

Mossaan, the beautiful young Serere woman who seeks and fights for her freedom both physically and spiritually. Carrying herself well is standard and following the norms in the village as a believer is revered. In Saassaara, the proud young serere woman could not stand living with her parents any longer. It is not for any appalling reasons, but a better future as she claims of the life people can have in towns and cities.

Mossaan hated the fact that she was not able to be one of the contributors, i.e., the young women who are seen doing beautiful things for the people of the village. She wants to start pulling her weight too which is very good of her. She detested the idea of being looked after by everyone around her even though she had her allotments in the orchard, but that was not enough for a modern girl. She despised the idea of being around without having a means of income to contribute towards the family day to day expenses just like any other young woman. She wanted to be like the girls who are already working in the cities. She is aware that many of them do work as a house help to sponsor their education and help their families home. It is common to see high school/secondary graduates who do not find work, nor apprenticeship to receive a bit of cash to contribute to the village.

Most of our school leavers nowadays do not turn their backs on the first offer to work as house help – domestic workers or even travel through the back way. Working as house helps does help them earn money in a most legitimate and non-risky way. Nevertheless, working as house help mostly or often is a choice of those who do not think that education was their thing.

Mossaan always wanted to go to the city to study, gain knowledge and return home to help her people achieve more than what they are already doing. She knew from the beginning that she could do well in academia. Her only predicament was being born a girl in a village where most women get married at a very early age but not as a child bride. At eighteen, it is normal for girls to get married. Mossaan was already twenty-two which means no one was forcing her to get married. Lucky for her and friends; Marie Ndebb and Jokel Mindis.

Most of the young men have already tasted the city and work life in big cities like Kaolack, Dakar or Saint Louis and even travelled beyond Senegal in the neighbouring countries such as The Gambia, Mauritania, Mali. Also, when they marry a girl from the village, they take them to live in their respective new homes/cities. Only a few of them leave their wives behind to stay with the in-laws, which is custom.

The piece of the puzzle

Mossaan is fit to work, educate herself, boost her people's repertoire by sharing earnings, knowledge, and skills she will gain once in the city. Her native village of Saassaara is in Senegal where, at one point, she couldn't stand living in anymore. She feels trapped. Mossaan developed a habit of writing down any memories that came to the surface and any storyline formed in her mind.

The life of the woman living in a patriarchal environment where chauvinism, early marriages are never erroneous, Mossaan wishes not to be anyone's property, even though there isn't much she was able to do to change the current narrative. Without the consent of those she was under their guardianship, this young woman will change that in a very respectable way. There are many young women in the village. Most of them in their early twenties and never for once been forced to marry anyone that they are not courting.

With Mossaan, everything must be exceedingly ethical in an enlightening way. That is the kind of person she is. She desires to remain that reasonable person, the darling of the community, everyone's sweetheart to her elders.

She did not have the chance to travel to the city, but she had the patience and waiting was all she did with a lot of complaining but not to the extent that those guardians of hers would notice. She did not anticipate anything happening without her plans. However, the last thing on her mind was to be a renegade which none of the elders in the village would have accepted for her to do. To whom was the broken vow made? To her friends? Did she hurt anyone of her nearest?

Mossaan feels unfortunate, but she is not. She has had her struggles, but she has never disappointed anyone nor taken anything that does not belong to her. She has not lost her will to live. Nonetheless, she gets desperate by the day and eager to start making money. Success is all she thinks, but she also is aware that patience and honesty would lead her to heaven as they teach us. The sense of having failed can render you burdened with sadness, illness, depression, and dread. It can also keep you stuck in the way of life that does not come close to your potential.

There is nothing wrong with having the liberty to do what you want to do. The only predicament that comes with it is the lack of having the desire to identify what is good or bad. There is this main thing that costs us something that we tend to fail to address. It is our modest way of thinking. When you think that what you have does not meet the standard of what your friends have, you begin to be ungrateful. As I have always mentioned, the opposite of grateful is not ungrateful. It is the worry. This worry can deny you a lot. It is ever so important to be mindful of the blessings that did not just come down to you to keep you company. They happen to you because you deserve them.

As for Mossaan, being emancipated means being able to see beyond the small box in which she is put in a pigeon hole and abandoned without the freedom she coyly asks for herself. She is a polite young woman who knows so little about the outside world beyond the parameters of the village of Saassaara. Associating women liberation with feminism is quite a reasonable thing to do, and if it is to give all the best attributes in the world, we can take it and celebrate without hesitations. What is not allowed is the negative connotations that many people; men and women like throwing at women who claim to be as if it is a bad thing. It is something that does not call for negativity, and anything ugly said it should not be taken light-heartedly. Feminism is about loving yourself as a woman. To be one fully-fledged feminist, you need to find time to recharge your desires and whatever you had before. You do need to show how fearless you are but modestly. Simplicity is about one of the influential personalities that come with being one strong woman who understands what she wants. When you like yourself, you look after yourself, your environment and be part of every bit of advocacy, decision-making processes and political participation and progressive society.

The Smidgen

Letting others be in control does not mean giving away your power. As it proves to be difficult to break the chain of responsibilities and care from our elders, only marriage or rebellion can separate a daughter, girl child from her parents. You see a liberated person the same gender as you in your town or village, accepted by all, respected by peers, and you wish to be like her. What do you do? What do you want to become? If you are wise, you become inspired, closer, intrigued to understand her journey and learn from it. This young woman Mossaan should meet with someone who is not going to be her nemesis but a person who will give her all the gist of life and ways of fathoming out challenges as a woman growing up in Africa with less contact with the outside world.

When you go through rough times, good habits are not enough. It only takes a few small practices to hold you back no matter how little they might seem to hold you back. Feeling angry and sad is not comfortable habits to have and resenting another person's success cannot help you grow. The people we cannot wish well would control how we feel. It is our own choices to love the person we are rather than wanting what another person is or have.

According to Mossaan, what she wants to be is a craft she has already mastered. She knows it. It is only those around her who turned a blind eye to what she was crafting. Her attributes are very telling. She is as responsible as a household leader amongst her peers. Never relent in making yourself somebody that matters. As the elders preach, "A believer who is around another believer or in a relationship with a strong believer in any religion is like bricks overlaid on top of each other. They strengthen one another". Having the kind and happy friends around her was a gift. She saw an example of an emancipated woman in her village which got her inspired by the time she laid her eyes on her. Though they are relatives, what she saw, her cousin who returned to the village with her family gave her that kick to become independent in a society that will allow her and deny her what she wants at the same time. It is for her to start the ball rolling. She wanted it all, and no one could stop her from being devoted to what she thought was going to be the right thing to do for herself.

Mossaan wanted nothing but to be a liberated, an educated woman which is of course not forbidden today, but comes with a lot of challenges when living with elders who respect tradition more than anything. Being emancipated in our society today comes with a cosmic plenteousness, that you cannot talk about without smiling for that means, in another way, challenges one can translate as abundance for there is a way of coming out of them as the winner. Some impactful consequences as the silver lining in every area one is yearning to tackle and execute. Failures are not for those who do not try to achieve something. It is part of our life.

This different point of view does not fail to surface in her life and her environment. All these qualities of life women have today, did not just happen, especially for the African woman. It is an endless fight for one thing or another. The girl who inspires her the most is called Marianne Semou. Marianne Semou Djimmit was amongst the village girls who travelled to the Big Apple, New York to be with her husband. Things started changing for the girls, particularly Mossaan, the day she arrived to visit the village, her parents, after an extended stay abroad with her small family. It is every girl's dream to have a voice and become an influence.

Mossaan got this inspiration from Marianne Semou Djimmit who willingly shares her experience, and she expresses her wishes for the girls in the village. After a decade, Marianne Semou Djimmit returned home. With her family for a summer vacation. She could not hide the feeling of worthiness within. It is worth everything; the other girls thought she had achieved. Marianne was down to earth and encouraging. She was different in looks, and her way of thinking was way beyond what the girls could imagine. It is what being exposed does.

There is a field of energy between the Creator and the soul, a still point of perfect trust and infinite possibility that allows creation to occur. Mossaan is a smart young lady. Her idea of reasoning was baffling to the girls and her love for her people did not go unnoticed. Her lifestyle now and her husband's way of thinking are wholly and undeniably different compared what the men and her peers in the village. An endless story/journey. Good stories do not end. Good stories leave imprints that stay forever. Do you know why? Because, the desire to live a happy life is infectious and everyone needs it, loves it, aspires it and hopes it. Let us roll with them. As they say is Wolof. "Samma waadji…Samma waadji. Ndamang cha, Gaatche nga cha." No one receives praises in vain and for no reason. It does not matter how well you praise your buddy. There is always a double whammy to what is said; good and bad. C'est la vie.

They said that "Roff Yaakhout Djeun." It means that stuffing the fish with mixed spice does not take the goodness or taste out of it. It will only make it enjoyable. I want to provide you with something you can enjoy and even learn with me as my maiden literature. It is my 'Chef d'oeuvre' that I would like everyone to be happy to speak about and even agree to disagree with me on some things.

The best of all types does not spoil it one bit. In fact, it makes it tastier and palatable. It is mainly to give an insight to the readers that the story of this young beautiful African woman is multifaceted. It is a story that derives from the short film written some years ago before deciding to publish it as part of my childhood passage as the first step to the fantasy world of Mossaan the sequel. We draw inspiration from the top ten issues we find in the story which depicts Mossaan, and every facet of her life. Amongst them are the dreams, challenges, triumphs, failures, and strength.

Never try to compare your beginnings to someone else's middle. It will never do you any favours. The only way you can predict your future is by reinventing and continually reminding yourself that you have a guide showing you the way and that you have been created only to be judged by your Creator and no one else.

Unleashing the stillness in you sets you free. For Mossaan, her life purpose is not going to be in vain. The bounty is unlimited because she is taking things at a commendable pace, a day at a time. All She Ever Wanted is not the story she wants to narrate. All she has ever fought for is what it could be and should be. The many excruciating pains and waits will make her discover the novelty of dreams and the broad-mindedness of it. The sad moments, aspirations, the muse, ownership, the right characteristics, envy in a positive way, the mutation and all the thoughts in her, have ticked all the boxes in the life of every human being. The race in our world has become paramount.

It is about education, freedom, vacation, motherhood, guardianship, marriage, chauvinism, exertion, success, achievement, inspiration, aspiration, failure, misfortune, obstacles, bondages, beliefs, rescue and everything that makes life what it is with its myriad of challenges.

Fantasy

In between my thoughts, I always stop and gauge my level of understanding of issues, criticise myself, though positively, to be able to continue creating a vacation from which I can ponder on many areas possible to miss should I maintain the race without the multiple pit stops. If I were to put it down in a thorough storyline, dialogue, the scripted version using pictures or a storyboard, it would start with an outside event. It will begin with an exterior shot mainly because I initially imagined making this film where young women have set routines with less to do in a milieu that not just does not favour them entirely but care about them enthusiastically. This is because they are surrounded by loved ones where their every move is on watch. Luckily for the people who care for them, these young women are virtuous young maidens who do not have the guts to be any other way but good. The way these maidens are is commendable, on top of that they obey the elders of the village under the most monotonous circumstances. Life is dull for them but the choice to adhere to whatever is thrown at them is unquestionably what they feel is normal for them.

Being dependent, less empowered, less educated can be a predicament of young women in Africa. Mossaan's story depicts the challenges women face and their choice to accept no matter what. They have a slim chance to get away with anything. They haven't got a choice to do otherwise but adhere to their rulebooks. People around you create a space for you to be under control and options for you. You are left disempowered to rely on someone else's decision. Thus, arranged or forced marriage cannot be ruled out. Typical of us and the way we live in Africa. We are facing predicaments we keep fighting for endlessly to eradicate everything that is uncomfortable to us.

In the meantime, talking about the role of a noble young African woman is another thing where we need to switch our focus. It does not matter how old you are; you have a huge responsibility at home. That includes the different household chores and looking after your younger siblings and the elderly. It equips you for when you settle in your own home. That's the humdrum for every girl. From the time you are born, they tell us that we must do this or that for when we get married. You see, from the time you are born, you are being told to get ready for when your wedding day or for married life. Another stripe that nothing can efface. Will that ever change the fact about the freedom women ask for?

I remember how I used to enjoy going to market with my basket to buy stuff for mom. I cannot write this section without the mention of a perfect sister, a friend I fondly call Lily or Laly Sanneh now double-barrelled with Singhateh as her husband's surname. Our parents knew each other so well and always talked about the traditional values of Gabou Kansala and many other things. Laly and I used to walk to the market together, chit chatting our life away. It makes me giggle thinking about it. She is one pleasant woman whom I adore so much for her strength, her determination and I love everything about her. She too lost her mother at a very young age, and that did not stop her from excelling. In life, some predicaments and challenges if I must say are presented in your life to save you by moulding you. It is not often that you hear people say that they have all that they wished for in their life. That is very rare. We had to do our morning routines, especially during summer holidays. She is now a prominent entrepreneur with the aptitude to educate her daughters. She makes me feel so proud when she tells me how she wants to make her children have the education she did not have. Kudos to mothers like her. She had dreams, and I am glad that we can all remember our humble beginnings and smile with or without much cash. We can still laugh and be grateful for the little mercy.

In Mossaan, I see many of us. Although I cannot mention everyone's name, I owe it to my pen to just grease in these few people that I feel I have known for at least three decades. My sister Khadijatou has taught me a lot about patience and beliefs. Marietou is a gatekeeper and Fatou the mother hen who does more of listening to us than telling us what to do. She is lovely. Fatou is just like her.

Mossaan, her environment and the people allowed her to dream. Her belief in success and emancipation, liberated mind kept her going. It is about the people with whom you surround yourself, those that remind you of what life is about; in characters, in deeds, in conduct and in everything that matters. If you do not fantasise about what you want to become and the possibilities of becoming everything you put your heart into, you seek counsel with your path in every type of virtue. The people you once knew, met or know to date can help you in the process of recollecting what you said you wanted and how you are going to get it.

Gather your thoughts and revisit the journey you've once mapped out for yourself. It is allowed. The passing tracks can be relieved, mainly when they were good ones.

The arrival of Marianne Semou Djimmit, on vacation with her family, is a great moment. She inspires the girls especially Mossaan. The way she carries herself. From inception, she wants to impress the girls with her charisma. Throughout this story, we have been learning ways to access our intuition, release the fear and old tales that hold us back and reconnect with the point of origin. Everything that Marianne has learned while living in the USA is going to be beneficial to the girls.

Her connection with the girls is also an eye opener to her and the whole community. Marianne Semou Djimmit lives in New York. Though she is not the protagonist of this story, many critical issues cannot articulate without her inspirational self in a middle of nowhere, a place where she once called her lifetime sanctuary. As she always mentioned.

Arriving in the village from The Big Apple through the story is not centred around her, she has become key to this story because of her achievements and in succeeding to emancipate herself and what she has become. An emancipated young woman from Saassaara to New York.

It is mid-afternoon at a corner in the village known to be everyone's meeting point during the day, Mossaan, a 22-year-old young woman, ordinary looking, slim-built, feels the need to speak to her friends about her desire to become a community leader someday. Someone who can bring change to her community, an already capable person who is now desperate to change the way she lives in her suffocating environment. Mossaan in her poised demeanour is all that is mentioned above. She never wishes to hurt anyone's feelings by repeatedly saying what she wanted to do with her life. She confides to her friends because she knows that they are loyal to her even though they have their girly moments with a personality like Jokel Mindis in their midst.

As we fondly call her Moss, she remains the Mossaan we all fall in love with because of her beautiful aura and characteristics. Pseudo is often used to show our appreciation to someone, and I am sure everyone is familiar with this. Marianne Semou Djimmit inspires Mossaan. She is one of their village sisters who now live in the United States with her husband and their young child. She is always thinking about work in the city as many of the sisters who are dropouts. Going to the city to work as a house help was an option knowing that she can turn her life around with the guidance of Allah.

Mossaan does not just desire to work as house help. The new trend is that those young women who are eager to educate themselves, work and pay for any training they wish to undertake. Mossaan's goal is to become economically empowered, to be well informed and be aware of what is happening around the world. She needs the exposure that all the girls working in the cities talks about in their evening gatherings every time they are home.

As a young lady, she is not dating anyone; she is not working for her education is primary level. She never had the chance to go for further education in the nearby town. But she is still a brilliant young lady. She participates in every event in the village and takes part in everything elders want her to be. That is how they trusted her.

Mossaan never fails to show her leadership wits. She thought that it would be interesting to know how her friends see things in their environment. Although they are well taken care of, she genuinely is baffled that no one thinks the way she is going on about life in Saassaara. Her attempt to have a chat with them went well. She had an exciting, heart to heart chit chat with her bosom buddies; Marie Ndebb and Jokel Mindis about everything that was bothering her. One of them was about the reason behind the elders' decision for not asking them if they would want to go and work in the cities as many of the sisters in the village did. It was all about their lives. Somehow, she felt she could instigate this kind of talk to gauge if her friends did not have any hopes of making their lives better even though they had a good experience compared to many people they know. Between them, their families are rich in wealth with farms that bring in a lot of money, orchards and many allotments from which their livelihood depends.

The Switch

Once upon a time, one of the daughters of Saassaara by the name of Marianne Semou Djimmit travelled to the west to join her husband. It's been a decade since she moved to New York. Now that she has been away for a long time, her coming home was a big event. It means a lot to her. She returns with her husband and her young child. Marianne's visit to Saassaara is layered within powerful moments in the lives of the young women in the village. These are young women she knew before leaving for the Big Apple. Mossaan is amongst these young and beautiful women. If anything, she always has a better life, and the arrival of her role model has added to what made her feel so sure about the urge for city life.

All that she sought for in a role model was everything that is in Marianne Semou Djimmit. A good role model she is indeed to Mossaan.

Voila, here is Marianne who was once just like them, in her new mindset for looks is not what the whole saga is. It is about steady life. The young women usually gather in the afternoon to go to the wells or boreholes to fetch water and filled the canaries, bottles of water to put in the fridges. Most villages have now become modernised with TVs in their homes, electricity served by generators, nicely built homes. The sons and daughters of Africa take pride in bringing back what they've worked so hard for to the village. They produce many places. Homes are taken care of by all members of the family, especially brothers and women had their part to play that has nothing to do with finances. That is what the demand was before, but women do their quota too in everything that needs their input because they have become economically empowered. The reason why the fight to become emancipated has become an anthem.

It starts here with Marianne Semou Djimmit commonly known as Marianne Semou. Her vacation in the village from The Big Apple although the story is not focused on her. She became the key figure for a moment. The story is about Mossaan and her ambitions, inspirations and her motivations towards the life-changing experience she will encounter. Marianne's achievement is what every girl wanted, and Mossaan was no exception. She is emancipated, opinionated, savvy, civilised, polite, kind and very helpful and encouraging to her young and novice peers. An emancipated young woman from Saassaara who owes her success to the big city she went to live in for a decade and with the support of those that supported her throughout.

She, Mossaan, is to leave the village to go to the city to do something for herself.

She also shows how she is encouraged by Marianne Semou, one of their village sisters who is residing in the United States and her young family. She is inspired to try different routes based on what is available and easy access to her. Mossaan wishes to go to the city to study to achieve her goals and become economically empowered and to learn to be aware of the world around her.

Going back to the expressive young woman's life, Mossaan feels that it is the only way she can make herself useful, be a contributor and become someone who can earn the respect of her community members. She emphasised gaining the respect of the man she will marry one day. As a young lady, she is not dating anyone, nor in any relationship. She is not working due to limited resources in the village. Her secondary education is not enough to help her through, especially when she does not see any connection apart from the cousins, half-brothers working in nearby big cities. Living in the village did not give her many choices which are standard. She would love to get a good education because she is for learning and a brilliant young woman. Her chances to get employed would also mean going to the nearby towns to work as a house help.

Most of the young women who are older than her work as house helps do not choose the small towns. They prefer going to the big cities where they can earn much money. Besides, many predicaments are working in the small towns that are nearby as many have mentioned. The people will be those you are familiar with, and they can take that for granted and not pay your dues. So, they always preferred working in cities far away from their native villages. What has become in fashion is the way these young women, house helps, pay for their education or training with the money they earn. Some also go to the university and work as home helps just to have accommodation. It is courageous of them. Mossaan is aware of how her older sisters challenge their predicaments and make ends meet has inspired her way before she set eyes on Marianne. She has always been a dreamer. With her positive aura, she never let anyone, or anything stop her from pursuing her noble dreams. She is already a community leader in her rights. Her stance was visible, and the elders in the village always prayed for her to have what she wanted in life. In her heart, she was unemployed, but in her mind, she was doing more than what she could, even though the mission is not paid to do what she does. All of this prepared her on her journey to excellence.

Marianne Semou Djimmit is one of the women leaders in the community who has a voice on anything vis a vis women and decision making. She participates in everything, very respectable and highly praised young woman, barely 34 she already is a responsible community developer in her right. What the girls like about her was her ability to speak and her courage to listen. Very laudable and commendable. Mossaan wants to be just like Marianne Semou. She is not asking for much, but to have an education that will help her change her life for the better and become empowered financially. However, she would need the right support for her to get to where she needs to be.

Mossaan and two of her friends Marie Ndebb and Jokel Mindis were having very ambitious and exciting talks about their life in the village and particularly Mossaan who is eager to leave to leave for the city. There were no plans, but the hope for a way has never gone out of her thoughts. Being optimistic about everything can be a game changer.

Marianne Semou Djimmit is already in town. Mossaan is aware of it already, but the other girls, Jokel Mindis and Marie Ndebb have no clue. They do their afternoon chores together every day. The most exciting moment of their lives in the village in the afternoon when they all walk to the wells and the gardens to get some vegetables, water and feed some of their cattle and take care of the horses in their stables. They used to hear people say that it is a man's work, but they enjoyed doing it anyway. The conversation about Marianne Semou Djimmit commenced.

From the time, Marianne Semou Djimmit stepped into the village; poor Mossaan had not stopped being engrossed about her urge to become the one people will look at in the future and be inspired by just the way she is to this beautiful holiday-maker. Very often, she mistakenly called one of the girls with the name of the person she is obsessed with for many reasons. She mistakenly called Marianne and hell broke loose. The girls love her but worry that she might think less of herself, which is a danger to her character. But to Mossaan, it is normal for life is filled with surprises and she is truly surprised by the sight of one of their sisters in the village who is now better off and able to change her life and others. Marianne Semou Djimmit inspires her, and she does not hide it.

A knack forgot mistaken by calling Jokel Mindis, Marianne Semou, which indicates how eager and desperate she was to talk about her to her friends. Under the tree, the conversation about Marianne was echoing. Mossaan did it deliberately since she is all about the positive things women do and what they can do in society. Her life is way beyond those buckets filled water though, as she had secretly made it known to those closest to her. She did what she did for everyone. Making sure that her environment is clean, her chores done and her role in the house means doing what she lived in and what she believes can make a significant difference in her life. She is very responsible which has been core to the persona she has happily embraced today and what made her. The girls chatted their time away. Wherever Mossaan, Marie Ndebb, and Jokel Mindis meet, you can expect close fights, endless teasing and a lot of argument. They grew up together, did a lot together too. However, they cannot be the same in personalities but understand each other.

Self-Discoveries

On a journey of self-discovery, anything can happen. It is afternoon time, near the gardens on the way to the wells, the girls and other women in the village head out to fetch water from the bow holes. Part of their afternoon routine is to go to the gardens and get the fresh vegetables, fruits and evening walk. Their evening gatherings 'Ngonals' are never dull. They cook all sorts to pass the time through the night until bedtime. The vegetables they harvest is usually to add to their nutritious dinners and lunches. Though it is life in the village, they live they get the best nutrients if I may say. Very healthy in every sense of the word.

During the gatherings, they discuss anything and everything concerning them; about the village stories, lifestyle, children, education, health, and living condition. The goals are not just about stories. Some make it a habit of bringing real-life stories and events for people to learn. It is spent in the yards to discuss anything and everything about life with friends and families. It is a custom that is enjoyed by everyone. Young and old. Personally, I used to love those moments and still talk about them in Gnolanem pronounced Nyolaaneym, a village situated just after Thioffack in Kaolack.

Reminiscence

I never missed out on the Gnolaanem's Ngonals on Saturdays. My aunt knew how much I loved going there. She sent someone to pick me from the city of Kaolack every Friday evening when possible so that I can go and spend the weekend at hers with her in-laws. I usually travelled with her husband's driver or with the chariots (Borrom charrettes) when I finished school on Saturdays.

Her father in law was the Big man of the village. He was well off, had a lot of money from his farms and raised so many people children in his big compound and multiple buildings in it. He was named Mame Mbaar Faye though I am not directly related to him, Mame called me his granddaughter from the Gambia. He talked to me so much about my ancestors and loved listening to him speak about Salmon Faye. I once asked him if he was known to him. He responded by saying, everyone is proud of that old man and said the Faye family is one huge one. I have never seen anyone like Mame Mbaar. He was an interesting character, very family oriented and a kind as well.

Mame Mbaar was not tall, but remarkably he was looking healthy for his age. His children were working in Dakar, and the oldest was already in his late fifties. What a generous human being he was. That is what I liked that about him, and I respected him for that, and I know everybody did. I enjoyed him at lunchtime when he told his daughters in law; my aunty Ndey Diouf, Ndiaye Saar and other women in the house, how to dish the food. Mame would bring the dishes himself, and you could hear his voice from afar asking women to dish out a lot here and there. He wanted everyone to eat well. He oversaw everything. I always asked him why he was still involved in everything. You know how young people think. I was thirteen by then and bold. I feel bad when everyone keeps reminding me of the things I used to say or do. But I guess it was the way my late father empowered me. I always said to Mama Diouf that I am the way I am because of Papa. My mother was such a natural, a noblewoman. She never liked to awkward situations to herself and her loved ones. What we loved most about her was her ways of having her interpretation of every moment. Nothing was too cumbersome for her to tackle. She worked herself hard to avoid troubling moments. She was the catalyst that any family would need. Her interventions were alluring. I felt protected whenever I was with her, and that was noticeable. I kept quiet whenever she stepped out. That meant something to my cousins and the elders in the house. You can hear my voice as soon as she steps in.

Everybody laughed when I asked questions too many questions to Mame Mbaar. He also smiled so much, but he never took it hard. He knew I always said that I was from a different planet which spared me the hostility. I did not mind at all. I just wanted to get to know the Mame Mbaar that everyone respected. I eventually became very close to him to everyone's surprise. He was my old friend. Things that no one dared do in his home were what I did without fear. I often put my other young cousins in trouble for following me. I was this happy go lucky girl in his home, and no one dared make me feel unhappy. He was the grandpa that I never had, and I was one his favourite little ones. I could ask him anything. The few times I experienced my aunt tried to cover my mouth so that I did not have to say what I was about to say. Mame Mbaar adored me, and I knew it. I even had to name one of my sheep in my mother's home after him. 'Mbaar' had the character of his namesake. He wanted to be everywhere in the house. I remember my late mother told me many times how Mbaar is so much like his namesake. I always laughed about it, especially when she said, namesake. My good-looking Mbaar, the sheep, was so much like a human being. I spent the whole academic year in Senegal. Being away from my parents never bothered me. As a middle child, I thought to impress my parents; I had to do something extraordinary. I had to do what pleased them. I had my strategy, and I used what I knew best to win their heart. I succeeded in doing that. Everything that I needed was given to me. There was not much but more than enough to make a child happy to learn.

Senegal was my home for nine months every year. I hardly missed the Gambia where my parents lived but enjoyed travelling back in June for summer holidays with a lot of stories to tell. It was always nice coming home to stay with Papa and Mama Diouf.

The sad part still kicked in during the last quarter of the third month which was all about the planning of heading back home to Senegal to be with my grandmother Aminatta Diouf for another extended academic year.

Characteristics

I always wonder why Mame Mbaar was not the head of the village because everyone came to him for help even the head of the village came to Mame Mbaar for support. He referred people to him and profited from his generosity. I miss the good people I already knew.

Many people that know me will be able to see the character of Mossaan in me because of how I relate some of the events to what her activities are. I lived and loved the life of the village. It is exciting, educating and enjoyable. Of course, it is how I got inspired to pin down a story that melts my heart. This story makes me relive those experiences and exciting moments. The evenings in the villages are priceless. With a little comfort, people get by and enjoy their precious time with families and worshipping their Lord. What more can one ask?

None the girls liked missing the Saturday 'Ngonal', chatting the night away until day breaks. Customarily, it is the time when we hear a lot of storytelling and different role models who are the heroes and heroines. Mossaan enjoys coordinating these evenings at home.

Because of her generosity, everyone likes attending her Ngonal. She provides all sorts. Everything she gathers from the gardens are prepared to share with the attendees or guests. In the evenings, she gets the pancakes ready, doughnuts, roasted peanuts, fruits and the attayaa (green teas) that is part of our beverage, though the drink is called Chinese green tea, it is consumed excessively in Senegal and Gambia. Oh yes, people love it. The perfumed tea has an inviting smell. The evening Ngonal is usually a platform for learning as well.

The girls enjoy those moments a lot. It is a garden of good and bounty. But before every Ngonal, Mossaan and the girls got themselves busy and engaged in their mundane routine. They involve themselves in their afternoon routine of getting their chores done and put in order whatever they needed for following day. They usually woke up early for their Fajr prayer, then breakfast for the little ones before they went to school and made sure that too much time was not wasted in the morning to cook the 'fondeh' porridge or 'Cherreh' couscous with milk from the cattle. It includes going to get the best vegetables to cook dinner, some fruits such as oranges, mangoes depending on the season and some 'Mboxha' corn on the cob and all. At times, they added all sorts; music, dancing or any entertaining instrument around.

The evenings in Saassaara are always fun packed with beautiful moments. In the late afternoon before cooking dinner, everyone in the village, men and women, file towards the gardens. The noise is always so loud you will think they have visitors from nearby communities joining them. Everyone is happy. They walk towards the wells in groups supporting one another with their watering cans, heavy buckets/barrels and big jugs of water to take home and baskets of goods from the gardens. Happiness is always what you can describe those moments. Mossaan, Jokel Mindis and Marie Ndebb in the middle of it walking happily as usual.

Everyone talks loudly, but Mossaan in her calm demeanour always smiled, she crept in quietly but listened to every gist shared. She still looked carefully and never interrupted others when they talked. She will occasionally say a few words, and that is all. She made it clear that she would not be bothering herself talking over the noise. She is patient, and she could wait. Wherever Jokel is, you must brace yourself and listen more because she does all the talking. Mossaan chips in when she needs to, and that is when they mention something that sounds interesting to her or anything that excites her. She always waited for the best opportunity to say something since Marianne came into the village. Her inspirational moments never failed to show, and the other girls knew it. It is without a doubt that Mossaan and the girls are different. However, it never got in the way of the harmony they shared and the great relationship they had they were growing up. She gets along with each one of them even though at times, feisty Jokel and her never-ending nags get into her.

The girls and other women amongst them in their journey were engaged in some talks, about other issues concerning their life in the village and everything that is happening. Most times they worry about their crops and what they will have for their work after harvest. They are all business-minded young women who are very serious about their work. They produce the best of vegetables as well as fruits such as mangoes, oranges, plums, satsumas and other exotic fruits that attracted the attention of many buyers. So, you can understand why they make it their worry and discuss a lot about whose turn it is to get most of the money after selling. Their evening trips to the gardens show how determined they are too. One hot late afternoon, on their way to the vegetable allotments, everyone was talking about whatever was of interest to them, but no one paid any attention to what Mossaan wanted to say. It is not that they did not notice her. It is because she was always respectful and timid. She is not a nag at all. She is very polite, and the respect she has for others does not do her much favours being in a group of lousy young women. It is something else when dealing with her naughty peers who do not always feel the need to listen for they lack the skill.

Mossaan had no choice but to learn from her friends and badge as and she needs to have her turn. They never listen to her when they are all yapping at the same time. She had to muscle her way in, forced herself into the conversation to say what was of interest to her. Mossaan and Jokel had the most beautiful relationship. You can't help it but stare when these two have a heart to heart conversation. Jokel understands Mossaan so well and knows how to get on her nerves. The good thing is that she does not get angry. But, with Mossaan, her short-tempered nature is the only predicament that needs omitting from her personality. It is funny enough that people only see that side of her when she is having a chat with Jokel who feels the need to toughen her up as she claims. You can always hear her say to her "Mossaan you need to be tough and understanding my antics would do you good. You get upset about everything I say. Why?" She laughed and just continue her conversation with others to annoy her.

Mossaan at some point wanted to interrupt Jokel. She wanted Jokel Mindis' attention and pretended to have made a mistake by calling her Marianne Semou. She knew what was waiting for her. That was the only way she could get Jokel to stop talking and listen. It was not a surprise that Mossaan wanted to talk about Marianne Semou Djimmit who is also Maar, a name that many people call her.

Everyone, including her husband Latir, called her Maar. Her parents named her after one of the noblest women whose father was called Semou. She too was given the same name coincidentally. Her father is also called Semou Mbacke Diouf.

'Marianne Semou! Said Mossaan. She abruptly interrupted one of the women talking to Jokel Mindis. Oops! She pretended to feel embarrassed to say the name of a person whose name had nothing to do with their afternoon trip and current conversation. She put her hands in her mouth, covered it. Mossaan was wise to interrupt. What she wanted she had which was Jokel's attention so that she can speak about her role model. "Oh, I beg your pardon Jokel. My mistake". She laughed, but Jokel did not find it funny. She just looked at her and rolled her eyes. Mossaan continued." I meant to say Jokel Mindis and not Marianne. I beg your pardon."

The eye-rolling did not stop Mossaan talking. "Have you seen Marianne Semou?" Said Mossaan. "What about her?" Jokel Mindis responded.

"I wanted to say that Marianne and Latir look so good. They are my ideal couple. Huh! We should hurry Jokel. I do not know why we are wasting here. It is true this is our destiny for now, but we have to keep praying harder my sister."

Jokel Mindis allowed her to continue and enjoy her excitement and never disrupted her knowing how mesmerised and infatuated Mossaan was about this newcomer lady in the village as she said with sarcasm. After a while, she began addressing her "Believe me, if I tell you this. I did not know that they were in town. Who are they by the way?". Jokel Mindis knew there were visitors in the village but had little interest in them. Seeing her friend's show so much attention in another person was not something she took lightly, the reason why she was always sarcastic towards Mossaan.

As always, she loved herself and very content with her village environment. She is not one of those girls who press on things. It is not because she is not ambitious. It is just because it is in her nature to take things as they are. Many a time, Mossaan accuses her of bottling things in because she knows her friend very well. When Mossaan asks Jokel Mindis, she talks about her love of bright ideas and her ability to show how much patience she has got. However, she yearns for bigger things and that everyone has a way of showing their emotions. Jokel Mindis does not complain, but she is a go-getter in her way. She is an enigma that is the simplest way to describe her. She can surprise you with innovative ideas you will never think she had in her head. That is the kind of person she was.

Jokel Mindis showed a bit of interest in Mossaan's question and a topic of interest. She asked with curiosity if they were back for good with a naughty facial expression that can quickly make someone keep quiet and not say a word.

But, because she was always interested in nothing much but talking about the couple, Mossaan responded in the same tone as Jokel and the expression she used. Mossaan's responded looking straight into her eyes to gauge her mood.

"Oh, I saw that they came with many suitcases but what I do not know is the length of time they are going to stay in the village. I hope they stay forever. I have not asked but I will when I get the chance.

They are strangers too to me. I have just been introduced to them not long ago. So, I greeted and welcomed them" Mossaan continued talking while her friend was in a 'Depeche Mode', mainly in a hurry to shut her up but at the same time eager to hear all the gist.

"They arrived on Friday. That is all I know. I wish you were there when they arrived. Everyone was looking at them with admiration" Said Mossaan.

Knowing how Jokel can be. She could go on nonstop. She went on wanting to continue the conversation. "Hmmm, I wonder what happened when they arrived. I bet you were there looking at them like you are less of a person than them."

Chores

The random things that Jokel Mindis utter from her mouth

put Mossaan in shock and awe. It is the same to everyone who knows her. It is still mind-boggling. That is the look Mossaan always gives her. The good thing about their relationship is that they understand each other. In an annoying manner and tone, rolling her eyes, Jokel Mindis was trying to pull Mossaan's leg. Poor young woman. She is a happy go, lucky soul. She never took Jokel Mindis' banter seriously. They've known each other so well. She tolerated her a lot with all the things she said and did, but that is a healthy relationship for us to know. It did not matter what Jokel Mindis told her. Mossaan always took it in her stride. She loved her friend so dearly. Nothing can come between them including Marie Ndebb.

"Going back to the question asked Jokel. Mossaan reiterated. "Nothing happened. I just loved smart looking people. I always look at myself and crave for a better life. That's all I imagined looking at them. I do not know what kind of life they live abroad but looking at them, I know they have it better than us. That is the truth. Who'd compare living in the West and living locally? We may have it easier than them. Who knows but the opportunities there are far much better than life here" That is what I think. Expressed Mossaan.

"That is what everyone thinks" replied Jokel Mindis, in brief.

"I know you may think that I am not with my senses, but I am thinking straight. Call me foolish, but it is what it is

Jokel Mindis. You might not like the admiration I have for Marianne Semou, but you must live with it. It is my life, and I can admire whoever I like. Besides, you need someone who inspires you in your life. It is normal my dear" I am not a jealous type of individual. I want good things to happen to me too, but I cannot allow my life to be lesser than anybody else's. I do not want to be closer to people because they lived abroad. Living in the village is as valuable as living in towns or big cities, that I guarantee you. It does not matter how much wealth you have got; I can never make myself lower than anybody.

Who would have thought that Mossaan could straightforwardly convince Jokel Mindis without the two of them tearing each other apart in a non-violent and non-malicious way? They always had heated debates but end up excellent.

The following day, as usual, the girls were together doing their chores. Their homes are a stone throw away from each other. So, it is apparent to see that they cannot be apart for too long. Marie Ndebb was not yet with them, as she was walking towards her home, she sighted Marianne Semou Djimmit and went into her home. She had a talk with few of the sisters in the village. Marie Ndebb needed to come and share the gist with the rest of the crew. In the community, from the time Marianne came for her vacation, all they talked about was Maar Semou as they called Marianne; the baby, the husband, the clothes she wears, her perfumes, her looks and the plenty materials she had with her. It is normal to have so much stuff when going back especially after spending over a decade abroad.

The three beautiful, helpful and responsible young women are inseparable. Their chin-wagging session about Marianne Semou Djimmit intensifies by the day. Marie Ndebb rushed in, eager to talk about Marianne Semou. Oh yes, they seemed to be the talk of the village. It is mainly because Marianne Semou Djimmit has not visited since she got married and travelled to New York to be with her husband, Latir.

"Listen! Listen! Listen, girls! I couldn't stay away. I had to go to their compound to see them last night. I am so happy for them. It is so wonderful to see people so happy together. She speaks well and about everything she did in her first years. So, inspiring. Marianne talked to us about her adopted home" The life of a twenty-year-old is never a dull one. It is interesting how they think. We have each been there, done that and lived in Utopia for a moment then realised that 'Life is a journey.' It is everything but some parlours in which you can chill and let things happen to you without sweating or fretting.

These young women are at that stage where everything they see that impresses them should be a grab for them because they are just beginning their adulthood and that their parents still have them under their wings. The ones who think fast and can gauge their environment always have it better because they've prepared themselves mentally. It is easy to get trapped by the care that is enjoyed when in a situation where everything given to you on a silver platter seem surreal. I know many would think that there is no silver platter in the life of a girl living in an environment that doe does not have much to offer. In contrary that is what happens to young people in the village. African parents are not aware of the western system, and the way they raise their children. Any child that takes an attempt to leave home will have the army of village members out to hunt you. You will never forget it.

Our culture does not allow a young woman to leave home at the age of Eighteen or even at Thirty/Fourty if you are not married. Luckily, with evolution and the emphasis put on education, many parents send their children to boarding schools, girls included.

Jokel Mindis, Marie Ndebb, Mossaan are all in their 20s. There is not much gap between them. Adulthood comes with a lot of responsibilities. Anything that shines impresses them especially things that they want but cannot have.

Marianne visit is something they wake up to and talk about every day. One can identify their different attributes, their wants and what have you. Being a role model presents no harm to them. She could have been different, but the girls loved her for her achievements even when the likes of Jokel Mindis did not want to show it in the beginning, but she eventually realises that Maar is everything every young person wants to be. Anyway, the irony is that Jokel Mindis had it in her head that Mossaan was the only one smitten about this new couple and their baby. Hearing Marie Ndebb spoke about the couple left her in awe. She just smiled and shook her head. Marie Ndebb continued in her excitement and never wanted anyone to lift her joy. She went on and on because she wanted to get Jokel's attention. Now it is her turn to be in the same book that Jokel placed Mossaan. She could not escape and must accept that it is the Marianne Semou Djimmit effect all over the village. Every person woke up to singing praises about Marianne from dawn till twilight.

They looked so good together and different compared to when they lived here" Said Mossaan to say what Marie Ndebb wanted to say. That did it to Jokel. She tried to run away, but the girls held her back forcing her to stay and listen to them by force.

"Aaaah! Someone is so eager to speak about something dear to their heart. It must be something vital (laughs Marie Ndebb). But Mossaan, how interestingly I took a U-Turn. You cannot help but love them. No way, you cannot dislike them." I like people that show humility even when they do know a lot or have everything in the world that should make them proud. Marianne is the business. Oh, wow!" Marie Ndebb waited to see the other girls' reactions. But Jokel Mindis who is always ready to tease with her endless banter, threw in her questions, eager to hear answers/responses flowing in from every angle.

"Why? Marie Ndebb, you cannot tell us what Mossaan has not said yet about Marianne. You can relax" Mossaan knew what to do and did not hesitate to let them hear what she has had in her heart all along. Her admiration for Marianne Semou Djimmit is beyond control. It is just lust. She will soon forget about Marianne if another woman or girl comes to the village for a visit. Marie Ndebb had the chance to be present when Marianne was talking about some interesting issues that happened where she resides in the New York and the work she does.

"Marianne Semou Djimmit was talking about issues on women. She is what we should emulate as young women. I have never heard of anyone in this village approach issues like she did. I have never heard of women talk about these issues in my life." Continued Marie Ndebb.

While the girls were debating or having friendly chats, somewhere, Marianne Semou Djimmit had the urge to speak broadly to the girls in the village. She noticed that there were many young women in the community and they have had plenty of time in their hands. Knowing that she was going to stay for an extended period, at least more than three months, she took the opportunity to coach them.

Suddenly, Marianne had the knack of coaching women of the village. In that brief period, she showed a bit of what she has learned or had been exposed to living in the west, far away from the village.

"She is going to be coaching us about how to value ourselves in society regardless of gender." Marie Ndebb made the girls feel like getting closer to Marianne especially Mossaan. "Marianne went through some changes, and I do want to know all about it. I can't get enough listening to her. I am sure she did not look like how she is now before travelling abroad."

With a deep breath, she looked up and the other girls especially Jokel Mindis looked dazed. She laughed in a very sarcastic way. Her relationship with Mossaan though very friendly sometimes makes her feel uncomfortable.

"Huh…Of course, anyone would look and behave otherwise if they lived abroad for this long. How many years again? She asked.

"I don't remember but they are here, and Marianne Semou Djimmit looks exceedingly gorgeous. Trust me; she is knowledgeable and smart too. Said Mossaan, trying to remember when the last time was she heard of Marianne Semou's name mentioned in the village.

[Marie Ndebb laughed and joined in the conversation again knowing what to get out of it when Jokel is present. She already knew what was on Mossaan's mind from the way she had been talking about Marianne's arrival. With an aspiring look and smile and tone]

Many of the village inhabitants felt proud of their new

visitors. Even the young children around have felt the difference in the mood. As usual, when someone comes to visit, they take turns in inviting the guests for dinner or lunch to hear their stories. Of course, exciting stories shared and what was inspiring was that the well-wishers are filing into the compound to greet their daughter and her family. It is a typical thing to do. It still happens even in the cities. It is normal to go around to randomly go to someone's home without invitation especially when guests are visiting from foreign lands or neighbouring countries, towns or villages. It is a sign of respect to go and meet and greet visitors without an invitation. That is the beauty of our way of life.

Marianne Semou Djimmit and her husband Latir were overwhelmed with visitors, but they enjoyed the busy compound as they jokingly tell each other. "Let us enjoy the attention while it lasts because we do not have this in the US." We do not usually get visitors at home" They laughed; Marianne and Latir. "This is epic," said Latir.

Marie Ndebb's many attempts to stir things up never ceased. "Haven't you noticed that Mossaan's dream is nothing but to go to the city, be like Marianne Semou. She even called you Marianne Semou, haven't you noticed?" Said Marie Ndebb. But Mossaan took no notice of what Marie Ndebb was saying. She knew that the girls were always onto her in an amicable way although quite annoying at times. Mann addressed her words to Jokel Mindis, but indirectly teasing the only one fan of Marianne. At some point, Mossaan interrupted Marie Ndebb so that she could move on to her next topic and put a closure to the current one.

"Marie Ndebb, how do you know that going to the city is my only dream? She continued. 'I happen to have had a dream, wanted good things to happen to me and everyone around me. Just face it. There is nothing wrong about that. Is there?" Mossaan does not get angry, but she knows how to respond to her critics especially when they are sarcastic.

"There is nothing wrong about that" retorted Marie Ndebb with a hint of sarcasm in her voice and demeanour. Knowing how Mossaan is, she never allowed her friends' words to overshadow her, and her high personality always kicked in. Her viewpoint is not easy to outshine. She worried little though her appearance did not show that.

Remembering how not a while ago, Marie Ndebb came in rushing and talking excitingly about Marianne, Mossaan asked if that was the same Marie Ndebb talking. She was baffled at the same time worried about her double personality. She laughed at her sudden switch. "It is not easy."

"What is not easy" responded Marie Ndebb knowing what Mossaan was on about but pretended that she was not addressing her. She was right. It is not easy to show the kind of admiration she had for Marianne before her friends. She was a secret admirer of Marianne. At least, there were to down, and one was left acting up. Jokel Mindis did not show too much enthusiasm. The reason is known to Mossaan because she teased her all the time and always acted with sarcasm every time the name of Marianne was pronounced.

Marie Ndebb does not have the strength to be trapped in a dream that would send her crazy as she always said before Marianne's visit. It was not the first time they talked about their goals for a better life. The tour of the family intensified it, but it was a dream that was there. Going to the city was their only option because not much happens in a village like Saassaara.

Being negative does not solve any problems. It is what Mossaan had learned from inception. The reason why she could do all she did and kept her hope alive was due to her beautiful mind. That was her secret. Many of them worried that she is holding things in. But she could manage her feelings. Nothing lasts forever she always said to herself. Of course, she was right for thinking like that. She was aware of the many dreams the other girls had. All they could do was not to listen to her, and she could keep her to herself. But, like any other young person, sharing their experience always helps them move forward. There were things they could not discuss with elders. Their bond allowed them to support one another.

Marie Ndebb was silently gauging what next to say to finish or seal the conversation about their inspirational lady in town/village. "Mossaan, you certainly do make us feel like we are dream free and that is not the case. We all have got dreams and would love to make it somehow." Marie Ndebb was not happy at all. The visit of Marianne did make these young women more cognizant of life. How to get it better was the common challenge they shared. "Marie Ndebb, you have to be careful what you say. I am for achieving better things in life. That does not mean I see less of myself and my native environment. I am confused, and that is wrong". "Hopefully someday you will understand why we need to move on swiftly. Our families here can only give us what we ask for within the village. We are already in our twenties and being fed, clothed and given incentives coming from people from here working in the cities is shameful. I find it difficult taking gifts when I can be the one giving. That is all I am trying to rectify about my life." "Our younger sisters here need role models." Besides I want to do my best to achieve something in life'. I hope you get what I am getting at" The lengthy discourse of Mossaan was an eye opener to Marie Ndebb. While the two talked, Jokel Mindis made herself unavailable. She did not want to take part in their little pep talk.

"I understand you Mossaan." Said Marie Ndebb. "I am glad that you do. Besides, you know what I mean, and I want to remind you that I am an African girl and I believe in what I found here centuries ago. But that does not deter me from showing what inspires me and from dreaming. I will keep dreaming until I get my wish." Mossaan cannot be kept in the dark and away from what she thinks is best for her. From her response, one could hear her eagerness.

With gentleness for the first time towards Mossaan, Jokel Mindis listened and asked. She felt that Mossaan was getting a bit upset due to the severe tone of hers responding to Marie Ndebb whom she gets on better with compared to her. Marie Ndebb rarely teased Mossaan which is quite surprising to Jokel Mindis. She speaks compassionately to Mossaan. "Why do you say that Mossaan? We do know that you are a dreamer. Aren't we all? It is because yours is obvious, but we do empathise with you. So, do not get mad."

As always, Mossaan understood where the girls are. The teasing is normal but should have a boundary. So much familiarity can cause havoc in a relationship. But that is what happens with friends especially girls of this age.

 "From what I know of, every woman, wherever they are today fights for liberation. To those who understand the cause very well, it t is not about showing how strength. It is about removing the predicaments. It is about having access and the right to do what your heart desires decently. I must emphasise, a decent way. We are raised to make our parents proud. We cannot derail." Jokel made a clear point. In her words, she even mentioned the possibilities of running away that many young villagers did previously. That is not their style. That running away has had a repercussion on anyone that did it in the past. It is a no-go area. The girls never thought of that. Though many would love to live in the city, accommodation is not what it seemed. The living space it is what an innocent person living in the village would think.

"We are where we are at this particular moment because it is where we should be. What tomorrow holds, we do not know. Let us take it one daytime. It is how I interpret it in my humble way. It is not a terrible thing to be inspired" Jokel Mindis affirmed and continued talking "I am not talking about Marianne Semou Djimmit and don't ever think that I mean she is better than me. I am also inspired by her and what she has achieved. That's all. I do understand your point Mossaan.

Mossaan is very eager now to share about the kind of life she thinks is worth emulating and the need to be supportive of the elders in the village. These elders speak highly of their girls; Mossaan, Marie Ndebb and Jokel Mindis. They run the show with their savviness and caring nature especially Mossaan. These young women have had the best upbringing. People might think that living in the cities means more privileges, but that is not the case. These girls have had the best of both worlds. It is just that with their age, they need more exploration for everyone believes that the city is the deal. They always want to show to their elders that they owe to them to do what will keep them in their proper books and to show that they are ambitious too. Going away to work in cities will give them what they need to make them happy as many youngsters do. They want to go away to work and bring home their earnings to look after their parents and even their young siblings.

Mossaan, Marie Ndebb, and Jokel would do all their best to make everyone around them happy. They feel that they owe it to them by proving that they can hold the fort. They are lucky not to have been forced into marriage, early marriages

It is not just women who are vying for emancipation today. Every parent would want their child to become somebody in their rights. Gone are the days when in that village, girls are given away so young. If anything, these elders should be given a tap in the back for believing in their daughters' destiny and not use them as objects that can sell anyhow. They have given them the right to choose.

Looking at them and knowing their age, they had gone way past the usual age when their mothers got married. Women got married at sixteen. Things have changed now even in the remotest areas; most sensible parents do not force their daughters into marriage.

The girls agreed that the dream they have all along was about having a good education at least to a level that can help them earn a good living, good salaries. 'It is all about training ourselves to become influential. That is a dream of every living person. In their humble and small village life, where they were born, these girls took pride living in their lovely space, big and breezy, noiseless. It is where they will always feel proud to come back to no matter what. Everything they get in life and the future will be brought back to their native home to develop it further.

"Correct me if I am wrong girls. I do not have to go on and on about how I will be doing things. I hope you know what I mean. Excuse me, but sometimes I should make my voice heard. I have been dying to share my thoughts" Laughed Mossaan.

Jokel Mindis and Marie Ndebb were surprised at length Mossaan always talked. Apparently, a very articulate and meticulous young woman. She speaks her mind when she has got a lot to say. Having these two strong personalities as friends is not always easy for her. What makes it beautiful is the genuine bond they've forged over the years. Who would notice otherwise? These three grew up together.

"We are good friends and listening to each other is very important. Mossaan, I do not tease you because I want you to be upset. I know you understand me very well. [Jokel Mindis laughed] She continued. "Believe me Mossaan; I sometimes wonder why we are trapped" Whenever you speak about the things that can happen for us in the city, I go to bed thinking how I am going to stop this girl talk about these possibilities that have no chance of becoming possible when I am around." I want to stop thinking of the impossibility though I am optimistic, I cannot see myself escaping the life we have here." Like many others in the nearby villages before Saassaara. Maybe someday a miracle can happen.

"Ah! I always knew you were pretending. That is interesting Jokel Mindis" Mossaan is not the usual type to be sarcastic but being with these almost so unbearably naughty friends, she gets in the mood of teasing too from time to time. It makes their friendship exciting.

"It shouldn't be that way. I know you Jokel Mindis. You have always been keen on having plans in place. People like you and even Marie Ndebb are my friends because we think alike. We are different in personalities, but that is what makes us get on well, Said Mossaan. But Jokel made a good point. She replied and said "Well! We do have our diverse ways of thinking. I don't have to be interested in everything that catches your attention. It would be copying or being your archetype. Something you make, fix and change as you wish. Wouldn't it?

Everything centred around Mossaan unknowingly. In all the conversations, Mossaan had to be in because the dream is known to be hers from inception. The personality clashes and everything about her inspirations etc. "Sometimes, you need to try and back off though. Listen to what I must share with your usual sarcasm. That is where things go wrong, and I get crabby which I do not enjoy Jokel" Mossaan laughed, but Jokel Mindis just kept quiet for a moment. "You do get carried away though Mossaan, and I am only trying to tell you that we all have our values and self-respect that we must embrace. Our situation will change one fine day. I believe in destiny. Thinking about where we are at scares me. We seem to be stagnant here, following a single routine day in day out. It is scary."

Marie Ndebb did not say much, but from what Mossaan saw, she didn't think that she was with them. She was in deep thoughts. Although she seemed very confused about Mossaan, who kept going on about her role model, Marianne Semou.

Dreams

Emancipation, empowerment are unfamiliar words but listening to what the other girls have been ranting about awoke her secret dream she did not dare to share because of her lack of trust in securing the support needed from any one of the elders in the village. She did not dare to dream. She just followed on. Well, at least for now.

She blames it on the lack of sharing their feelings about issues that affect them. Each one of them has an inner voice that tells her the impossibilities in their dreams and not sharing consequently. Mossaan, still so quiet, is not bothered about sharing. She knows that girls would love to get on with Marianne even though they aren't saying anything about her. She knows them very well. She knows they have got dreams too. Having Marianne Semou Djimmit in the village on holiday is an opportunity for them to be mingling with someone they can learn from about life.

Now and then, they remind each other of the many opportunities they could have possibly had beyond their imagination. They gauge their level of understanding of the world daily. They also watch the way others working in the cities and everything they do in the village when they come visit monthly. That is how it works. Those that work in the towns owe it to their families to attend them every month. They bring monthly groceries to the village and a bit of fish money that can help to buy necessary things when needed. If you want to find humble persons, visiting as one of the sons and daughters mentioned to friends who were with them referring to the hospitality they are good at providing. You don't have to feel like a queen not because you have more than they do. It is because that's the way people live in tight, neat communities. They share everything they have and care about one another. It is seen clearly in their offspring. They are always together, supporting one another and looking out for each other.

Everyone shares the goods and leave again from the beginning of the new month. Socialising is core to our families in Africa. It does not matter where one is; your extended families matter a lot. It is traditionally a requirement and your family especially parents, take pride in having a son or daughter who takes care of not only their immediate families but almost everyone in their community when they can.

While the girls are dreaming and talking about what inspires them, other elders are taking care of the younger girls and boys who haven't reached that stage yet. The neighbours have their young boys in the 'Mbaar' (where the circumcised young kids stay with their mentors or coach for the period of four to six weeks). It is summertime, the young boys got circumcised, and many of the village sons and daughters in the city are back to spend time with families. Some of them brought their children to join the group of boys already circumcised. Others without children follow their regular routines of visiting monthly. Generally, by the time the child is fifteen or sixteen years of age, he is taught values and etiquettes to last a lifetime. A child should greet elders, help parents with household chores, avoid foul language, and list to the wisdom of elders. They are also trained to understand societal norms.

In their early years, boys and girls play together. The gender roles become sharply defined as they grow older to become young men. Girls remain more with their mothers to learn household chores. In almost all ethnic groups, boys are supposed to undergo the practice of circumcision as part of the process of reaching maturity. It is different for women for the FGM practice has now been abolished due to the many health hazards that surrounds it. In fact, it is all tribes that do it on their daughters. There is a lot of controversy around it. The practice of female genital mutilation is now a criminal offence.

Muslim children attend Koranic schools until they are six or seven at which time they start a formal education which is essential to their upbringing. The Koranic learning is compulsory for every child to learn the necessary things about Islam. With Catholics and Christians, learning the Bible is vital and receiving communion when they reach adolescence. Teaching religion in the lives of young persons is imperative. They grow up to understand themselves, know the Almighty and acquaint themselves with life's principles.

In every community, we find people who are always ready to serve. Mossaan, Jokel Mindis, Marie Ndebb make it their point of duty to lend a hand to the men of the 'Mbaari Njulli' where the circumcised boys are secretly kept, far behind the village where their sanctuary is for the whole period with their mentors. It is their moment of initiation. Women are usually not allowed to go in the sacred place. Credit to the 'Bortal Mbaar' who is the head of the Mbaari Njulli during the entire process. Usually, they take their food halfway, and one or two or three of the 'Selbehs' coach will meet them halfway to collect the treats and food for the little boys. It is a moment of festivities because the village is usually lit up, rays of light everywhere, drumming and the sounds of 'Kassack' songs and meanings trained to them. It is a perfect initiation for them.

The discussion on emancipation takes over the girls' chores wherever they are. In a way, it keeps their minds busy. The boys in the village tease them about their monotonous banter. No matter how intense their chores may seem, often, they pause and continue with their talks on women on liberation, freedom, equality and equity. Some great leaders do encourage young women in Africa, informing them of their sacred positions in society and that they should never try to be equal as men because what they are can never be matched to what men represent in society. It takes us back to what the scholar said about the position of women in society. The story of Barakah got shared, and that alone was inspiring to the girls to understand the status of women in society. Mostly, for us to laugh about that. The girls think that is a way of calming them down, but it should not stop them from fighting for what is in their best interest. Jokel Mindis is the hyperactive one. She gets overexcited. Once they engage on a topic that interests her, she goes on nonstop. Even when the others have enough, she wants to carry on. Who wouldn't want to engage themselves in such topics that can only show you the way? Such issues are educational, an eye opener to every young woman. They know very well that Mossaan has her heart attached to emancipation and advancement in women.

'We indeed are not time wasters at all girls. Have you noticed how we get ourselves busy throughout? With us, there isn't any dull moment. Thank God, we are here for everyone especially you Mossaan. I sometimes get vexed when I need to rest, and you come up with something like this. "Aunty x, y, z wants us to help with this or that."

'Who are you referring to Jokel Mindis? Laughs Mossaan.

In response to what Jokel Mindis just said. 'You know very well that I am talking about you Mossaan. Who else does that? However, I think it is alright I guess. I complain, but I see the reward in it. It cost us anything to be there for those who took care of us. These people did from the time we were toddlers'.

Jokel's response sounded harsh, but Mossaan prefers to pay less attention to the tone which she has used responding to her.

[The village and many community settings in Africa is the envy of every community. There is no such thing as paying a nanny to look after your child. Neighbours, parents help you raise your child.]

'I am so proud of all of you girls. We could've been different, but we do for the sake of our Creator. We must not stop, and we must not be tired of doing good. That is how our mothers were, and they raised us to be the same. We must follow their footsteps. Besides, we can easily regard us as bad as rotten potatoes should we disobey our elders. We are always expected to do what they want. They are saying good things because we are doing good. If we were not doing what gives them satisfaction to say wonderful things about us, they would never have found the need to say good things about us. Trust me, and they do not beat around the bushes' Said Mossaan.

'I grew up in this village, and I know every bit of our tradition. We have no choice but to do good and wish for the better' agreed Jokel Mindis.

'All I can say is that it is not difficult to emulate good things done by the ones before us. We are the luckiest young women in the village. I am not saying that we the best, but we do our best, and we are known for that. Thanks for the encouragement Mossaan's Marie Ndebb stated.

Marianne Semou Djimmit is going to be impressed with us. That, I am sure of that. She happens to be luckier than us, but we should be happy for her. Besides, she is older than us as well. We must remember that. Maybe when we reach her age, we will be in her shoes too. Laughs Jokel Mindis.

'Jokel Mindis, she was married when she was our age. Remember that.' Mossaan reiterated on it because they had a hushed discussion about that. Marianne Semou Djimmit is now thirty-three years old. She left to join her husband Latir when she was almost twenty according to her calculation and had spent ten good years in the USA before her visit. It had been a decade.

'So, you are saying that we are 'lamba' not courting or because no one has shown interest in us to marry?' That's sad Mossaan. Don't you think that it is time for us to open a shop and send out application forms for good guys to apply? I think that we should do that. Should we open a shop and write down? These Trios want to get married.

Any candidates!!!! They laugh about her antics. Oh, there is never a dull moment with Jokel, I reiterate. 'You are right Jokel Mindis. Said Mossaan, we should think about that. We are way overdue for marriage'. Marie Ndebb approves. These young women reflect a lot on their usual ways whenever they have a moment of peace and tranquillity. They also ponder on their current lifestyle bequeathed to them. But, they remain grateful and accepting their faith makes life easier.

Daily routines in the village are what motivates Mossaan, Marie and Jokel and nothing else. They all use the same line of expression to show gratitude to the Lord of Mankind that patience is a virtue and one day, they will enjoy receiving what they have been praying for every time they put their hearts at something. It is what they do daily in the village for their families that motivates them. They are lucky to have been surrounded by elders who understand life in their very humble way. It is proof that only knowledge that gives you everything and puts you up there on the map of virtuous deeds. There is nothing they would not praise. Even things that should not wait for praises. However, recognition is something people do until their situations change. The seniors of the community; men and women make it their point of duty to train their sons and daughters on things such as etiquette and how to live as a community. They remind them of their respective responsibilities.

While walking home from 'Mbaari Njulli' for the deliveries

of goods/groceries, Jokel Mindis released a big sigh. She has had a fruitful day. Most of the things they did were productive as she mentioned.

'We have never had a futile moment. Our people know that we are the three Musketeers always ready to serve. But I do not complain compared to tayal mbaiy /lazyJokel Mindis.' 'Marie Ndebb stop it right now! Says Jokel Mindis. She knew that Marie Ndebb was talking about her. It is not that Jokel Mindis is lazy as that is what Tayal Mbaay means in Wolof. She just wanted to dilute the conversation. It is a bit of laugh that keeps them going. Mossaan was not paying too much attention to what they were saying. Suddenly, she saw a car coming through from the main footpath, the 'chantier' which is the road to the village, full of sand and stones.

'That must be Marianne Semou Djimmit and Latir.'

'Maybe, let us wait and see who is in the car, Says Jokel Mindis 'Here we go again.' Smiles Marie Ndebb.

'Oh, of course, it is Marianne. They must be tired. I think that they have been out all day. It is late in the afternoon. Let us go home and freshen up. Maybe later we can go and visit them.

While walking home, Mossaan threw in a question about education, marriage and domestic work in the city.

'Would you like to go to college or get married? Asked

Mossaan.

'Who are you asking the two of us or all of us including you' responded Jokel Mindis with another question.

'Jokel Mindis, I am asking a question. Why would you respond to another question? You could have simply answer and asked me what I would want in life.' Mossaan in a tetchy voice is not always on the same page with Jokel Mindis. She does it deliberately for not answering. She wants to hear what Mossaan would say first.

'OK, if you insist Mossaan. Personally, I am not fussy about anything. I am with anything my parents decide. I know that they must have wanted something good for me, reasons why they have not given me away to any of my cousins'

'I bet they know that we are not for sale' as Marie Ndebb was so eager to throw in her pinch of salt, making Jokel Mindis feel so proud of her parents.'

'I am so happy that they do not see us as objects. I have never been told to introduce a boyfriend to any of them' says Mossaan.

'They will not joke about that. Mossaan, don't you that if they ask you to introduce you to a boyfriend, it means they are approving you seeing someone. Hell no. These people do not joke with that. They will rather watch you rot than ask. All they are waiting for now is for someone to come and ask for your hand in marriage.' Marie Ndebb and Jokel Mindis show how they trust their village elders in sharing few stories about one of Marie Ndebb's cousins in the city. She was living there, working in one of the main government offices. She did not get married until she turned 35. Well overdue as they fondly tease each other. Marie Ndebb teases Mossaan for being twenty-two without a husband. 'Sans Mari' is the term used at times when addressing Mossaan. They laugh about that every time she mentions the word. Well overdue. It is the standard age now which is four to five years added to the usual period most of their mothers got married.

It is not by force now to marry at an early age. Our elders have now become mentally liberated. Don't think that because they are in the village, they have never lived in the cities. They are pensioners, and some are homebound due to illness. But, their brains function more than anything you can imagine. They do us proud.

'Anyway, what is the plan tonight girls. We need to do something. I do have an idea. We can go to visit Marianne together. What do you think?' Asked Mossaan as she is about to enter her compound.

Hopes

Every girl needs someone to emulate, a role model, a coach and someone onto whom to confide. These three, even though they have never had significant arguments, that does not deter them from finding a friend they can talk to about anything. The familiarity between them is a predicament. Therefore, having Marianne to be their coach is advisable. The way Mossaan discusses Marianne has finally inspired the others. Didn't she just win in the end? Of course, she believed in Marianne, and that has helped her win the hearts of her friends. They want to hear it from about all the things she can explain to them about life. There were many people in the yard. It is the usual evening prayers at home. Mossaan walked in to greet the elders already seated while the others were about to head home.

Mossaan, it would be pleasant for us to have the chance to go to the city to study. But I do not think that I am ready for all the challenges. Says Jokel Mindis out of the blue.

'That is a topic for another day Jokel Mindis or later in the evening. We can discuss all the possibilities. Why is the change of heart now? Says Mossaan in response to what Jokel Mindis had said.

'I am just thinking Mossaan. I know that at some point it is going to be necessary for us to move away from all these things that we do. Our younger sisters are going to be the ones in need of inspiration, and they will seek no further than from us. They will look up to us and think of us for inspiration as you can imagine already. They do listen to us and watch our every move. Said Jokel Mindis.

'You are so right about that Jokel Mindis' Marie Ndebb says in a very reaffirming tone. She is a good listener and what

Jokel Mindis noted has touched her too.

The girls agreed to meet at Mossaan's later in the evening for the usual short Ngonal. When it is weekdays, the Ngonal are not too long. But the weekends like Saturdays are mostly until day breaks.

Usually, leaving home can only happen when you get married, or you head to the city for further education if allowed. To go to the city to study, especially if you are of a female gender, your parents, call your uncles, aunts, and elders of the village for their blessings. That is a tradition that is fading anyway, but most people do now to ask for them to pray for you. That does not stop some of them from having your family as

'It would also be agreeable for us to have the opportunity to go to the city to study too if that is what we want or get married and head of the town but what we have in the village is part of us, and no one can deny that. We must accept life the way it is right now, and we must take it as it is. It would be best for any one of us.

'we are all different in characters Jokel Mindis' I guess it is just the beginning for us to see that we can do better in life. I am glad that we are engaged in these kinds of topics. What a pleasant afternoon.'

'This is what good friends do Mossaan. You know that we owe it to each other. It is better for us to have our little fights and makeup before the sun goes down. It is never a dreadful thing. We always mean well. We owe it to our parents. They've taught us the best ways.' As for me Jokel Mindis Diouf, I will never take you for granted. I just enjoy pulling your leg. Besides, it helps you to come out of your shell. I will always be by your side. No matter what.

'I never take you seriously Jokel Mindis. In fact, both of you although Marie Ndebb does not tease me that much. Sometimes, I laugh about how you just go on and on. You two are on a mission. You are an anti-Mossaan, aren't you? But I am not going to fall into your traps. You want to see me lose myself in your pettiness. You should grow up. Jokel Mindis, I do miss you a lot when you are away. You are just a crazy little lady. Look at you!'

[Jokel Mindis laughs]

'Huh, it is alright for friends to agree to disagree sometimes. Not always though. I am glad that our conversations make a lot of sense. We do not talk about futile issues. We talk about topics that concern us and that helps a lot.' I know that hearing my name does make you jump Mossaan's knowing how much of a nagger I am to you.

'Never Jokel Mindis. You think that I cannot do to you what you do to me? You must be in denial. Listen to yourself if you are the Boss Lady. I just love you that is why I can tolerate your nonsense. Who would not want to embrace Jokel Mindis? Ha? Said Mossaan. In an amicable manner.

She continued.

'See you later. Meet me here if you are not tired. If you would like us to still go to Marianne Semou's, I would be glad to organise it. I can send Salima to go to her house and ask if she is available tonight'.

When it comes to Marianne Semou's affair, Mossaan never relents on it. She confirmed sending someone to hers. Jokel Mindis and Marie Ndebb agreed and parted nicely.

While the two young women walked home together, Mossaan entered their house and tiptoed into the living room. She needed to finish up her late afternoon chores. She found her sister Salima and asked her to run to Marianne and ask if they can visit her tonight with the other girls. Salima also had a message to deliver to her. One of their uncles knew how much Mossaan loved the idea of meeting women she wants to emulate and make them her role models. Uncle Sammy Saine, says Salima, told me to meet him at Marianne Semou's later, Mossaan.

'What about the meeting? Asked Mossaan. 'I do not know Mossaan's He only asked me to tell you to meet him there.

Uncle Sammy officially wanted to introduce them. He has already told Marianne how much Mossaan hard Mossaan works. Marianne already loves Mossaan due to the excellent things she has already heard about her. She cannot wait to hear about Mossaan's quest for a better life. Looking at the village setting, Marianne knows that some of these girls though need to be near their parents, but further education would do them a great deal of good. It can change their lives. However, she was into meddling in their affairs. She was very meticulous. She did not want to interfere in other people's lives. Jokel Mindis expressed her feelings to Marie Ndebb about the way she sometimes treats Mossaan. She felt terrible and told Marie Ndebb that she really would like to change the way she goes on attacking Mossaan every time she tries to say something productive. Marie Ndebb being the loyal and fair person she does not want Jokel Mindis to feel bad. She reassured her that Mossaan does not take her attacks seriously.

'Jokel Mindis, Mossaan is not the type that holds grudges. She is such a sweetheart. Don't lose your sleep over that and whatever you have ever said to her. She would've confronted you. You know her. She is that kind of person who quietly says her peace and gets on with things. She does not have time nor space to keep grudges against anyone.' They both laughed.

'Thank you, Marie Ndebb for this peaceful approach. Trust me; I do feel bad.'

'Just say sorry for her next time we see her. If that makes you feel better. I am sure she will call you crazy for thinking that you mean any harm.'

'She is her mother's daughter. My mom tells me how long

they've been friends for and never had a single disagreement.' I am Jokel Mindis. She will never forget about me wherever she is. Do you think she will ever want to take me to the city if she gets that opportunity she craves for?'

'Stop it Jokel Mindis; you are sarcastic. You are talking behaving like a toddler looking for someone to adopt you. I do not have the patience that Mossaan has for you. OK! Goodbye. I have now reached my destination. See you later.'

Laughed Marie Ndebb.

'See you later Marie Ndebb. You see, I will never change.' Said Jokel Mindis

'You are so right Jokel Mindis. You will never change. But it is all good. It would have been boring without you. We thank the Almighty for blessing us with such a character. You are so full of life.' See you sister.

Jokel Mindis murmured looking like she was talking to herself.

She was thinking about what good it will do to her to change the way she behaves around her peers. Not that she disliked what happens, but she believes that she makes them feel uncomfortable and upset all the time with her expensive jokes.

As natural as it seems, is to be jovial. It is also good to respect other people's opinions. I am lucky to have these young women as my friends. I never complain about them. How does it always have to be me teasing everyone? I will have to reduce the way I joke. Too much of everything is not good. I should keep quiet more often and listen. That is the only way I can learn. Mossaan possesses a good personality.

Marie Ndebb too thought she attentively listens to me too much; she gets carried away when Mossaan is in her element. Huh, they make me feel like the joker of town. I should change my attitude from now onwards. Otherwise, they will never take me seriously.

There was one thing Mossaan was trying to explain to me, and I never paid attention to it. She talked about predestination. Not sure but I think she meant, what we are to get out of life and that our Creator has already designed what each one of us will become…

I think it is time to get serious. I will ask her when we meet this evening if possible. That Mossaan never wastes her time on the useless thing. I trust her judgment too. She is a smart cookie. Let me end the daydreaming and get on with things.

All the time Jokel Mindis was talking to herself, her cousin brother Essa was listening to her. Ah! Jokel Mindis, that was classic. I would have been upset if you were talking to yourself about another man. They both laughed.

'Essa, you were listening to me all this time?' Asked Jokel Mindis.

'Yes, indeed Jokel Mindis' What is the matter? Are you having any issues with Mossaan and Marie Ndebb?

'No, not at all. I just feel guilty about how much I tease Mossaan. That's all.

'Jokel Mindis, you can do something about it. You know that she would have told you where to get off if she was upset. Right?

'Yes, I know.'

'To avoid talking about it with her, just do yourself a favour. Never mention it and see what she will say when she notices that you have changed your attitude towards her.' That could help says Essaa.

Essa's wife Maremma walked in looking so surprised and ask making a gesture that seems like she was asking what happened. But she knew that Essa always talks to Jokel Mindis about life. He adores his young cousin sister. She greeted them and went straight into her bedroom. Essa gave Jokel Mindis some brotherly advice which he hopes she will add to her wisdom.

Maremma, his wife, asked what the conversation about was, he explained how Jokel Mindis was talking to herself about the way she treats Mossaan. Maremma shook her head.

'That is Jokel Mindis for you. I hope you have told her not to take it to heart. Mossaan understands her more than anyone in the village' Says Maremma.

'Anyway, how was your day?

Hope everything you went to sort out in in the village went well.

'Everything went well.' My husband. Said Maremma.

She called Jokel Mindis to tell her who she met. Maremma met Marianne Semou Djimmit and wanted Jokel Mindis to go over to her to greet her as well and introduce herself officially. They all want their younger women to meet Marianne. It must be a good sign for all of them. Instead of them meeting Mossaan at hers later, they will all be at Marianne's in the evening.

Marianne Semou Djimmit is the talk of the village. She did not come empty-handed. She came to visit with a vision and aims to encourage younger women around to stick to their dreams.

Mossaan, Marie Ndebb, Jokel Mindis happened to be the ones people refer to when talking about advocating for causes. Maremma taught of Jokel Mindis, Mossaan's uncle gave Halima a message to pass onto her. It is not by accident. Marie Ndebb was delivering a letter to her uncle, Djogoye fa Maag. On her way home, she went to meet the girl Jokel Mindis sent to her. It is a date for them to meet

Marianne for an evening chat. The Ngonal at Mossaan is now at Marianne's.

It is Marianne's welcoming party. The whole village is getting ready for it. The words are already out. Yes, it is normal to have family members organise parties for their sons and daughters when they come visit from abroad and even from the cities nearby. The family has not had time to welcome her officially introduce her to the inhabitants especially the new ones. Usually, the kids follow their car whenever they see them. Many of their age mates; Marianne Semou Djimmit and Latir, have heard of their visit and made the trip to the village. So, a great weekend is on the card. It is a feast.

It is the first day of the preparations so meeting everyone and asking for their help is vital. Marianne is not aware of it. All she was being told for now that she needed to know all the girls and who is who in the village. Many she knew, but most of them are new. Her generations of girls are either in other cities or abroad with their partners and studying too in Dakar, in Kaolack and few in The Gambia working and teaching.

These sorts of events do happen everywhere. Somewhere, someone will not be able to attend because they of a wedding they are to participate. Whatever the situation, a gathering is being put together to welcome Marianne, Youssu, and Latir officially. They have travelled with the American friends they left in Dakar and were planning to renovate some of their rooms in the village to invite them over. Of course, when they know of this event, they will invite them over. But they are not yet in the know.

Tama, the talking drum & Djembe make up the sweet sounds of Afro Manding, and mbalax vibes that Africa prides herself with for it are used to inform, entertain and has inspired western music of all times, old and contemporary music.

There was a wedding in the nearby village not too far away from Mossaan's village. The sound of the drums is something you cannot ignore because it was also loud. Some of the small children danced to the loud noise even though it was not inside the village, but one could hear it. Children danced happily to the sound of the Sabarr on the sandy road. The 'Sabarr, Gamba and Tama' are the musical instruments used in African weddings and history has taught us that this instrument 'Tabala' was used to inform nearby villages when something happens. It is a medium used according to the account of events.

The small talking drum aka Tama is the noisiest of all of them. The Gamba is in the form of a big calabash that exudes beautiful sound one can undoubtedly think that it is a mixture of water in a vase or canary shaken around. The Gamba players are usually women, wearing huge rings on their four fingers. It gives a lovely but loud sound when the women tap on the calabash. It is a unique effect that cannot be made up with any contemporary instrument.

It does not matter how poor people are; their wealth shielded for days such as weddings 'Takka, and Nguenteh' Christenings. It is important for they represent union and happiness, which is 'Mbekteh' spending their all is inevitable. People mix and mingle and chat, eat, dance the evening away. Many guests from that wedding will sure pass by for Marianne Semou's welcoming party.

The girls get on well now. As they say, three is a crowd. It is difficult to be in a friendship that comprises of many and usually the number three is the spoiler. That is what people say. For those that live on an understanding of association, it is good to heed to that.

Reflecting what they used to talk about and how they addressed Mossaan whenever she spoke about Marianne, both Marie Ndebb and Jokel Mindis try to take their words back. It is guilt. But, whatever the misunderstanding that was, they have moved on. What is left is the words said, the conversation had, emotions caused, and reconciliation made. The rest is history.

Our lives seem to be like the story of the Musketeers. I remember reading their stories throughout my childhood, different from ours. I am sure the girls have read the story of Tintin as well. We have also watched clementine, Maani le Libero and many other stories. Jokel Mindis is now a reflector, Marie Ndebb, Mossaan, Jeggaan Wassyla, Marianne Semou have made an impact on this story and what I have realised is that they are all in for change coated with a lot of shocking moments. But, we can all agree that at the end of the day, these are things that make up stories of whatever we go through in life. There are so many things we cannot comprehend at once more reason why we need to do follow ups always. This applies to every situation. It takes a brave heart to dream. Many people do give up so quickly. But, that is not the best answer to anything.

FINAL QUOTES

"Be a Bird perched on a frail branch that she feels bending beneath her, still she sings away all the same, knowing she has wings"

May the Eclipse Never Becomes Endless Nights.

SPECIAL TRIBUTES

In remembrance of two influential Gambian people in the lives of a growing nation. Sadly, their journeys were cut short to answer to the call of Allah The Almighty. We hold on to the helm of His Garment to ask Him for his mercy on them and grant them each a place in His most beautiful gardens of Heaven.

Doyen George Christenson

Proprietor of Radio One FM Media Outlet

Gambian Doyen of Broadcasting

Uncle of the nation, mentor, coach, educationist, Contributor

Consequently, they said that to make your mark in this world; you should be fierce, bold, daring, courageous and truthful. You must be a person who adapts quickly and willing to learn, to grow and to develop.

I have personally met a man called George Christensen in 1991 who despite the odds, gave me an opportunity to excel. He gave me a chance called JOB. Yes, a very cutting-edge job as a young woman growing in a society where men do the kind of situation I was offered to do mostly men did the job with few exceptions.

Radio Broadcaster/DJ/Presenter in training.

It is with sorrow that I am penning his name here to show my gratitude, for all I ever wanted was to send him or give him in person a signed copy and say a big thank you. I had plans to write...'Thank you George Christensen, our very own 'Alpha Ngoos' for the journey.' That is how I would have loved to pen it down on the first page with a huge smiley face personally sketched.

Since we were the kiddos and Boss was the Alpha Ngoos, we immediately became the Ngoos kids. Therefore, I would have written it this way to give him a giggle.

Mossaan Belle Djigguenn. Here is a copy specially for Alpha Ngoos, by' Neneh Ngoos of Radio One FM.

This is what I would have loved to see happen. Sadly, George left us on June 3rd, 2016. Since I am left with this void, giving you tribute in this book, my premier, is the only choice I have left. It was as if something stopped me from printing the book or finalizing it for publishing. I pray that your legacy stays with us forever and that your memory remains with us always. Nothing about you shall ever fade because you were who you were, and your imprints are enormous. You were a Legendary Man, and we will miss you dearly. The broadcasting world has lost a monument. You were the one and only one Boss.

This is a tribute to you, and I want you to smile down on us. We are impacted by your sudden demise but knowing you George, the action man in you is turning into the blood that runs through our veins. You were always on the move, top form and top of your game. You have come into this world to do some work and left. Many might think that your life was too short. But to those who knew you, you did more than what a hundred-year-old person could have done. You will be continuing your work, and through us, it is going to be completed at least by doing our bits and passing it onto others to get a go at it.

You have left the proof here for all to see. Not just in and with your family members but the nation and the whole of West Africa. You were an exemplary man.

I am not sad anymore. I am smiling because I can do this for you. I can pen your name down in a book that has got my name in it as the writer, and I am sure that you would have found this thrilling and laughed with me. Yes, I love my clan as you can see, I did not need to add other names outside the Serere clan. The name of my heroes; my great grandmothers' the Guelewaar of Sine and the beautiful lineage I always talked to you about are mentioned in all the books to follow this sequel. This is I know you have always said to me after meeting Njaga Mbaye at Radio whom we chatted with about my late father. I know exactly what you would have said if you were here to read this book. Exactly, what you would have said, I told you kid. You see how much I knew you. Boss! Thank you!

Life is what you make it. You have made us understand that it is not the amount of money you have or material you can show to the world, but the person you are and the characters that complete you as a human being. The myriad of lessons and blessings can only be learned and experienced by observing the good people around and taking away the best from that and whatever you learned through interacting with them. We equally learn from people of evil characters so that we can avoid being what we do not like in them.

We are told to stop feeling sad and asked to add you to our prayers. That is indeed what we have already started doing. Your Torch will never be put out. You are the star we see at night, the brightest in the sky that doesn't move places because you were the same proud man we all knew. You beamed with joy every time you spoke to us. I am going to be that person who will not blow your horn silently. I am proud to have been a mentee to you. All I should say now is this.

The Broadcasting world is going to miss you deeply.
THANK YOU, GEORGE CHRISTENSON!

Adieu Doyen!

Rest in Eternal Peace.

Rest In Perfect Peace Doyen

Dr. Harr Freeya Njai
The Doctor of Humanity.
Mother, Scientist, Writer
Daughter of Senegambia, the darling of the nation

It gives me immense pleasure to give a special mention to this special lady who has always been an inspiration to me. I will be addressing you in this book using the present tense as you are still alive, living my heart and I do indeed see you in everything I do Harr.

I would like to take this opportunity to say thank you for inspiring me. Giving tribute to you is nothing more than telling you that I am continuing the journey you loved so much. You encouraged others to be the best they can be. Did I just add some of the attributes to the main character in the book? Hmmmm! I think so, Harr. With a grin on my face, I smile knowing you would have loved to say…" Don't you dare choose another publisher? Majaga publishers are yours too." You used to scare me off from posting my write-ups on social media. I often said to myself, Harr is going to see this and will not stop to ask me to pen something down. Well dear sister, I was not ready then, but I am now, and I am prepared to do you proud. I know if you were here it wouldn't have been this late. The book is ready since April, but as the perfectionist that I am, I was not courageous enough to publish it. It is now or never, come what may. I would also like to whisper something to you…'I prayed for confidence, audacity first before sending it out. Hope it is alright.' You are no longer with us, but the thought of you always makes me smile. You were here for a purpose, and you have done all you could, your possible best and return to your Maker. We cry not because you are gone. It is the void that reminds us that you are not coming back. You did well with your life and the people around you. You shall never be forgotten Ms. Harr Freeya Njai – Rest in Perfect Peace.

You believed in many of your sisters and me. This is what supported the idea of me accumulating all the notes I have written about the first book of etiquettes which I have shelved already, but this script/film turned into books in sequels. I add a lot of Chossaan and Humour in it because I know a bit about your wits for traditional stuff. I wanted to tell you that I have listened to you. I was not ready, but now I am. So, with the etiquette book to follow, I am trying to do the finishing touches on this sequel that has taken too long and hopefully, you are already proud that I am pressing forward with what I am about to present to you my good sister Harr. You did say that you want to read it first. Yes, we are going to read it together. Every night will be for you to hear the echo of my voice, reading out loud to you so that you understand and even whisper to you about some of the funniest bits, asking if you to find it funny so that I can listen to your laughter we all miss right now.

Here is Mossaan Belle Djigguenn. Thank you for the many years of support and encouragement. Everyone misses you. You have written few books before your demise, and everyone lauded the idea and gave you props for a job well done. I learned from you that critics are like BENZIN. Your human' sciences worked well as a scientist, a mother of three and a career woman. You have never ceased to inspire us. I always laughed when you say that I am your inspiration. I know what you wished for the sisterhood. We are at it. R.I.P.P

Just one other thing to add...You know how I like making people laugh and I know that you will be smiling down on us as well. "Harr Freeya Njai I know that if I read the story louder at night and have my eyes closed, I will imagine/see you smiling right back at me with your white teeth as bright and twinkling like the star that you are. You the star in our eyes."

This is not just a tribute to you Harr. It is us showing gratitude for knowing you and all that you contributed to our community. I want to tell you, Harr, that it is just the beginning. The stories you liked reading, putting together are going to be rewritten and rewritten. Your humour is still alive with us. Your legacy is what we have got left of you, and we cannot go without remembering you every day we are faced with issues to tackle and events to celebrate for you my lady, you were always in the middle of everything that our community is about. Remembering is a task because you remind us of so many things. We emulate you and your ways.

Rest Well, my sister. You have run your race very well. Adieu to the darling of the nation.

You, my dear, we miss you too much. But we are continually smiling because your tracks remain with us, your aura felt around us, and we often revisit the days and time spent with you just feel your presence again. We know that you are okay where you are, and we are here trying to do just like you did. Thank you, Ma'am. We miss you too much beautiful soul. Thank you for all you did in your short life. Your untimely death gave a shock we shall never forget.

"*Yesterday is but today's memory. Tomorrow is today's dream*" Khalil Gibran

THANK YOU, HARR!

Rest In Perfect Peace

SPECIAL THANKS

WAMBUI WAMWERE FOR PROVIDING ME WITH THE MOST SIGNIFICANT PHOTO OF YOU AND YOUR BEAUTIFUL DAUGHTER FOR THE FIRST BOOK.

NOTES

Smile in The Mirror To Change Your Life.

"Life Is a Voyage"

Find the Beautiful Things Hidden Underneath The Thorns

"To Love Another Person is to See The Face of God"

I want to take this opportunity to do a chronicle about these two famous words that we take for granted. We often speak about them, and we know so little about how we can have them as virtues. I used to think that loyalty is all that I needed to show my gratitude to everyone who has contributed to my journey. The experience had growing up is what inspires me to write this story which is the *beginning of the sequel. Most of it is my childhood and a great portion nicely inserted in it to use as a contrast to the life of the protagonist. It is a world we live in where we the people are only loyal to convenience.*

What I have learned is that, people are loyal to opportunity, to your potential and nothing else. If you see loyalty for what it is, then you can never be misguided. Loyalty is transitory, and that is not how we should go on about our daily lives.

I choose integrity therefore because it comes with moral values. What is your pick?

Integrity comes with morals, and your words are your bond.

Neneh LouL'anne Khan

nee

Faye

NOTE Three

"Forty is The Old Age of Youth, Fifty is the Youth of Old Age"

NOTE Four

"He Who Opens a School Door, Closes Prison Doors".

Every Professional Pianist Needs Page Turners.
Mossaan Silhouettes – Steps & Thirst
Mossaan on a Voyage – Power of Lineage
Mossaan – Revival of a Kingdom

As we discover the door within doors, a wider gateway is created where every journey begins. Voyage is ng

PROFILE OF MOSSAAN

Character profile of Mossaan 1 (the centre of attraction/protagonist),

Protagonist: Mossaan

Sex: female

Age: 22

Physical distinctions: brown eyes, darkish, brown hair, tall, slim, well built

Movement: not too fast and not slow at all - She is balanced

Verbal expression: none (but sighs a lot because she is despairing but shows a little of it)

Tension / Pleasure: always smiling and a bit temperamental

Upbringing: raised to respect herself, her boundaries and to adhere to the typical norms that elders impose on young girls growing up in Africa.

Intelligence and knowledge: Elementary school graduate. Very smart though but lacks opportunities for further studies. She loves her freedom but respectable to the rules set out within her family. Fear of losing her balanced family life and everything she has going on even though little but content while dreaming for the best. Practises a lot with others - Does not like hurting people she loves.

Relationship: Relatives, friends, aunts, cousins, nephews, local elders, community, husband, and kids, mentor (in the city)

Birthplace: Africa

Spoken language: Serere, Wolof, and vehicular French

Personal history: Charismatic, Humble and down to earth.

Effects of Mossaan's life: Marriage, Career Prospects, Travels, etc....

To me, the story is a chain of events that will end up meaning something that impacts. So, I would follow this saying...

I did this.... Then I did this.... Then this happened.

SYNOPSIS

It is based on a true-life story though fictionalized, of a young woman, a 22-year-old GIRL/Woman (early age) called Mossaan.

It is never about what a woman can do or cannot do when it comes to liberation. It does not matter whether young women's dreams of becoming is not lauded. It doesn't matter where a young woman's life takes her. What matters is that she attempts to take herself to another level to contribute towards change.

Mossaan yearned for so much, and so many things went from good to bad, but she will not give up for this is the beginning for her to spread her wings like a phoenix. Her perseverance and determination became her solace. She wanted a different experience not just to enjoy life to the fullest in the city, but to be part of societal norms as EMANCIPATION became the norm for the African woman. She yearns to keep rising above all the grouches that have managed to pull her down. She tried and failed, and she has come back with force simply because she has moved away from being a human being to a human becoming. Therefore, her contribution in this life is something sanctimonious. She worships every step of hers to make her mark. In failing she learned and has become fully empowered beyond what she dreamed for.

She has always wished for a better life for all women, herself and the generation next. Mossaan is a DOER.

ABOUT THE AUTHOR

Neneh LouL'anne FayeKhan

Qualified Lecturer in the lifelong learning sector, Social Development Expert with a massive interest in Global Entrepreneurship. CEO and Founder of EclipxSpace Charitable Foundation, Women International Networks Online, Emancipation of African Women Online Television Advocacy Program. I am a Journalist/Broadcaster, Entrepreneur, Feminist, Influencer, Contributor, and Educationist.

International political affairs, Global Advocacy, African History, Arts & Culture, Empowerment of Women, The Girl Child, and family welfare are my current areas of interest. I am Prone to the development and currently involved in community enhancement. Sociolinguistics, Humanitarian work, Activism, Social Development Initiatives Expert.

Visit the following website to contact Neneh LouL'anne Faye Khan

www.LouLanne.com

God is King, and HE lives forevermore. I wanted to add that we need to live with each other no matter the race, color, gender. Love each other and share whatever the Holy books teach us.

As for me, God the Almighty Allah has opened a fountain of love in me.

God shares His compassion with me.

My humble mission in this world is to share the compassion from the fountain of love in my heart that God has implanted in my heart.

We will always have the strength to hold on to Him.

Thank you!

Printed in Great Britain
by Amazon